Other books by Dan Stark:
Silence of the Bunnies *Tales of Life, Love and Survival* 2007
Gelding Goliath *An Insider's Account of the Destruction of AT&T* 2012
Izzy & Oscar 2015

Tewksbury Tales Press, LLC.
19 Wandering Oaks Way
Asheville, NC 28805

First Tewksbury edition 2019
Original published in the United States by arrangement with the author.

Book and cover designed by David Stark
Set in Adobe Garamond Pro
Cover art by ShutterStock and www.123FreeVectors.com.
Manufactured in the United States of America

ISBN-13: 978-1-934160-04-6

VAMPIRES

A Novel About The Legal Profession.

DAN STARK

Disclaimer

This is a work of fiction. The characters are made up, as are the events that occur in the story. I cannot say, however, that the things or people described bear no resemblance to things or people that I have observed in the real world. They do - particularly when it comes to the lamentable behavior of members of the legal profession. The sharp tactics, the avarice and the incompetence described in the book all are rooted in observations of lawyers made during my twenty-seven years practicing law, or after I retired in 2004. Every profession has its knaves I suppose, but in few professions do these lesser lights have the ability as in law to drain so quickly the resources of their victims.

These bloodsuckers are enough to give vampires a bad name. Keep your distance from these creatures, and if you cannot avoid them, watch your back, your neck, and your wallet.

Finally, I am aware that normally judges will not handle both state and federal matters. The judge in this story handles both in order to simplify the cast of characters.

Dan Stark

Chapter 1

Tuesday was cool. Sam Chapman had worn his typical "ensemble" for working in the auto plant on cold days – an old, thick corduroy shirt that buttoned up the front, faded blue jeans, socks that were too stretched out to stay up all the way, and work shoes. He had a problem with his fingers he'd noticed some months ago but didn't want to worry his wife about – they were very stiff in the morning, and he found it difficult to thread the tiny buttons on his sleeves into the matching buttonholes. As a result, he had stopped trying to button the sleeves.

It was his left sleeve that became caught in one of the gears as he leaned forward to re-engage the punch press he operated.

At first, he was more annoyed than concerned. He hoped he didn't need to rip his shirt in order to remove it from the gears. It was when he pulled on it and it didn't release that he began to worry. He yelled at his co-worker, George, who opened his eyes briefly and closed them again. Sam yelled louder. This time George opened his eyes and kept them open. Sam next took off the earmuffs worn to protect workers against the incessant factory noise, motioning with his free hand for George to do the same. George did so, perhaps not as neatly as Sam, but he got them off. "George, can you hear me?" Sam shouted above the din of the plant machinery.

"Loud and clear, partner," George said. Sam felt the shirt being pulled tighter across his chest as the punch press continued to ready itself to make the next bumper. He wasn't yet panicked, nor did he want George to panic. Sam spoke deliberately, shouting, "Okay George, this is very important. Got that? Very important! My shirt is caught in the machine. George, I need for you to get up, and use that lever to turn the machine off."

George stopped smiling. He tried to stand up but didn't quite make it. He next tried using his right hand to help push himself up. He did manage to stand, but like earlier that morning, he became dizzy and this time – without Sam to help – he fell, with one of his legs going in one direction, the other going in another. "It's no use. Sam, I'm too drunk. You'll just have to get someone else to turn it off," he said.

Sam had already realized that and was waving frantically at Joe Franks, the one other worker who he could see clearly. He waved at Joe, and shouted, but Joe was wearing earmuffs as well, and the distance, the factory noise, and the muffs all conspired to make Sam's words unintelligible. Without the words, the waving failed to convey a sense of desperation, so Joe did what he thought Sam wanted: he waved back. Sam finally turned to his shirt, and ripped at the buttons holding him prisoner. But he was too late.

The left sleeve was now totally trapped in the machine and his hand was being drawn steadily towards the gears. His shirt had become a straightjacket, imprisoning him. He managed to buy a few seconds more by pulling his arm frantically as far up the sleeve as possible, curling his fingers away from the gears. With those seconds, he screamed at Joe and at George that they must help him. Joe seemed at last to realize something was wrong, and turned off his own machine so that he could take a look at what the problem was. George, who tried and once more was unable to stand, whimpered, "I'm sorry, Sam" over and over.

Time ran out on Sam. The gears now clamped on his fingers, crushing them up to the knuckles in their first pass. Pain more excruciating than Sam thought possible wracked his body and caused him to scream louder than he could ever have imagined. The random thought flitted through his consciousness that he hadn't been to Church much of late, but that didn't stop him from moaning, "Oh mother of God, Sweet Jesus…"

The merciless gears were ready for another pass. This time they pulled and crushed his arm a few inches past his wrist. Again he screamed. This time the scream lacked the energy of the first one, not because the pain was less; to the contrary, the intensity grew with every moment. He simply lacked the energy to scream as loudly. He looked at the gears as they inexorably rotated into place to pull more of his arm into the machine. Sam thought of his wife, and how she'd be alone if he didn't somehow escape. "Sarah!" he cried, in a voice filled with anguish and pain. Then, as the machine crushed his elbow, he passed out. Blood was everywhere, even before the machine severed his mangled fingers from his body with a "thwack-thomp-thomp."

Joe finally came running over, and turned off the machine. He called Sam by name a couple of times, and getting no response, came closer to see whether he could pull Sam out of the machine. He could not. As he stood back up, he noticed blood spurting from the mangled mess that had been Sam's hand. He watched, morbidly fascinated, as the fountain of blood gushed lower and lower. There wasn't enough blood left in Sam's body to keep the fountain going. Tearing himself away, Joe ran to get help.

It was at about then that Sam Chapman died.

Vampires

Chapter 2

Steven Karansky stuffed the remnants of the chocolate glazed donut into his mouth, brushed his hands together to free them of frosting and crumbs, and then literally ran up the courthouse steps. He checked through security and began looking for his client, who at the last moment had asked to meet with him prior to going into the courtroom for the first time.

He didn't begrudge Sarah Chapman the time. He had come to respect the frail woman for dealing with the death of her husband in such a dignified way. Besides, it shouldn't take that long to brief her – they were here to work out the pre-trial order before his Honorable Joshua Lehman, the judge to whom the case of the Estate of Samuel Chapman v. the American Automobile Company was assigned. Once issued, the order would set the times at which various events would occur – for instance, when depositions would be taken, discovery be completed, the trial commence, etc.

It was unusual to have clients attend such procedural skirmishes. Karansky had asked her to attend in order to start working the judge. He suspected that Sarah's thin façade of self-control would fall apart during the proceeding, and as far as he was concerned the sooner the better. Karansky wasn't being heartless; he was reasonably certain that his Honor would feel the same anger towards the auto company as he himself had felt the day he'd first heard the story of Sam's death. In the long run, that would be in Sarah's interest.

Judge Lehman had a reputation for being "emotional," based on his penchant for trying to "do equity." This translated into interpreting the rules to favor the litigant that Judge Lehman thought was in the right. He wouldn't stray so far that he would be reversed, but in the hundreds of little discretionary decisions that a judge makes that make it more likely one of the parties would win, he would act in favor of the party who the judge thought should win. Karansky couldn't have been happier with the judicial assignment.

He looked at his watch. He had told Sarah to meet him at 12:15. It read a bit shy of twelve thirty. It was not like her to be late, and he wondered whether everything was okay. Finally, he saw Mrs. Chapman approaching with her stepson in toe. She was trying to hurry, but had to keep pausing to wait for the young man, whose legs were longer but seemed to move so much more slowly. Karansky had seen him previously only in photos. Karansky hadn't liked him before, and he didn't like him now. There was something about the expression on his face that seemed to suggest the young man knew that those around him were less than what they aspired to be, and that it was his lot in life to let them know it!

"Hello, Mr. Karansky," she said, as she walked up to him. 'I couldn't say no. Sam was his father."

"It's okay," Karansky said, not wanting to make her uncomfortable. "Please just ask him to sit in the back of the room when we're before the judge. I want the judge's focus to be on you. Right?" He got a nod of assent, and continued, "Good. Let's go talk somewhere." He escorted her to one of the rooms near the entrance to the courtroom designed for just such meetings between lawyers and their clients or witnesses. The stepson followed. Once inside, Karansky held out his hand, saying, "Hello, Will. Your mom has told me about you. I am Steven Karansky. I'm very sorry for your loss."

Despite Karansky's instinctive dislike for the young man, he was still not prepared for the response his expression of sympathy evoked. "I doubt that Mr. Karansky. Did you know my dad?" Will asked.

"No, I did not know him," Karansky answered quietly.

"Didn't think so," Will said. "So spare me the fake sympathy, okay? All he is to you is an opportunity to make money."

Karansky stared at the young man but said nothing. Then, to the widow, he added, "I'm sorry, but it's nearly one o'clock and I absolutely must go prepare. We can talk afterwards."

Karansky entered the courtroom, and walked up to the desk reserved for plaintiffs. He began to take from his briefcase the papers he thought he would need, when a familiar voice said, "Ah, then you must be Mr. Karansky."

"Mr. Cayhill," Karansky said. "I wasn't aware this was your case."

"I'm sorry," Cayhill said, his voice evidencing surprise at Karansky's familiarity. "Do we know each other?"

"Yes," Karansky responded. "We were on opposite sides in a divorce case a few years ago."

"I see," Cayhill said. Then he smiled, if one can call a mean smirk a smile just because the ends of the mouth turn up. "I take it you lost?"

"Yes," Karansky said. "Then you remember the case?"

"No, not really. But I am not in the habit of losing. I would have remembered you had you won," Cayhill said. "Ah well, now you will have another chance." Cayhill paused for a minute, then added, "And to answer your question, yes it is my case as of today. It seems you were somewhat rough on the young man we had assigned it previously. I have reviewed the files, and I have advised my client that we should pay something. Very tragic. So long as you don't force us to spend a lot of money defending the case, I see no reason we can't be very generous. Say, ten million, so long as we come to terms within ten days."

Karansky was stunned, though he did his best not to show any reaction. "I'll need to check with my client," he said.

"Obviously," Cayhill said in response. "In the meantime, we will do whatever we can to remind you that I can bring the assembled talents of the more than four hundred attorneys of Dunlop and Schmidt to bear on this case. If you continue, your effort will be as forgettable here as it was the first time we met."

Karansky looked at Cayhill to see if he were joking. There was no smile; only a confident, even arrogant, look matching the words. Karansky's thoughts about his opponent were interrupted by Judge Lehman who entered the courtroom, banged the gavel, and told the clerk to call the next case.

"The Estate of Sam Chapman versus American Automobile Company, case number 09-441," the clerk read dutifully.

"Thank you," the judge said. "Now, let's get to the pre-trial order..."

Cayhill stood up, interrupting. "Excuse me, your honor. There is a preliminary matter before we get to the pre-trial order. Your honor, with respect, Defendant moves that your Honor recuse himself, and that the case be assigned to a different judge, on grounds of bias."

"That is preposterous, counselor. Denied," said Judge Lehman, testily.

"Move to reconsider, your honor," Cayhill said, choosing to go toe to toe with the judge. "Your honor, we have gathered a number of papers or statements that were authored by you at different times during your life. Together, they create the unmistakable impression that your Honor is prepared to use the judicial process to practice "social engineering," of the Robin Hood variety. You know, taking from the rich and giving to the poor."

Judge Lehman kept his temper under control, but Karansky could nonetheless see him starting to fume. Cayhill must have found something, Karansky guessed, because this was not a fight you would want to start unless you were pretty darn sure you'd win.

Lehman must have thought the same thing. He was cautious in his response, saying, "I don't know what you're talking about. I want to have every piece of evidence you rely upon to justify your claim of bias on my desk in ten minutes. Otherwise…"

Cayhill interrupted, "Your honor, I don't need the ten minutes. You will see a reference to the evidence we rely upon at page 27 of our brief we are filing today." Cayhill walked to the clerk and handed him a copy, then walked over to Karansky and handed him one, as he finished, "…and the actual text of the statements in Exhibit A." The clerk promptly handed the brief to the judge, who (along with Karansky) thumbed through the pleading and read the text.

"Gentlemen, chambers," the judge said, seething. Cayhill and Karansky followed the judge back to his office, where the judge resumed his inspection of the material. Listed in the pleading were two documents: a paper the judge purportedly wrote when he was a twenty-year old political science major, and a signed affidavit of one Honeysuckle Rose. The paper was benign; it was the usual left-wing blast from a very smart but alienated young man, talking about taking the wealth from corporations and "sharing" it more equitably. Such statements could be explained as the intemperate exuberance of youth; acceptable if no longer espoused as the path the adult would take.

The affidavit from Honeysuckle Rose was a different matter. The woman, a self-acknowledged prostitute, stated that she and Judge Lehman had been seeing each other for nearly two years. She attested in her letter, addressed "to whom it may concern," that in addition to giving him "the best oral sex a man could want," she had had discussions with the judge, during which Lehman had gone on wild tirades insisting that corporations were evil, and the right thing to do was to separate them from their assets.

The beauty of the thing was that it didn't matter whether the claimed discussions had taken place; to continue handling the case would be ruinous to the Judge, a married man. If Judge Lehman and the prostitute had been involved, fighting the motion with the attendant publicity would be tough.

Karansky decided to raise a bit of a fuss so that the judge would have time to think. "Your honor," he began, "I object. The rules of civil procedure require notice, typically ten days, to the other side, between the filing of a motion and the hearing on it. I recognize the defendant had proposed an order in this case cutting that to five, but even then it isn't zero. It's outrageous for Mr. Cayhill to withhold this pleading, which they've obviously been working on for some time, until the moment they make the motion in court. This is trial by ambush."

"Trial by ambush," Cayhill repeated, chuckling. "I like that." Cayhill stared at the judge, and said, "So? What's it going to be, your Honor? The only response I would give to Mr. Karansky is that we in fact wrote the brief this morning, dividing it between four lawyers to get it done." Then, looking at Karansky, he continued, "It is one of the things you can do when you properly staff a case." Turning back to the judge, Cayhill finished his argument, "I am sorry if Mr. Karansky is surprised, but there was no effort here to ambush anybody. Look, if you want five days to think about this, your Honor, you've got it. Frankly, my only concern is that Ms. Rose is a very talkative person and is likely to discuss this matter with some member of the press while we are waiting around for a decision."

"I am touched by your concern," the judge said sarcastically. "Okay, let's cut the crap. Cayhill, what happens if I do remove myself from this case?"

"Then the pleading is withdrawn. The matter is over. Done," Cayhill said.

"And Ms. Rose?" the judge asked.

"I obviously can't speak for her, your Honor. But it would be my guess that she would forget all about it in a day or two," Cayhill said.

The judge took a deep breath, and said, looking over the top of his glasses as he did, "Very well, Mr. Cayhill, I withdraw from the case. Let's go back in there, and put this on the record."

"But your Honor," Karansky started to protest.

"I'm sorry, son, but I need to do this," the judge said to Karansky. He leaned towards Karansky as the two walked from his chambers to the courtroom, and added, "If you shake hands with this asshole, which I don't recommend, count your fingers afterwards."

Once back in court, Judge Lehman was very efficient. He told both parties, on the record, that he was withdrawing from the case, and that it would be returned to the case pool, and assigned a new judge. That was it. Karansky stood up, disgusted at the turn of events. A smiling Lester Cayhill came up to him, and said, "Don't forget, you can still look like a hero," he told Karansky. "The offer is ten million dollars now, but will be reduced as we expend time and money defending the case."

"You mean like today? Was that 'defending the case' or blackmail?" Karansky asked.

"Defense of course," Cayhill responded. "By any means necessary." Cayhill then strode from the court, four of his attorneys following in his wake. Karansky wanted to wipe that smug look off his face. If Mrs. Chapman wanted to take the money and run, that was fine – it was her right. But if she didn't, then he was going to find some way to beat that son-of-a-bitch.

Chapter 3

Laura Simon had that look of cleanliness and order those too young to have made a mess of their lives can have. Her face was open and honest. Her clothes were neat, professional, and fresh from the cleaners. She hoped it would make a difference. She needed a job.

She had been interviewing for months and still had not received a single offer of employment. Her early interviews had been with the large law firms, the ones that paid top dollar and looked for the best students in each graduating class. Her grades were excellent. She had a legitimate chance to graduate Seton Hall Law School as valedictorian, the honor bestowed on the student with the highest grade average in the class. For all that, she hadn't received a single job offer, and now even interviews with the mid- to large-size firms were becoming scarce.

Laura couldn't figure out what went wrong with her interviews. She had tried different looks and different clothes. She was attractive, or at least she thought she was, with a slender figure, complemented by long, dark hair, a Mediterranean complexion, and bright hazel eyes. Sometimes she smiled and sometimes she was very serious. She seemed, though, to have an intensity about her that made people nervous. Laura Simon believed in integrity, honesty, and helping the little guy. After all, those were the main reasons she had wanted to become a lawyer.

Seared into her brain was the sight of her father signing over his business to his partner, a man she had detested from their first meeting when he had tried to fondle her bottom while her father had been looking in the other direction. Laura had been fourteen. The two men later became embroiled in a dispute over her father's insistence that the partner had been siphoning money improperly from the business. After two years of increasing legal bills without resolution, her father had sold his share to his partner for a fraction of its worth when it became clear the alternative was continued litigation and legal bills he couldn't pay. Laura had decided to become a lawyer, one who would do better for her clients than those who had represented her father had done for him.

Her beliefs about what lawyers should be, which nearly all of her peers said they shared, seemed, however, to set her apart in a way that was anathema to most law firms. Law schools made ethics courses mandatory, but that didn't really seem to change the behavior of her fellow students outside ethics class. To her, they just seemed more careful, not more honest.

Laura recalled her interview with Dunlop & Schmidt. She had been escorted into a conference room to wait for the partner who was to interview her. The room exuded wealth. There was a custom-made, highly polished, oblong table large enough to seat thirty people. The chairs were of matching wood, a dark mahogany with a lighter wood used as a decorative inlay. On the floor was a large, ultra-modern rug, obviously expensive but not at all warm or comforting in her opinion. Nor did it match the Kandinsky print on the wall. At least she thought it was a print. She leaned closer and was looking at the brushwork when Lester Cayhill, walked into the room. "If you're wondering whether that is real," he said, "it is. We don't deal in fakes, Miss..." and here he paused while checking her name on his legal pad, "Simon." He looked again to make certain he had it right, and said, "Miss Laura Simon, how do you do, my name is Lester Cayhill." She held out her hand, which he looked at but ignored. Laura felt awkward as she raised her hand to her forehead, pretending to brush a strand of hair behind her ear.

Cayhill then started the interview by asking what she thought was the best attribute she would bring to the firm were they to hire her. She answered decisively, "Integrity," before seeing him fighting a smile.

"Really?" he said. "Not hard work? Intelligence? No? Those are lesser qualities?"

She felt uneasy at his reaction, and responded with her voice now less firm, "Of course they're important. But isn't integrity the foundation for everything else?"

"I don't know. You tell me. How would you handle this situation?" He paused, and then after thinking a moment, went on, "You and I are working together on a case. I have answered interrogatories saying we don't have a certain document. You know we do. But you also know the document was written by a disgruntled employee of our client, and contains false statements that will be difficult to disprove. Assume also that our client deserves to win the case, but if this document is produced, there is a good chance he will not. What, Miss Simon, do you do?"

She swallowed hard and said, "None of the facts you offer justify failing to produce the document. I would have to tell the court that we did in fact have the document. Then I would seek to use the mitigating facts to explain the document to the judge or jury."

Cayhill shook his head and stood up, saying with evident disappointment as he did, "Well, Miss Simon, if that is the best quality you would bring to this firm, I shudder to think what the others would be. Your approach would certainly damage, and could possibly end, my career. Our client, who should have won the case, most likely will lose it now even though, as I asked you to assume, he deserved to win.

Vampires

In the real world, things are not always black and white. Judgment is necessary, the sort of judgment that you seem to lack. Good luck with your job search; we have no place for you here." With that, he walked past her down the long hallway into the bowels of the firm. She was shocked and, walking unsteadily to the elevators, wondered what had just happened. Her hand shook as she pushed the button.

Laura went to classes each day in business attire so that she would be prepared for any interviews that might arise. She was close to being out of options. She didn't want to be one of those who, graduating without a job, worked as waiters to support themselves while looking for a legal position. Employers were reluctant to touch students who had been passed over by every would-be employer during the last year of law school when it was customary for students to find jobs. Each day when Laura arrived at school, and again just before she left, she would pass by the placement board where those looking for lawyers posted notices advertising their positions. That day, she had seen the note on the bulletin board in the morning; indeed it would have been hard to miss. At the top of the notice in big bold letters was the promise that the job offered "Long Hours/Low Pay." Beneath the headline, the text stated that Steven Karansky, class of 1996, was looking for one attorney, giving as a starting salary a number that was about one-fifth what the big firms paid. She had heard the other students laughing at the poor schnook who would end up working for Karansky, joking about his taking on and losing big cases. "Man, can you imagine working for this guy? What did the paper say, that he hadn't won a case in three years?"

"That's probably why he can afford to pay top dollar," another student had said, the sarcasm palpable.

She had waited until the crowd outside the placement office had all gone, either to class or in search of some adventure or other. Then she had quickly jotted down the number, and called from her cell phone.

Karansky answered the phone himself, which startled her. She apologized for interrupting him and asked to speak to his assistant. "What is it you want that you think I can't help you with?" he asked.

"Oh no!" she exclaimed, wondering how she managed to get the conversation off on the wrong foot. "I wanted to make an appointment and didn't want to bother you. May I speak to your assistant, please?"

"What do you want to see me about?" he asked, ignoring her question in favor of his own.

"About the job," she replied.

He sighed, asking if she had seen the salary. She said yes.

"And you're still interested?" he asked, sounding surprised.

"Yes," she said.

"What's wrong with you?" he asked. "I assume I wasn't your first choice, which means that you've tried to get a job at a better paying place and not succeeded. Right?" She said yes. He continued, "So what's wrong with you? Are you stupid? How are your grades?"

Laura was offended by his questions. Her voice rose a bit as she answered. "Mr. Karansky, I am not stupid and my grades are excellent. I am likely to finish among the top ten in my class. I resent your questions. What does it say about your job position that you assume anyone who wants it isn't smart enough for you to consider?"

Karansky chuckled, and thought a moment. "What are you doing now?" he asked.

"I'm going to the law library," she answered. "I have an hour or so before my securities class and I was going to do some reading. "

"Well, I don't want to encourage you to cut class, but I have time now. Can you get here in twenty minutes?" he asked.

"Thirty, maybe," she answered.

"Good. It's now ten after eleven. I'll see you at eleven thirty," he said, and hung up.

Laura arrived at his office at eleven thirty-five. She looked for a receptionist, and not seeing one, wondered what to do. She couldn't help but notice too that the furnishings were very different than at most of the places that she had been. The couch in the waiting area was visibly worn, and the leather on the arm nearer the window was cracked and dry. The walls looked freshly painted, but the paint from the walls had spilt over to the ceiling in spots when it had been applied. Laura guessed that Karansky had painted it himself rather than use professional painters, in order to save money.

Laura turned around, startled, at the sound of Karansky's voice. He walked in, talking on a cordless phone. He had wavy brown hair, and was overdue to have a haircut. His brown eyes were deep but looked tired. He was wearing the trousers of what was probably a suit; it was well cut (or at least it made his butt looked good, she thought, smiling) but was very wrinkled. She was trying to assess whether she would have called him handsome when he abruptly brought his conversation to a close, "Listen, you go back to Mr. Cayhill, and you tell him that you tried to sell that bull-shit story about how tough it is to do your job. Tell him also I ain't buying, and unless I get an inventory of all responsive documents by the end of the day, with the documents within three days after that, then I will see him in court."

He hung up, glanced absent-mindedly at her, then focused and looked at her again. "You the legal superstar?" he asked.

She smiled in spite of herself, nodding, "I guess that's me. You look busy," she added as the phone rang again. "Is this a decent time for an interview?"

"Absolutely," he answered. He thought a moment, then asked, "Are you good?"

"I'm not certain that I understand," she said, puzzled by the oddity of the question.

"Let's skip all the chatter, okay?" he responded. "I don't have the patience for it. Are you good?"

She stared him and decided that she wanted the job. "I think I will be very good," she stated. "And I want the job."

This time Karansky smiled. "Fine," he said, "You're hired, provided you can start tomorrow. What do you know about motions to compel?"

"It's something you file with the court to compel your adversary to do something he should do. Like produce documents covered by a discovery request."

Vampires

"Good," Karansky replied. "The case is Chapman v. American Auto." He handed her a binder with pleadings. "We need to file a motion to compel tomorrow morning, addressing their failure to provide any of the documents we have requested in discovery. Since you're not yet an attorney, have it on my desk tomorrow morning at eight; that way I can review it and we can be ready to file when court opens at nine. Oh, add a request for attorney's fees on account of the fact that these guys are assholes. Any questions?"

"Mr. Karansky," Laura protested, her composure shaken. "I need a job. I've come too far on student loans to give up becoming a lawyer. But…" She paused and looked around, before deciding to say what she had been thinking. She sighed, took a breath and continued, "Look, the office is shabby, the furniture is worn, you don't appear to have any other employees, and I'm told you haven't won a case in three years. Now you ask me to have something on your desk first thing in the morning on the first day I'm supposed to show up for work. To do it right would take several hours. At least!"

He stared at her for a minute before answering. "I suppose this is a good first lesson that things are not always as they appear. True, I haven't actually won a case in the last two, not three, years. I take very tough cases against very rich opponents, Miss Simon. Still, things are not all bleak. That statistic you mentioned doesn't include the three cases I've settled during the same period when it became clear to defendants they were going to lose. As to other employees, I do have one other but her sister is sick and she's visiting her. You'll meet Pam. She is office manager, secretary and paralegal all rolled into one." He paused for effect, and then gave her a big grin. "Finally, as to your assignment, yes, to do it right would probably take you three to four hours. You have to read their condescending pleadings in the case for at least an hour to get angry enough to write it. But you start your job tomorrow, and tomorrow starts at 12:01 a.m. I figured I was giving you eight hours to do a job that would at most take four." He saw her start to protest, and cut her off, "I know, you prefer to sleep rather than work. Well, perhaps I was a bit harsh. I'll give you until 9 a.m., but please, no more delays."

Chapter 4

Karansky arrived at his office at 8:00 the following morning. Pam was back and opened his office door for him. Handing him the envelope she had found propped against the door when she'd arrived at the office at 7:00, she asked, "Do you have something to tell me?"

Pam's questions always made him nervous because inevitably he failed to tell her all sorts of things, not because he was trying to keep secrets but because he just assumed she knew everything about him without him saying a word.

"What?" he asked. "What did I forget to tell you?"

"Miss Simon?" she prompted.

"Yes, um, I hired another attorney," he said, waiting for the blast to come. It took about five seconds for her to react. Pam didn't yell, but Karansky found it worse than yelling. Her voice dropped to a level he could barely hear, something that happened when she was truly exasperated with him. "Steven," she said, "How will you pay the poor thing?" He started to speak, but she interrupted, "And don't tell me the Chapman settlement. That woman is never going to decide. Meanwhile, I haven't taken a paycheck in two months."

The problem with the Chapman case was that the same thing that made Sarah Chapman an ideal witness also made it difficult for her to decide whether to settle the case. Her stepson wanted to try the case and his recommendation had paralyzed the widow. He saw in his father's death the possibility of a new life for himself, one where he didn't have to work every day, if his stepmother didn't squander their chance by settling too cheaply. The last time Karansky had tried to talk about settling the case, she had begun crying. He had then proposed that they try the case if that was what she wanted, but Mrs. Chapman had shook her head "no" and cried some more. It was going to take time.

"Pam, I want you to make a reservation for three at Scalini Fedeli for lunch." The restaurant he named had a reputation for excellent food, but at exorbitant prices. To eat there was to make a statement that money was not an issue. He saw her face get red, and cut off the impending explosion by taking a wad of bills from his pocket and stuffing them into her hand. "Not to worry, Pam. This is just the petty cash. There is also this," and he took out a check made out to her for twice the amount of her missed paychecks, and another for one point nine million dollars, and change, with a deposit slip already prepared for the firm's account.

She looked at him, her head cocked to one side, not yet ready to smile. "They settled?" she asked.

"No, but they will."

"Then where…?" she demanded.

"I sold our interest in the future settlement," he said, a note of triumph in his voice. She was totally confused and her expressive face begged him to explain. "There are firms that pay cash for the future value of settlements. I showed them defendants' offer letter, told them it was just a matter of time, and convinced them it was going to happen."

"And they believed you enough to pay cash now?" she asked, incredulously.

"Well, they do shave the value to cover some of the risk. And," he added as if it was the smallest of inconsequential issues, "they also took a lien against the house as collateral."

"Steven! That house is all you have. It was your parents' legacy to you. You could lose it now!" she sputtered, her anxiety bubbling to the surface.

"Come now, have some faith," he countered. "Look, Pam, this will carry us for six months in style, easily. If I can't settle the case by then, or cash out one of my other big cases, then I'm going to have to close up shop anyway. This gives me a fighting chance. And I needed a second attorney to help. I decided to roll the dice one last time. Don't be angry; c'mon, let's kick off the firm's last six months on the right foot."

"May I ask how much you got?" she inquired.

"Now don't you start on me," he began, and then had a change of heart. She deserved to know. "I got two million; they kept the rest to cover their risk."

"What risk?" she replied with a snort. "Their risk is secured by your house, which is worth twice that!"

"True, but Pam, we really needed the money. Who knows what will happen in the future, but we now have enough money to take a run at the cases we have without worrying about making ends meet day to day."

Vampires

Pam sighed, deciding to drop it for the moment. She was silent a minute, and then asked, "Is she good?"

"Is who good?" he asked back.

"Ms. Simon. The woman you hired," Pam clarified.

"I don't know yet. I think she is. But we'll know soon enough," he responded. With that he ripped open the envelope, looking at the first page. In the short time before he flipped to page two, a smile played on his features. "Oh she's good," he muttered, "she's very good."

He said these last words trailing Pam into the reception area. Pam, a mischievous grin on her face, said, "Mr. Karansky, I believe you know Ms. Simon. I didn't have a chance to tell you, but she asked to see you before ten, and I added her to your schedule."

He looked over his shoulder at the wall clock. "About time," he said. "This is a good effort. Now come into my office and I'll tell you what you did wrong."

Chapter 5

The machine that had caused the man's death was made in China, from drawings created in the United States. The factory manager had called his American consultant into his office and asked the question that had been on his mind ever since he had first looked at the drawings. The factory manager was a competent engineer but he didn't understand the need for the costly electronics labeled "automatic cut-off." The consultant finally showed up, his face florid from drinking in the hot afternoon. The factory manager looked at the American with disgust. The man had no pride. But China had need for such people, at least for now.

"Mr. Frank," the factory manager said, using the man's first name to show disrespect, "this thing called automatic cut-off adds at least fifteen percent to the cost of this machine. I don't understand. Why include it? The machine seems to work well without it."

Frank Mahoney had seen better days. Too much alcohol had damaged his career in the States. He had lost the job he had working for an American company, and had bounced around before landing a job with an international consulting group, through which he had gotten the current assignment. Though he drank too much, he knew his trade. He also knew the mentality of the factory manager, and knew his advice would be futile even as he gave it. "Listen Jiang, it's a very important safety feature. The automatic cut-off shuts the machine down if it detects that something like an arm or a piece of clothing has gotten caught in it. Without it, a worker could be pulled into the machine and crushed."

"I see," the factory manager said. "Tell me, Mr. Frank, do the Koreans equip their machines with automatic cut-offs?"

"No," Mahoney said, "but their stuff is crap."

"Crap, maybe. But it is priced very aggressively, Mr. Frank, and if we don't get our costs down, we will not be able to compete. I talked to my superiors and I'm sorry, but the automatic cut-off must go. It is a luxury that I would like to include but I must compete. But I will, how you say, "go the extra mile." We will add a sign in big red letters that says; "Warning! Please keep hands and clothing away from the machinery." The factory manager looked very satisfied with the solution and with himself for thinking of it. Mahoney started to protest, but the factory manager held up his hand, and said, "Thank you, Mr. Frank, you have been of the greatest help. And now if you will excuse me, I have work to do."

Mahoney had few illusions left. Thinking he might prevail upon the factory manager to change his mind was not one of them. He searched his brain for what he could do. The thought of these machines being sold to factories around the world, and the horrible deaths that would ensue, depressed him. He sat down at his computer and began writing an email to Jiang, with a half dozen cc's: two were Ministries in China, one went to his supervisor at the consulting firm, another to the U.S. Product Safety Commission, one to a friend he had at the AFL-CIO, and the last to the New York Times. After writing introductory paragraphs talking about who he was and what he had been doing, he got to the issue at hand. It took him three tries because he was not naturally a writer, but at last he had something that satisfied him. He read it one last time:

"Producing machines without automatic cut-offs in order to save money is going to have tragic results. We know that factory accidents will happen. A number of workers will not only be killed, but killed in the most ghastly manner, pulled slowly by an arm or a sleeve into the machine, where the worker will suffer an incredibly painful and gruesome death. The only thing that distinguishes this situation from firing a gun into a crowd is time. The gun kills immediately whereas this machine will get its victims more slowly. But get them it will." He admired it for a while, and then decided he was going to wait until 4 in the morning to send it, after which he would leave. He doubted Jiang would do anything, but this would give him a head start. Just in case. He also decided to make everyone outside of China a bcc, meaning that the recipients would not know it had been sent to others.

His work done, Mahoney packed a bag, looked at his watch, and seeing he had a little more than six hours before the four o'clock time he had selected to send the e-mail, he broke a promise to himself and took out his last bottle of bourbon. He had told himself not to drink until after he was safely away, but that meant leaving an almost untouched bottle of Jack Daniels for Jiang and his underlings. After one drink he had another. And just one more. He woke a little late, remembered to send his email, but then took more time than he had planned getting going. He had a splitting headache and dug around his bag, finding his bottle of aspirin. He took four and waited a few more minutes for his head to stop throbbing.

The delay wasn't long but it was enough. He had failed to factor into his plan the fact that the Ministries he copied on his message monitored email traffic from Westerners working in the country around the clock. His message was seen immediately. Unhappily for him, the employee of the Ministry of the Interior who saw the message was eager for promotion and diligently brought the message to his supervisor within a few minutes of its receipt. The supervisor, who spoke enough English to recognize the document as hateful and dangerous, promptly called his superior, waking him up, and read him the document. After screaming at his subordinate for waking him, the supervisor calmed down enough to listen. He was immediately concerned; he had a colleague whose career had been damaged irretrievably by similar unfair criticisms appearing in the foreign press. He looked up in his computer the name of the factory manager involved, and was pleased to see that he knew him.

He picked up the phone and called him, enjoying the man's initial sleepy response. He wasted no time. "Jiang, you know this Frank Mahoney? Yes? Well, he has crossed the line. That goddamned memo will end your career and mine. You should have prevented him from writing it!"

Jiang stammered an apology and began to promise he would talk to Mahoney, but the man from the Ministry cut him off, "It is too late for that. The Ministry will have to follow procedure and interview him. It's too late for talk."

"Then what can we do?" the factory manager asked.

"I cannot tell you that," the man from the Ministry said. "I can only say that if he is still around and capable of talking to the investigators by the end of the day, I will need to replace you with a manager who cares more about worker safety."

Jiang said he understood and hung up. Then, knowing he was opening a door that he would never be able to close, he called a local triad leader who had approached him several times offering to do favors for him. After a lengthy exchange of pleasantries, the factory manager said, "I need a favor."

Mahoney walked towards his car in the still dark morning, an hour behind his intended schedule. As he fumbled in his pocket for the keys, two men stepped out of the shadows, machetes in their hands. He looked at them, realized he was in trouble, and tried to run. He was, even at his best, not in shape to run quickly. This morning, though, he wasn't at his best. He hadn't taken more than two steps when he felt the first cut, a deep gash in his right leg. He felt one other before he felt no more.

Chapter 6

Large organizations are notoriously bad at preserving and organizing records. The New York Times should have had a field day with the story – had it reached anyone who might have realized its importance. But the news organization receives so much paper each day, much of it from people crying wolf about everything from food additives to aliens, it can't be blamed for overlooking this single document, which is what it did. The news that week had focused on the presidential campaign, and a letter complaining about manufacturing standards in China just didn't seem that important.

Similarly, the AFL-CIO, failed to recognize it as anything important. The union, whose membership was reeling from cheap or Chinese prison labor sucking almost all the manufacturing jobs out of the country, was not really focused on complaints about the quality of the products made there. They did try referencing it in a political speech, but an argument that the Chinese were making inferior manufacturing equipment really didn't play. After a week, the text was replaced with allegations that Chinese-made baby food had lead content three times the FDA limits. Now that caught people's attention!

The consulting company for whom Mahoney worked at first didn't know what to do with the report. But when the Chinese Ministry for Industrial Production complained about it, it did what any customer-focused organization would do: it agreed with the customer that the report was not in its best interests and answered all further inquiries about it with the response, "what report?"

Vampires

The final copy sent out of China went to the United States Product Safety Commission, which had jurisdiction to act when dangerous products were introduced into interstate commerce. Here it was reviewed by a junior attorney who brought it to his supervisor. The supervisor sighed when he read it, and asked, "What about this Mahoney? Is he a nut?"

"We don't really know," said the attorney. "He worked for a consulting outfit, but I talked to his boss, and they claim not to know anything about the memo, nor to have heard from him since it was sent. I had one of the paralegals try to track him down, but without success. The factory where he worked in China says he's disappeared. They gave an address in Thailand, and said that it's last place they knew that he'd gone. After that, they say they have no idea."

"Did you check on the address?" the supervisor asked.

"Of course," came the response. "It appears, according to our contact in the Chinese government who checked on it for me, to be a place of prostitution, a place specializing in the provision of pre-pubescent girls to westerners."

The supervisor was silent for a minute while he digested this piece of information. He shuddered at the thought, and it took him a minute to re-focus on the issue before him. Finally, shrugging off his nightmarish thoughts of a girl in that place with his daughter's face, he told himself to breathe deeply, deal with the issue and then go home early to see her. When he finally spoke, he was back on course. "Well, I tell you one thing. We aren't going to stop what few manufacturing establishments have survived in this country from getting necessary equipment at competitive pricing. Christ, do we even know whether there's an existing American company that makes these things?"

"So far as we know, the answer is no," the attorney said. "The last U.S. company making this type equipment closed last year. Now it is only the Koreans and the Chinese."

"Shit," the supervisor said. So if we act against this equipment, we lose more factories because the Chinese or some other country won't have any qualms about their workers getting killed. We're damned if we do; damned if we don't."

"So what do we do? Ignore it?"

"No, we can't do that," said the supervisor. "All we need is for some poor sap to get chewed up by one of these machines and there will be hell to pay. Members of Congress absolutely love to act horrified about such things once they happen, though they rarely provide us the budget and tools to prevent them. I'll be damned if I'm going to put this agency in a position to let them eviscerate us. No, here's the plan. You know the letters we send to company's advising them of dangerous chemical compounds or other things they use in manu-facturing? You've seen them, right? Well good! Draft up a cover letter using the same format, and advise all U.S. manufacturers of the dan-gers of machines without automatic cut-offs. Lay it on thick. Tell them we recommend they don't use such machines but if they do, to make certain they take precautions like having another employee around so that the second employee can stop the machine if necessary."

"That's a great idea, boss," the attorney said, half flattering his boss but half believing it. "Do you think it will work?"

"It depends on what you mean by "work," the supervisor said. "Will it stop workers from getting killed? It might prevent some, but not all, deaths. We're going to read someday about a man, with a wife and children, who gets chewed up by one of these machines. But when that

Vampires

happens, no one will be able to say we didn't do our job. We issued a strong warning and so on and so forth. Hell, our warning might even save some lives."

The product safety commission dutifully sent out thousands of copies of its advisory called: Caution: Dangers of Certain Chinese-Made Manufacturing Equipment Without Automatic Cut-Offs. Most of the recipients took a quick look at it and tossed it in the recycling bin because they didn't have such machinery, and had no plans to get any. At the few companies that did have such machinery, the American Automobile Company plant in Linden, New Jersey, was fairly typical in its response. The head of Quality read it quickly, and tried to do the right thing. He got approval for a policy change that required a second worker to be on hand near the machinery in question whenever it was being operated. Having done what the product safety commission recommended, he felt satisfied that he had done what should be done. He filed the document in a folder marked "product safety," and went about his business.

The document stayed right where it was, and probably never would have emerged had it not been for the lawsuit following the death of the worker, Sam Chapman. Karansky had filed some very routine document requests asking the other side to produce documents they might have relevant to the accident, including documents "pertaining to the safety of the equipment or the company's knowledge of any such safety issues relating to the equipment." Attorneys representing American Automobile in a routine sweep of company files found the document. The associate who first came across it, a fresh young graduate from Yale Law School, whistled when he reviewed the document, and promptly called the senior associate working on the case. The senior associate looked at the document and asked the junior associate whom he had told about the document. "No one!" the junior associate protested, almost truthfully, figuring he did not have to count his fiancée to whom had mentioned it in passing over the telephone. The two of them were engaged to be married, and he would call her at the first opportunity and swear her to secrecy. The senior associate pressed, "Are you sure?" The junior associate had made his play, and couldn't change now without admitting that he was a liar. In a testy voice, he said, "Look, I said I hadn't told anyone about it but you. I meant it!"

"Right then," said the senior associate, himself a Harvard man. "C'mon, let's take this up the line." They went to see the junior partner, who began reading the document absent mindedly while chatting on the phone to a young woman. Suddenly, his face went ashen as comprehension hit him. He tried to speak, and then raised his voice, talking loud enough to be heard over the voice of his girlfriend, saying, "That's great honey. Tell me later; I've got to go."

The junior partner hung up the phone, then immediately picked it back up and redialed. "Les, we've got a problem," he said. "May I come in?" He hung up the phone, and told the two other attorneys to follow him to the offices of senior partner Lester Cayhill of the firm Dunlop & Schmidt.

Cayhill saw the three attorneys coming towards his office through the glass wall. The offices were designed to let the maximum amount of light into each attorney's space, and were not more than a year old. The expense of the redesign and construction had been enormous, but the firm had had three very good years in a row, even in a down economy. That's the thing about lawyers, Cayhill thought to himself: if you're good, there is no such thing as a bad economic situation. Hard times mean desperate actions by many companies and that just means legal bills go up. Good economic times means companies want to expand and that makes legal bills go up as well. Up is good, mused Cayhill.

"Well, Mr. Hooper," Cayhill said as the three men entered his office. "This must truly be important to assemble this much brain power. A meeting will cost our client two thousand dollars an hour. And since our minimum charge for a conference is a half-hour, opening the door will cost our client one thousand dollars. You sure you need to come in?" Hooper nodded yes, so he said, "Okay, let's be efficient. What have you got?"

The man he had called Mr. Hooper, Lawrence Hooper, cleared his throat and said, as he handed the document to Cayhill, "Take a look at this."

Cayhill read, keeping his face without expression. When he had finished, he asked his visitors what they thought they should do. The youngest associate, Matt Thomson III, the one who had found it, answered first. "I don't see the problem with producing the document. It is obvious hearsay and can't be introduced into evidence. In fact, we could draft a motion to that effect, filing it at the same time we furnish the other side with the document."

Cayhill looked at the young man with unwavering eyes, and then turned to the junior partner. "Say Larry, what was I thinking? He's right; it is hearsay. Anyone know what happened to the author, our Mr. Mahoney is it?"

The young associate once again answered quickly. "No one seems able to find him. And we have tried!"

"Well, Matt, that seems pretty good then, doesn't it? Can we just furnish the document and then exclude it from evidence?

"Yes sir," came the response. The younger associate was starting to think he had earned his salary this morning.

Cayhill continued, "So that is what we should do, right? What's the harm?"

The older associate looked uncomfortable but wasn't sure enough of himself to participate in what he saw was a dangerous conversation. The junior partner, however, was seasoned enough to enjoy a good lynching. He jumped in, saying, "You're joking, right? I mean it would be a fucking disaster!"

Cayhill, who delighted in teaching young attorneys about the real world, suppressed a smile, and asked him, "And why would it be a disaster Mr. Hooper? I have it on good authority that the document is hearsay, an out-of-court statement without the author being able to appear in court to withstand cross-examination. So what is the harm?"

Hooper answered, "Well, once the plaintiff's attorney sees the document, he'll put our client's senior executives on the stand and ask them whether they thought the equipment was safe. If the answer is no, we're dead—they won't and can't say that. Any other response and plaintiff's counsel brings out our document, and uses it to impeach our witness. In other words, he asks something like how could Mr. X think it was safe? And then he reads the document in little pieces to the witness, stopping frequently to ask whether he wants to change any of his answers in light of it. The law is that even though the document is hearsay, and can't be introduced as evidence, it can be used to impeach a witness."

The young associate didn't yet know when he had lost. "But," he interrupted, "that's all it can be used for. At the end of the day, it still can't be relied upon as evidence. And we would be entitled to a direction from the court directing the jury to not consider it for anything other than judging the credibility of the witness."

Vampires

Cayhill exploded. "He doesn't need to introduce it into evidence! Jesus! Look, the case is being tried to a jury. Do you really think a jury of our peers gives a flying fuck about anything the judge might say once they see that document and learn we had it in our files for several years and chose to use the machinery anyway? I doubt Fort Knox has enough gold in it to pay the judgment that would result." He glared at the associate, who looked like he was about to throw up. Cayhill went on with his lesson. "Now, Mr. Hooper, let us consider our client's actions here. They really tried to do everything right, didn't they?"

Mr. Hooper knew his role. "Yes sir," he said.

Cayhill continued. "The Product Safety Commission says that they should have had another person stand around for safety purposes and they did it, right?"

"Yes sir!" said Hooper.

"Yet this doesn't help them, does it, because the goddamned second worker turns out to be a drunk! He watches the poor employee get chewed up but he is so inebriated he cannot stand, much less turn off the machine. So why didn't American Auto get rid of the guy? Surely they knew he had a drinking problem."

This time no one said anything. Cayhill continued, "I'll tell you why. In the state of New Jersey, alcoholism is considered a disability. As such, employers are prohibited from firing anyone because they are an alcoholic. The company in fact tried to fire the son of a bitch for showing up drunk at a customer meeting. He sued, and this firm properly advised American Auto that they didn't have a leg to stand on. They had to reinstate him. The law says the company must make efforts to accommodate his disability, giving him a job where he can succeed notwithstanding his disability. So they take this asshole and they give him the job of just sitting there. His only job is to turn the machine off if something goes wrong. And he blows it!"

"American Auto was not negligent," Cayhill asserted, and there were none to argue with him. "They really did try to do the right thing, and if there is any justice, they should win. But what happens if we play by the rules and provide the document?"

"American Auto will lose," came the response, this time as a chorus.

"Right. I will not let that happen. What we need are strategies to avoid causing an unjust result. And to keep our options open it is vitally important that we not broadcast the fact that this document exists." He glowered at them one by one. "Got that?" One by one, they said yes. Satisfied, he sent them off on the unnecessary assignment to come up with strategies to prevent such an injustice from occurring. It was unnecessary because he already knew what had to be done.

Chapter 7

Preston Dunlop's name not only was on the door; it also was the first name listed on the venerable firm's doors, its stationery and even the warm-up suits the firm thoughtfully provided to its new associates in lieu of health insurance. His firm, as he proudly thought of it, was counsel to many of the major corporations, including American Automobile. In the case of the auto company, the bond between company and firm was further solidified by the fact that William Gamble, a former partner and friend of Dunlop's, was general counsel to that company. Gamble had been the first lawyer hired by Dunlop and Schmidt when the two founders had finally had generated enough business to support other attorneys. When the CEO had asked Dunlop to join American Auto as its general counsel, Dunlop had declined but had recommended Gamble for the job instead. Now, years later, with Gamble as the general counsel, you would need dynamite to sever the relationship between company and firm.

It was only natural that Gamble turned to Dunlop for the biggest project in American Auto's history. Gamble had outlined the deal – a massive investment by the Chinese to buy 20% of American Auto at twice the current market twice, with options to buy another 13.33%; a joint venture in China, majority-owned by the Chinese government, into which the auto company would transfer technology necessary to manufacture 5 million cars a year, initially for sale in China. "Look, the alternative to this was bankruptcy," Gamble summarized. "This will make us number one again."

"I appreciate that," Dunlop said. "That is truly incredible." He thought a moment and then decided he had to ask. "But aren't we creating a monster that will, in a few years' time, come back and destroy us?"

"You worry too much," Gamble said, dismissively. "First we have to survive the short term; then we can worry about the long term. Besides, if we didn't do this, someone else would."

Gamble then asked Dunlop to fly to Lucerne, Switzerland to negotiate the terms of a detailed memorandum of understanding. No one else from American Auto would attend to avoid suspicion, though Dunlop would be tethered to Gamble by phone.

Dunlop took an immediate liking to his counterpart. He was an older man with clear eyes peering at the world from behind a stony expression that gave away nothing. He told Dunlop that he was a mid-level administrator from the Ministry of the Interior, though Dunlop suspected he was much higher ranked. The man smoked incessantly. Dunlop tested him early by asking him if he minded not smoking during the negotiations. The man looked at his cigarette, knocked some ash into his coffee cup, and said, "I don't insist that you smoke; so you should not insist that I don't."

That comment set the tone of frank and tough negotiations. Within three days they had hammered out the written document. The deal gave each what they wanted: American Auto, whose priorities like most American companies were all short term, would reap immediate profits despite the current world auto downturn. The five million cars produced by the joint venture would need engines and other critical components that would be sourced from American Auto plants around the world, at least at the beginning. And the sale of the minority interest in

American Auto for an above-market price would generate immediate cash and a short-term windfall that would impress Wall Street.

For the Chinese, the benefits were longer term because that was the only thing that interested them. The technology infusion would enable them, assuming that they assimilated the technology as they intended, to develop an export auto industry over the long term that could best the hated Japanese. The Ministry had concluded that with labor content averaging about two thousand dollars per automobile, the huge advantage the Chinese could bring to bear in such costs was still not enough to overcome the technology advantage the Japanese possessed. The Chinese required a technology partner. The Europeans were too arrogant and old fashioned, and that left the Americans. They were the perfect partner, since their technology was first rate, but their business focus was incredibly short-term and naïve.

As they were preparing to leave to return to their respective homes, the man from the Ministry approached Dunlop, his hand outstretched, and a smile on his face. "Farewell, friend. You are one tough negotiator. I don't know if I should show my face to my superiors."

Dunlop laughed. "I think it's safe. You got what you wanted. And then some," he replied.

The man smiled, content that Dunlop was correct. He took a puff on his cigarette, then threw it down and stepped on it. "There is one small matter, trivial really, that you can help me with. I almost hate to mention it, because of its insignificance, but it troubles one of my colleagues."

Dunlop put his arm on the Chinese man's arm, and said, "This is hardly the time to start beating around the bush. Ask, and if it's in my power to accomplish, then I'll do what you ask."

Vampires

The man smiled. "Thank you," he said. "There is a lawsuit in your country. The same manufacturing equipment we plan to use in the joint venture factories killed a worker in your country. Quite unfortunate. My colleague feels that this could become an embarrassment and could give potential enemies of our deal some small opening to attack our alliance if the lawsuit proceeds and attracts news coverage. He asked me whether there isn't some way to make the lawsuit go away. I understand that one of your partners is representing American Auto in the case – a Mr. Cayhill. Perhaps you could talk to him."

"Consider it done," Dunlop said. "The case will soon be history. You have my word."

Chapter 8

Dunlop met with Cayhill two days after his return. He was in a buoyant mood. The American Auto Board had readily approved the agreement, the company had issued a press release outlining the barest bones of the deal, and the stock had surged.

"Congratulations, Preston," Cayhill said upon entering Dunlop's office. "And here I thought you had broken with old habits and actually taken a vacation."

Dunlop smiled and gave his usual answer. "In time, when business slows down. How are things with you? Speaking of taking it easy, I understand you're once again on a pace to win the award for most billable hours this year." He fished around on his desk, picking up a memo, and continued, "Here it is. It says that you are on a pace to break your old record of 3100 hours. Les, that's absolutely nuts. That's why we hire associates. Ruin their lives, not yours."

Cayhill responded only with a professional smile that signaled he was waiting to learn why Dunlop wanted to see him. Dunlop obliged. "Les, you are handling a wrongful death case involving manufacturing equipment made in China, aren't you?" Les nodded his head in the affirmative. "Yes," he answered. "The case is Chapman v. American Auto. The goddamned Chinese stripped the safety features from industrial equipment they made, against the advice of their American consultant, who then disappeared. An American worker was pulled into the machine and died an agonizing death, and his wife sued our client." Cayhill had delivered this summary of the case in a monotone. As he finished, he brightened, and added in a tone unaffected by the facts he had just related, "Why do you ask?"

Dunlop winced. He decided he did not like Cayhill, though a firm needed people like him – tough litigators who took no prisoners. "Because our friends the Chinese would like the case to be settled. If it is a question of money, I have been authorized by Gamble over at American Auto to go as high as twenty-five million dollars."

"It's not a question of more money," Cayhill said. "I already have a gen-erous offer on the table. "When I talked to plaintiff's counsel, he was having a hard time getting a decision from the widow. The last thing I want to do in such circumstances is to sweeten the pot without getting a response to the offer on the table. It would delay, not hasten things, to bid against my own offer."

"Well, you know best, of course," Dunlop said. "How long do you think it will drag on before settling?"

"A week or two. Maybe more," Cayhill said. When he saw the pained expression on Dunlop's face, he took from his jacket pocket the copy of the recently discovered Product Safety Commission memo he had brought to the meeting. Sliding it in front of Dunlop, he added, "Of course, the timing could be affected by whether I produce this document."

Dunlop's face flushed as he read. When he had finished, he looked at Cayhill, and said, "Geez, Les, we can't have that document come out. Or is it already out?"

"No, not yet. But they have filed a motion to compel and I will have to do something."

"Les, I don't need to tell you…" Dunlop began, but Cayhill interrupted.

"I know," Cayhill said. "I will do what I can."

Vampires

Chapter 9

Karansky had never been good enough at basketball to be a star, but he loved the game and played two nights a week when he could. It kept him content more or less, and it kept him fit. He had met Olga about a month earlier when he and three of his friends had gone to a bar for a beer following their usual Thursday night game. He had showered quickly but was still perspiring as the four of them, all in high spirits, pushed their way through a crowd and got close enough to the bar to order a round of drinks.

She was hard to miss. She was blonde and quite tall, and appeared to be by herself at the bar. He guessed that she was or had been a model; she was striking but looked to be about thirty. "You have got to be a model," he said. "Am I right?"

"I am a model, yes," she said with a slight accent. "But I do it because I like it, not because I have to."

He laughed, assuming she had been making fun of his question. But her blank and puzzled stare convinced him otherwise. Perhaps English was not her first language, which would explain her response. "You have an accent. Where are you from?"

"Pittsburgh," she replied. "My father is Swedish, though, and you can hardly understand a word he says." She smiled at him, and asked, "I guess I picked up some of his accent as I was growing up. Do you like it?"

"I adore it," he said. "Tell me, is there a Mr. Beautiful?" He for whatever reason was feeling brave enough to use what he thought was a very obvious effort at shameless flattery.

"I don't know. I don't know anyone by that name, but I don't know everyone. So I can't tell you whether he exists or not." Was she joking? She seemed entirely serious.

She caught his searching expression, and asked, "You are staring at me. Why?"

He smiled, and gave her an entirely honest answer, "Because you are very beautiful and I don't think I've ever met anyone like you before."

She smiled as well, and for the first time her features softened, as if she was letting down some invisible guard. "Thank you," she said. "You're very nice." They talked for another hour or so, during which he experienced a few more instances where she seemed unable to penetrate idiomatic expressions he'd used without even thinking about the fact that he'd used them. Still, the conversation was pleasant and he found himself unable to tear himself away. Finally, she gave a little yawn and asked if he would walk her home. He gave her a look, which she misinterpreted, but which prompted her to add, "Don't worry; it's only about a five minute walk." It took seven minutes, but they took their time. She finally stopped in front of a new building in which they still were selling units.

"This is you?" he asked.

"This is me," she answered. "Would you come up with me? I want to show you something."

He was unsettled. She was gorgeous but he had a nagging worry about their conversation. His delay in answering prompted her to add, "Don't worry; I'm not going to attack you. I really want to show you something."

He said "okay" this time without delay, and they went up the elevator to the eighth and top floor. She had a corner apartment. She took her keys from her purse and let them in. Taking his hand, she led him to the second of the bedrooms, which she used as a studio. As she turned on the light, he was surprised to see a large number of canvases both hanging on, and leaning against, the walls. "This is my studio," she announced simply.

He looked from canvas to canvas, his awe growing as he did. They weren't simply good; they were original and wonderful works, each one conveying emotion and each one penetrating the subject. The colors were brilliant. He didn't speak for several moments as he went from canvas to canvas, finally saying, "Olga, these are really, really good. I'm not just saying that. You have a real talent."

"I know," she replied honestly. "I wanted you to see them because I like you, and I didn't want you to think I was stupid." He started to protest but she interrupted, "Steven, I know I'm not book smart and I don't understand everything you say. But that doesn't mean I'm dumb."

He approached her and put his arms around her, part romantically and part in an effort to reassure her.

"Don't," she said. "Not tonight. There will be time for that if…well…" She let the sentence remain unfinished.

Vampires

He released her, saying, "May I see you again?"

She smiled at him. "Tomorrow night?" she asked, and the bargain was struck.

Chapter 10

Laura's office wasn't exactly glamorous; it had been and was still used as a file room, though it did have a window – a luxury that she'd likely not have had at a larger firm. Pam had actually made the room look attractive, cleaning off and polishing the large butcher-block table Karansky used as a work-table, putting a vase with a fresh lily in it on one corner, and a blotter and pen and pencil set where she imagined Laura would sit. It wasn't fancy but it looked like a place a lawyer could work.

Karansky stuck his head in about 8:45, asking, "Can I buy you a cup of coffee? I don't think I'm paying you enough for you to buy your own."

She smiled. "Where?" she asked.

"There's an old fashioned coffee shop near the corner." He looked at his watch. "At this time of day, the coffee is fresh. Don't try it in the late afternoon."

She grabbed her purse, stood up and said, "Love to." As they walked into the reception area, he repeated their destination for Pam's benefit, though he was certain given the proximity she'd already heard. "Pam, would you care to join us?" he added.

"No. Someone needs to stay to handle the rush of client calls I know we're about to receive," she responded.

Just at that moment the phone did ring. He smiled at Pam as if it were a small victory, while telling her to take a message, and giving Laura a gentle push towards the elevator. Before the doors could close, however, he heard Pam say in a voice too loud for the listener on the phone to be her only intended audience, "I'm sorry. You have the wrong number."

"Wiseass," Karansky muttered, but he smiled as he said it.

As they rode the elevator down the short distance to the lobby, Laura looked at him with a quizzical expression. He acknowledged it by giving her the same look back, and asking simply, "What?"

"I'm sorry, I'm being rude. I was really wondering about things that are none of my business," she replied.

"Like what?" he asked, curiously. "If you ask something I don't want to answer, I'll tell you."

She took a deep breath, thinking. Then, "Like don't you worry about whether you'll have enough clients to keep going? Like what do you expect to happen in the American Auto case?" She paused and then added, "Like I'm guessing that you're near forty years old. Have there been women in your life, and if so, where are they now?"

The doors opened and they stepped out. He laughed heartily, followed by a smaller chuckle. "Let's dispense with the first two questions, which I would guess you're not really interested in anyway." She started to protest but he held up his hand. "In any event, the answers are 'No' and 'I don't know.' We can tackle the third question once we get our coffee."

They didn't talk much until they sat down with two regular coffees. The owner who poured them their drinks didn't want to be bothered by what he considered "sissy drinks" despite the ability to charge two or three times as much. "I tell you what, Stevie," he had once told Karansky who had pointed out the missed revenue opportunity, "I pour an honest cup for an honest price. You want to pay double for the same thing with ten cents of syrup added to it, you're welcome to… somewhere else!" Since that conversation, Karansky always ordered a mocha grande latte and always happily accepted the regular coffee served in response. Laura started to say something when she saw the coffee cups they were given, but he cut her off, explaining why at the table.

"How strange," she commented. "You'd think he would want to make the extra money."

"It's not really that strange," Karansky responded. "There are people who do their jobs the way they think they should, and wouldn't do them any other way, even if they could make extra money. The fact that you are working for me tells me that you and he are a lot alike."

She blushed. "You're very clever, counselor, but we're supposed to be talking about you, not me," she said.

"True enough," he said. "Let's see, you wanted to know about the women in my life, right?"

Her face became a little red as she nodded yes but didn't speak. "I'm not really that complicated," he began. "I've been married once. Our love was only in one direction, which never works. She married me, I believe, for my earning potential, and ended up ditching me for a senior partner at the firm I was working at who had much greater earning potential. Hell, not just potential. He was already making more money than I ever dreamed of."

"That's horrible," Laura said, reacting as much to the pained expression on his face as he spoke as to the history itself.

"Well, it wasn't fun," Karansky admitted. "But it was therapeutic. I couldn't very well stay at the firm and have my reviews and salary dependent in part on him. I left that firm, worked for another one for two more years, then quit and started the firm you've now joined. I doubt I would've had the courage to turn my back on the wealth and comfort that my old life provided without the push my ex provided. She also prevented me from wasting even more years married to someone who didn't love me."

"I don't understand what attracted you to her in the first place," Laura said.

"Are you kidding? She was very sexy. I don't want to embarrass you, but there was a tremendous feeling of satisfaction in making love to her. I suspect, even knowing what I now know about her, that I would do the same thing all over again." He noticed her expression, and added, "You find that hard to understand?"

"Yes," she admitted.

"Your brain is wired differently than a man's, I think," he replied . "I'm glad I had the experience, though I'm even happier that it's in the past."

"And that's it? What about since your divorce?" Laura asked.

"I am going out with someone," he said. Her name is Olga Johannsen. She's very beautiful…" He paused.

"But…?" she prompted, trying to get him to continue.

"Yes," he said. "She has an incredible butt, but I think her beauty goes well beyond that." He laughed at his own joke, while Laura continued to look at him, waiting to see whether he would give a serious response.

"It's no fun to laugh alone," he said. "Look, if you're asking for my deep, dark thoughts on my relationship with Olga, I don't know you near well enough. And even if I did, I don't have it all figured out. I enjoy her company and I think she enjoys mine. That's already an improvement on my marriage. As for the rest, I'm trying to play that by ear."

They sat in awkward silence for a moment, while he thought about whether he should say something more, and she wondered whether she should ask anything else. His cell phone vibrated, and he fished around in his pocket, retrieved it and looked to see who was calling. It was Pam.

"After that wrong number, you actually did get a call from a potential new client," she said. "Are you available in an hour?"

"Sure," he said. "We're on our way back." To Laura he said, "Duty calls. C'mon, I want you to attend this meeting with me. Pam says we have a potential client coming in. Depending on what it is, you might want to take it."

"But I'm not even a member of the Bar yet," she protested.

"That's okay. You work under my supervision, and I am. But do me a favor. Don't volunteer that you're not yet a lawyer. It makes clients think they're entitled to reduced rates." And with that they began the short walk back to the office.

Vampires

Karansky resumed the conversation as they walked back. "Tomorrow is your turn, you know," he said.

"I don't know what you expect," she said. "I had one boyfriend in high school and one, a different one, in the first year of law school. I could cover them completely in about a minute."

"You may think you can, but I suspect you're missing some richness in the telling. No, let's wait until tomorrow," he said.

Chapter 11

The woman who wanted a lawyer showed up ten minutes early. Pam stuck her head in to let Karansky know she had arrived. "Well?" he whispered.

"Hard to call," Pam said, her voice muted. "She looks angry and like she's been crying. I don't know if she looks rich. Don't think so. I'd say her clothes come from J. C. Penny's, not Neiman Marcus."

"You're a cruel woman," Karansky said. "Lord knows what you say about me behind my back."

"The same thing I say to your face," Pam said, totally comfortable with saying what was on her mind. "I tell some people that you are eccentric and dress the way you do deliberately. Others I tell that you lost everything you had in your divorce except your ugly clothes. Which one I use depends on my mood, and the degree your choice of garments that day offends my sense of taste."

Karansky tried to look stern but failed. "Would you please do me two favors to compensate in a very small way for your insubordination. First, ask Laura to come in. And second, ask the lady whether she wants some coffee and if so go get her some. Then show her in."

"That's three," Pam said, before turning on her heel and leaving. He lost himself for a minute thinking three what, and then he heard the woman say, "Nothing, thank you." She walked in at the same moment as he figured out what Pam had meant. A moment later, Laura entered with a legal pad tucked under her arm.

"Hello, my name is Steven Karansky, and this is Laura Simon, my associate," Karansky said.

The woman seemed so uncomfortable that Karansky asked if something was wrong. "Mr. Karansky, even one attorney is going to be expensive. I know I can't afford two," she responded.

"Miss…?" he asked.

"Mrs. Parks, Susan Parks," she said.

"Well Mrs. Parks, I don't charge for an initial consultation. Depending on what you may need in the way of legal support, it may make sense for Laura to help you rather than me. I cost considerably more per hour than does she. But please don't worry about it now. I promise that we'll have a full discussion about fees before either of us does anything for which you'd get billed. Fair?"

"More than fair, Mr. Karansky. Thank you," she replied.

"Good. Then why don't you take your time and tell us why you're here?" Karansky asked.

"I want to sue the Coast Guard for the death of my son," she said. She bit her lip in an attempt to control her emotions, but lost the battle. Tears began forming in the corners of her eyes.

"Tell us what happened," Karansky said. "Include everything you remember even if it seems trivial to you. We need to have a complete picture."

"There's not much to tell," she said. "He was on a fishing boat out of Cape May that ran into a bad storm and sank. It was all over the news. Four fishermen died. One of them was my son. Mr. Karansky, they knew they were in trouble and they radioed over and over trying to get help. The Coast Guard admits receiving several SOSs over a three hour period when the boat was taking on water." She paused to blow her nose. When she resumed the sadness in her voice had been replaced by anger. "We also know that the Coast Guard didn't lift a finger to help them. They let those poor boys drown."

"That's hard to believe," Karansky said. "What makes you say that?"

"Oh, it's true all right. My husband is a cop, Mr. Karansky, and he talked to a number of people who knew the men on duty. They're irresponsible kids. They didn't help because they were having a party with two young women, under-age women on top of everything else. Their supervisor, who was supposed to be on duty, had a fight with his wife and spent the night in a bar, drinking away his sorrows."

"Mrs. Parks, did the Coast Guard do anything? Did they perhaps tell the people on the boat they were on their way?" Karansky asked.

"No, they did nothing. Nothing at all. They didn't even realize a boat had gone down until they read it in the newspapers the next morning. They then checked the logs and found the pleas for rescue. By then, of course, it was too late," she said.

"Ma'am, I am truly sorry for your loss. It doesn't make it any easier to tell you that we can't take the case."

Vampires

"But I've got some money. I can pay you," the woman said.

"It's not about money," Karansky said, as gently as he could. "The law is very unfair, but very clear." Karansky was silent for a moment as he thought about how best to explain it. "The Coast Guard," he began, "has no duty to rescue. None. They can stand by and watch someone drown and there would be nothing anyone could do. As long as they don't do something that actually worsens the position of those they are charged with helping, there is no liability. There was a case eerily similar to yours. Two families, including three young children perished in the Bermuda Triangle when their boat went down. You'll find accounts of it in the various books trying to make the boat sinkings in that area sound mysterious. There was no mystery, only under-trained would-be sailors betting that they could take on the elements and losing their bets.

"The people in that case also sent out repeated distress signals that were picked up all along the east coast. The Coast Guard rescue station personnel were having a Christmas Eve party and did nothing to help. The court ruled that the Coast Guard personnel were like "Good Samaritans," there to help if they want, but not liable if they did nothing."

Laura couldn't restrain her frustration with the injustice of it any longer, blurting out, "But that was one court. Surely when this matter gets to the appellate courts…"

Karansky interrupted her, shaking his head, "The decision I'm referring to was from the appellate court." He turned back towards the woman, and resumed, "Mrs. Parks, please understand that I think the law is wrong and that there ought to be some sort of compensation in situations like this. But there isn't. It would only compound the tragedy for me to pretend otherwise and take your money."

"It isn't right," Laura argued after the woman had left.

"I didn't say it was right; I said it was the law," he replied. "Here," and he jotted down the name of the case, "I don't remember the citation, but you can find it using this. Go read it and clear your head. Then, there is some research we need to do on the American Auto case to which I'd like you to turn your attention."

As he was writing down the name of the case, Pam came into the room, looking like the cat that had eaten the canary. "What's your problem?" Karansky asked.

"You have another visitor," Pam said. "And this one, unless I'm mistaken, is not looking for legal services." She winked licentiously.

Karansky was short on patience. He still had a bad taste in his mouth from the last meeting. "Pam, please. Just tell me who it is," he said in an exasperated voice.

"Her name is Olga Johannsen," Pam said, her grin now stretching from ear to ear. As usual, she refused to give into his moods.

"Oooohhh," chimed in Laura, "the girlfriend! Wait, let me take a peek!" She went up to the nearly closed door and looked out. "Oh, she's gorgeous!"

Karansky was surprised that Olga had come to his office. It was her first time, and he was a little taken aback. He liked to keep the two parts of his life separate. Karansky acted differently at work and at play; bring people together who knew him in the different settings and he worried whether he could satisfy their expectations of him.

Vampires

"Excuse me," he said, as he moved Laura to one side so he could leave his office and greet Olga. She looked nervous and was twirling her hair behind her right ear. "Is everything okay?" he asked. "I wasn't expecting to see you."

"I thought that I would surprise you and take you to lunch," Olga said. "I hope it's okay that I came."

Was it? He felt awkward certainly, but that wasn't her fault. Karansky looked at his watch. It was only a few minutes after eleven, hardly time yet for lunch. He was about to point this out, but was interrupted by Pam's and Laura's entry. "Aren't you going to introduce us to this lovely lady?" Pam asked.

Karansky acted like an awkward boy being reminded of his manners. "I'm sorry," he said, "Olga, this is Pam Horan, my office manager and that is Laura Simon, the new attorney I was telling you about." There were smiles and "how do you do's" and a few truncated attempts to make conversation. Most were banalities that none of them would have been able to remember five minutes after they were said. Karansky did remember Olga's comment to Laura that "Steven didn't mention how pretty you are," and Laura's response that "He did tell me that you were beautiful. But he didn't tell me that you were this beautiful."

What could be bad about two women telling each other how pretty each was? Theoretically there was nothing wrong with it, but Karansky nonetheless had a very bad feeling about the exchange. The problem was they were not simply telling each other they were pretty; they were sharing what he had told each privately about the other. That changed everything. He couldn't explain it logically, but he could feel the tension and knew this was not a healthy situation.

"So where do you want to go for lunch?" he asked Olga.

"Are you sure you have the time?" she asked. "I don't want to take you away from your work." This noble sentiment was expressed while she was looking at Laura.

At this point, Pam intervened. "For God's sake, would the two of you go enjoy yourselves?" As she said this, she pushed Karansky towards the door. He gratefully accepted the push, since his goal in the last few minutes had been to go anywhere with one of these two women. Olga's departure was more reluctant; she didn't want to go just yet. She wanted to know why Karansky had talked about her to that new attorney, but had not shared anything about Laura with her. She thought Laura was a bit short, and her breasts a bit too small, to be beautiful. But her face was cute, and if she dressed with more understanding of what made women sexy, she could be trouble! Olga gave him a big smile, and said, "Coming honey!" Then with a smile to Pam and a blank stare at Laura, she joined Karansky, who had already retreated into the elevator.

Chapter 12

"I don't like her," Olga said, frowning. They had just sat down at a table at the Grand Café, a wonderfully classic French restaurant.

"Who?" Karansky asked, hoping she meant anyone but Laura.

"Your new lawyer. What was her name?" Olga asked.

"Laura Simon," he answered, with an inward groan. "Aren't you being a little unfair? You just met her for an instant. She's really very nice. And I think she's going to be an excellent lawyer."

If Karansky thought that defending Laura would help defuse the situation, he was sadly mistaken. "Why did you tell her that I was pretty?" Olga asked.

"Because you are," he replied.

"I'm also an artist. Did you tell her that too?" she demanded.

"No," he admitted.

"Don't you see," Olga pressed. "Your Miss Simon is pretty but you described her to me as a good lawyer. I've other things going on too, but you describe me just by my physical appearance. You take me less seriously. Steven, has it occurred to you that you're sleeping with the wrong woman?" The question skewered him. She asked it not with anger, but with sincerity. He could have dealt with anger, but her sincerity deserved the same in return.

"I don't know," he said. "I really don't know." It was the best he could do. It wasn't enough.

"Well, if you figure it out, call me," Olga said quietly. She folder her napkin, put it back on her plate, and slowly stood up. Taking the few steps necessary to stand by him, she leaned over and kissed him on the cheek. Saying, "Goodbye Steven," she walked gracefully out of the restaurant.

Karansky felt a surge of affection and admiration for Olga that made him want to run after her and bring her back by telling her what she wanted to hear. He remained rooted in his chair, however, because he felt she was right. She was an exceptional and beautiful woman. But he wasn't in love with her, and she had realized it before he had.

Chapter 13

The following morning, Laura stuck her head into Karansky's office and asked, "Coffee?"

"Why not?" he said, getting up from his chair. They walked side-by-side to the coffee shop, once again not talking much along the way. Karansky again ordered two lattes. They collected their coffees, and sat at a table near the window.

"How was your lunch?" she asked. "Olga is a beautiful woman."

"She is more than that," he said. Then he sighed. "She broke up with me because she told me that I didn't love her."

"Well, do you?" she asked.

"No, I think she was right," he answered. "Lust, yes. Great affection, yes. But the love of Romeo and Juliet, no. I wish I did. It would make life so much simpler." Karansky's thoughts had been engaged in a comforting fantasy with Olga, where he was in love with her. He gradually focused on where he was, and realized that she had been staring at him. He shook it off, and said, "Today was supposed to be about you. So, what makes Laura Simon tick?"

"Well, I don't want this to sound corny but right now it's my job," she replied. "It's exhilarating to know that I could actually go into court and argue for something noble. You're probably so used to feeling that way that it doesn't seem extraordinary any more. But I am nearly walking on air!"

Karansky searched her face for hints of sarcasm but found none. "God, she means it!" he thought to himself. He tried to remember ever feeling that idealistic and couldn't. His personality had always been tainted with too much cynicism. He looked at her as a father would look at his twelve-year-old daughter who still believed in Santa Clause, finding it charming at the same time he found it disconcerting. He hoped knowledge of the way the legal system really worked when it came didn't crush her enthusiasm for the profession she had chosen.

He took a sip of coffee and changed the subject. "Okay, boyfriends," he said. "You are an attractive young lady with an income. Not a great income, but still enough of one to tempt your share of deadbeats. Where are the young men?"

She shuddered involuntarily. "The young men are chasing even younger girls who, as Springsteen sang, all "promise to unsnap their jeans.""

"And you haven't made such promises?" he asked. "Surely there have been…" he began.

"…two," she said finishing his sentence. "One was while I was in high school; the other in law school."

"What about college?" he asked. "Do you mean to tell me you tasted gay Paris and went back to live on the farm?"

She gave him an odd look.

"It's a generational thing," he said.

Laura didn't get the reference but continued anyway. "My high school romance lasted until the end of freshman year in college. He was sweet," she said, looking wistful as she remembered something she didn't share. "But he changed schools and while we wrote each other for awhile, it didn't last. We had agreed that there wouldn't be strings and he found someone else."

Karansky was silent as he waited for her to finish. She sat for a moment before continuing, "The romance in law school began the first day of my second year. He was a year ahead of me, and Editor-in-Chief of the law review. He had it all, including the looks of a Greek god." Laura blushed as she said this, and he thought to ask her something to get her out of an uncomfortable memory, but it was unnecessary as she resumed. "Everything was fine until he got a job offer based in Los Angeles. It was a good offer, which he accepted without talking to me. He asked me to dinner, told me he had accepted the offer, and proposed. There was a catch though. He wanted me to leave law school without finishing my last year, and move to LA with him that summer. He had the answer to the question that plagues most professional women: how to balance career and family. He told me I should give up my career and follow him and have his children. I wasn't ready to do that."

Karansky sat looking at his hands not knowing what to say. "I'm sorry," he managed at last. "It's a tough issue, but you did the right thing. For you."

"I think so, although there have been times when I was looking for a job or have seen a young mother with a baby in her arms when I've wondered," she said, looking him full in the face, pain showing in her expression.

Vampires

"I'm an optimist," he offered. "You're young, too young to give up on finding Mr. Right and to settle for Mr. Wrong, which this guy clearly was. Anyone who could have demanded that of you, knowing how important your career was to you, had to be incredibly shallow and selfish." Then, not wanting to end the conversation on such a serious note, he added, "Okay, the guy was a jerk, but look at it this way: by taking a job with me, you have solved your romantic problems. You won't have the time to worry about good and bad dates. In fact, you probably won't have the time to date at all."

She wasn't certain whether he was joking or not. She decided he was, and responded with a dry, "Thanks, you make me feel so much better."

"Now all is not lost. It's love that takes time; sex can be quick. It's love that your career choice makes difficult. Take a look at the private lives of most lawyers at firms, and you'll find fairly active sex lives. Some even with their spouses."

"Stop," she said. "You are way too cynical for me. Have some pity on me – I don't want to give up on love. Even as an overworked attorney. Sex is part of love; as long as there is love, the sex will take care of itself."

"It generally does," he mumbled.

"What was that?" she asked.

"I said that I agree with you that sex without love is empty and that even if you invited me to have sex with you I wouldn't do it unless I also knew you loved me," he said.

"You said all that, huh?" she said, laughing. "Well, cowboy, I suggest you keep your pistol in its holster. Yesterday, you were going out with Olga. I don't intend to be the next notch on your gun."

"I come in peace," he said. "Unarmed."

"More like armed and dangerous," she quipped, laughing again. Neither of them said anything further, but the discussion triggered thoughts in each of their minds about what a relationship with the other might be like. He was the first to smile, but her smile, when it did appear, lasted a much longer time.

Vampires

Chapter 14

Laura Simon's former neighbor and good friend could not have been more different from her. Laura was a life-long Democrat, liberal to her core. Cecelia was equally conservative and Republican. Laura was not exactly a slob, but was not a fashion statement either. Her favorite outfit was jeans with a man's cotton shirt, which always managed to pick up a stain or two from being worn when she cooked or ate. Cecelia had been partners with her husband in the fashion industry, in fact had been the genius responsible for turning their business into the success that it became. One morning Cecelia had awakened to realize she'd been totally outmaneuvered by her husband. She had left the business side to him; her strength having been in design, All the papers her husband had her sign over the years ensured the business belonged solely to him. She was left to claim the value of her shares in their divorce.

Predictably, the year of her divorce, the business – now run solely by him – suffered financially. Costs went up, revenues went down, and profits all but disappeared. Her attorney recommended a forensic accounting firm to her, which she had agreed to retain. Their report concluded that the value of her shares was, optimistically, a million dollars. Tops. Her divorce settlement had been based on that. Now, a year and a half later, the business had been sold for forty-five million dollars. She related all of this to Laura at the dinner the two of them were sharing to celebrate Laura's new job.

"Cecilia, how could this be?" Laura asked, incredulously. "Did anything miraculous happen to the business to turn it from the near-broken shell your accounting firm had said it was to the highly profitable design house a larger company had willingly paid a king's ransom in order to acquire?"

Cecilia thought for a minute, before answering, "Not that I'm aware of, although I have to admit that I know so little about accounting that I wouldn't have been able to spot anything that the accounting firm had done incorrectly." When Laura offered to look at the report for her, and to share it with a classmate who had an accounting background, Cecelia surprised her by confessing that she didn't have a copy of the report, had never seen it, and couldn't get it now.

"Cecilia," Laura protested, "that's your report. You're entitled to it. I assume you paid for it."

"Well, not exactly," her friend replied, sounding embarrassed. "My law firm told me it was better to have them retain and pay the accounting firm. Something about preserving the reports as privileged." Laura shook her head in agreement, explaining if counsel hired an expert, his work could be hidden from opponents if you chose not to use it by the attorney-client privilege. Cecilia continued, "That's what we did. The law firm hired the accounting firm, and I paid the law firm and they in turn paid the accounting firm. Well, the law firm says the report belongs to them and that they won't share a copy with me unless I bring my bill with them current."

"How much do you owe?" Laura asked.

"They say I owe another fifty-three thousand dollars for their services. That's on top of the quarter million dollars I already paid them. They also say they owe the accounting firm another twenty thousand dollars, which I in turn owe them, bringing the total to seventy three thousand dollars. And are you ready for the best part? Both the law firm and the accounting firm are willing to forgive the debt, provided I sign a release promising not to bring claims against them for anything they might have done, or not done. If I don't either pay or agree to the release, the law firm told me they will have no alternative but to bring a lawsuit to collect what they're owed. I suppose the cherry on top is their reminding me that the retainer agreement I signed with them stated if they do sue to collect their bill, I am responsible for their attorney's fees. They estimate that would be another fifty thousand dollars."

Laura was outraged and said so. Cecilia was frustrated, and asked the obvious question, "But what am I to do? I'd have to come up with more money than I have to fight this. I feel the same outrage as you, but I don't have the money to pay their damned bills. I even consulted with another attorney. He told me to settle because, as he put it, 'my chances are between slim and none to challenge the professional competence of a respected accounting firm.' He told me I'd be lucky if I could even find an accounting firm that would testify against another 'member of the club.'"

"How long do you have to make a decision?" Laura asked. "Do you at least have until tomorrow?"

"Yes, I'm sure I do," her neighbor said, "At least I think I do. Why?"

"I don't know. It seems pretty hopeless," she agreed. "But I'd like you to see the man I'm working for and see what he has to say. He seems to have a lot of experience. Maybe he'll know what to do."

"Will he see me?" Cecelia asked.

Vampires

"I'm not sure. But I'm having lunch with him and Pam, our office manager, tomorrow," Laura replied. "I will tackle him then."

Chapter 15

Cecelia returned home from dinner with Laura to find Larry Eagles in her apartment, slightly drunk. "Larry," she said, trying to keep the irritation from her voice, "what are you doing here?" She appraised his condition as he started to get up from the sofa where he'd been sitting. Larry had had more than one or two, she decided, as he struggled to stand up. She sighed, and decided she'd need to keep him there overnight for his own good. She put her hands gently on his shoulders, and pushed him back down. "Sit, Larry," she said affectionately, plopping down on his lap. She gave him a brief kiss, and asked, "So, how did the game go today?"

Larry Eagles was a baseball player. The son of a rabid football fan living near Philadelphia who had actually changed the family name from Patovsky to Eagles, in honor of the football team there, Larry had disappointed his father by choosing baseball over football, the latter being the only game played by real men. But Larry loved baseball, and was very, very good at it. Unfortunately, in the semi-finals of the high school state championship, he'd torn a ligament in his knee trying to steal third base. He'd undergone strenuous rehabilitation, not made easier by his father's recitation of how this or that running back would have been shaking off three hundred pound tacklers by now had they suffered the same superficial injury. He'd recovered, but word passed among the professional scouts that he'd lost a step defensively. This was enough to prevent him from being drafted out of high school. He didn't have the money or the grades to play in college, so he'd ultimately hooked up with a minor league team, playing in New Jersey.

Two things kept Larry Eagles from getting a shot at the pros: first was his knee, which though he'd recovered, still gave him trouble pushing off as he started to move to his left. The second problem was that he couldn't consistently hit a big league curve ball. Not too many pitchers in the minors could throw them so it didn't hurt him much, but this, added to the injury, was enough to keep him from reaching the major leagues.

Larry and Cecelia had met building a house for Habitat for Humanity. The baseball team and a local bank had co-sponsored the build, and while Cecelia didn't work at the bank she had a friend who did and persuaded her, now that she was divorced, to come help. Maybe, the friend had giggled, she'd get lucky with one of the ball players that were supposed to show up.

Larry Eagles had shown her how to hammer a nail. He had watched her struggling to assemble the rear steps to the house, and had offered to help. She was blessed with slightly larger than average breasts and an athletic, small bottom – an intoxicating mixture that left most men wondering how to attract her attention. He was wearing only an abbreviated undershirt, and his biceps bulged with each swing. This, and the fact he was volunteering his time had impressed her sufficiently so that at the end of the day when some of the participants went out to a Thai restaurant to celebrate the day, she'd accepted his invitation to join them.

Cecelia had an optimistic personality. It had developed over the years, in part as a result of the sort of attention a very sexy woman attracts. Men went out of their way to do things for her. She was gracious but not giving in return. Still, one tends to see the positive side of things when half the species would make fools of themselves for a chance to get into one's pants. Larry had made it clear that he was no different in what he wanted, but he had a sadness in his eyes that at first she thought meant he was "soulful." She didn't let him make love to her the first night, though there wasn't an inch of her that he wasn't familiar with by the time she finally told him to go 'because it wasn't going to happen on a first date.

It happened about five minutes into their second date. He had kissed her at the door, at first a modest kiss, but one that she prolonged by opening her mouth so that any sense of his exercising restraint went out the window. He tried undoing her pants first, but she was too busy kissing him to help. After a brief experiment with her belt buckle during which he made no progress, he instead slipped his hand inside her pants, creating enough room to move it around until he felt her wetness. They staggered to a nearby sofa, and this time she helped take her clothes off.

The sex, she had to admit, was as good as she'd had. But you can't stay aroused constantly and she became concerned about how to fill the rest of their time together. She didn't mind that he was an athlete, or even one who was for whatever reason had limited potential. What did concern her was his reaction to his situation, which was a pervading gloom. She didn't broadcast her own troubles, and was having a difficult time knowing how to deal with Larry, who wore his troubles on his sleeve for the world to see.

"I hit two doubles today," he said. "That lifts my average to .311, second highest on the team. But after the second hit, in the sixth inning with one out, the goddamned third base coach signaled for me to steal third! Can you fucking believe it? The numb-nuts called for me to try the same thing I tore up my knee trying to do once before."

"What happened?" she asked.

Vampires

"What happened?" he mimicked derisively. "What the hell do you think happened? I took off with the next pitch. I was thrown out by two feet!"

"I'm sorry, honey. Maybe next time…" she began.

"You don't get it, do you? It wasn't just that I got thrown out. He was testing me to see if I still had the speed and was willing to use it," he said. "I failed the fucking test!"

Cecelia sat not knowing what to say. Larry became restless, lifted her off, and threw her on the empty part of the sofa. He stood up, went to the refrigerator and took out the fifth beer of a six-pack he had brought with him. He opened the bottle, took a long drink, looking at her as he did. Then, putting the bottle down on the counter, he went back to the sofa and sat next to her. Larry tried to kiss her but she turned her head. He pushed her down on the sofa and got on top of her, pinning her with his greater weight. She felt him becoming aroused even with their clothes between them. As he pawed at her breasts, Cecelia brought her knee up as hard as she could. His exhalation of breath confirmed that she had connected. He rolled off her, crying, "I'm sorry, I'm sorry," over and over.

She stood up, looking down on him with her hands on her hips. Larry looked back, his face tear streaked, as if her forgiveness was the only thing that mattered. Cecelia softened a little, and taking that as a sign that he might make her forget or at least forgive him, he got on his knees with his head against her stomach. Placing his hands on the small of her back, he said "I'm sorry" one last time. She sighed, and relenting somewhat, put her hands on either side of his face, lifting it so that he was looking up at her. "Don't ever, ever do that again," she warned. "Is that clear?"

Larry shook his head yes, and started to rise, kissing her on the breasts as he did. In spite of herself, Cecelia felt a quickening of her pulse, and a pleasant heat began to envelope her. Before she succumbed to the mood completely, Cecelia made a promise to herself that this would be the last time, and that Larry was, or would soon be, history. She saw the violence in him, and knew that on some other night she might not be so lucky. Having made this promise, she moaned, leaned over and kissed him, and let herself live in the moment without worrying about the future.

Chapter 16

Karansky was in a foul mood. He'd hoped to get a quick hearing on the motion to compel, because he believed that American Auto was hiding something. Instead, the company's counsel requested extra time in which to file their response to the motion, which the judge granted, so that their pleading opposing his wouldn't be due for 21 days. With the judge's cramped schedule, they wouldn't have a hearing for over a month. Meanwhile, the clock was ticking on the settlement offer. Cayhill had put a ten day time period on the offer, after which it would expire. That meant whatever documents American Auto might be hiding wouldn't have to be produced until after a decision on settlement would have to be made. If they settled, no documents would ever be produced. If they didn't settle, then his sale of the settlement would be considered in default under its terms, and the company that had paid him the two million dollars could seize his house and sell it to raise the money to satisfy his debt to them. "God, what a mess," he thought.

He tried to clear his mind of such things as he walked into the centuries old home that housed the restaurant. Scalini Fedeli was a very charming smaller restaurant with the reputation for serving up probably the best, and almost certainly the most expensive, Italian food in northern New Jersey. He'd never been there before, but then he'd never had two million dollars before. He looked at his watch as he was ushered into the room, and saw both Pam and Laura sitting there. Both were dressed more carefully than usual. He had seen Pam dressed well before and was not surprised. She had lived long enough so that her face took on the character of the individual inside; hers was expressive and kind, with etched care lines around her eyes, to which he no doubt had been a major contributor.

Seeing Laura dressed elegantly was a first for him and he was surprised. He thought of her primarily as an attorney, one that billed clients at the rate of, hmmm, he would say two hundred and fifty hundred dollars an hour. He would raise it once she passed the bar. But she was more than an attorney; she was an attractive young woman.

As he sat down, he asked "Am I late?"

 "No, right on time," Pam answered. "Laura asked me to come a few minutes early." She looked at Laura and grinned, saying, "She wanted advice about how to approach you on something."

"And what did you say?" The answer was delayed by the waiter, a gracious and very serious person with a heavy Italian accent who came over and spent the next five minutes going over the specials of the day. Finally, he was done. Karansky repeated, "What advice did you give Laura on whatever she asked about?"

Laura answered, "She told me just to ask you directly." She paused. Karansky looked at her expectantly. "I have a friend…" and she told him Cecelia's story. "What do you think?" she inquired once she was done.

He sighed. "I think your friend has almost certainly been screwed. That happens in life quite a lot, I find. Here's the most troubling part of life in the big city," he said gently, "there is not a remedy for every injustice. Your friend's situation is just like the Coast Guard failure-to-rescue case, only here it's not a question of legal right and wrong, but the practical ability to get to the truth." She stared at him, her big eyes showing defiance rather than acceptance. "Look," he continued, "your friend is in a box. She has to come up with over seventy thousand dollars just to find out whether she has a case. She doesn't have the money, nor does she have the additional funds to pursue a case if she finds out she has one. Under the circumstances, she ought to take the offer and sell the case she can't pursue for relief from the fees that she can't pay."

He watched Laura as he talked, expecting her to look dejected. She didn't; she looked angry. She hadn't given up yet. "I don't accept your not-every-wrong-has-a-remedy speech," she said. "If that's true, then there is something wrong with our system of justice."

"There's a lot wrong with our system of justice," he interrupted.

"There is only if those participating in it let it be," she interrupted right back. "I would have expected that response from others. I had hoped that you would be different."

Karansky looked painfully at this young idealist sitting across from him, and said, "What would you want me to do?" He was exasperated. Lunch wasn't going as he had anticipated. "She doesn't have the money to start a fight. You know that! And I expect that she's up against some heavyweight lawyers and accountants."

"You're right," she said. "Cecelia doesn't have the money. But I can't believe that it's right to allow her to be bullied this way, in order to get her to waive her rights! I mean, you have plenty of money, judging by this lunch! Couldn't you afford to make her a loan that could be repaid out of the proceeds that she'd receive?" Pam, who had been taking a drink of water when Laura had started this last tack, sprayed it inadvertently over her companions when the statement about Karansky's wealth had been made. She'd started to say something but looked over at him first, and saw him shake his head "no." She instead contented herself for the moment with a mumbled apology.

Laura picked up on the by-play between the two, "Did I say something wrong?" she asked.

Karansky felt responsible for preserving her intoxicatingly naïve belief in the power of right over wrong. He answered, "Nothing wrong, Laura. You didn't mention the name of the law firm harassing your friend."

"Sorry," she answered. "But you won't be surprised. It is our good friends at Dunlop & Schmidt." Karansky felt twinges of anger. He was surprised. Dunlop & Schmidt was an elite firm, not one that he'd have suspected of playing hardball to extract a release from a young woman. There was more here than met the eye. He asked the next question, his voice very low and serious, "And the accountants?"

She rummaged in her purse and said "aha" as she emerged with a rumpled scrap of paper, on which she had written the name. "Scott Wendells," she said, "at Reliable Accounting, LLC."

Karansky's blood reached boiling point. He said simply, "Have her come by in the morning if she wants to pursue this." To Pam, he said, "Whenever you can fit her in." Looking at Laura again, he said, "You bring her." Then, pushing his chair back, he looked at Pam first and then Laura, "I must go do something. Please, it's very important the two of you stay and have a nice lunch. For one thing, a place like this will probably charge us anyway if you don't. I'm sorry I can't stay." And with that he left.

Chapter 17

Karansky was almost certain it was the same name, but he wanted, no needed to, eliminate any room for error. When he got back to the office, he went directly to Laura's office, which still doubled as the file room. Pam did a masterful job of keeping him organized and with her help, he could generally find what he wanted. The trick would be doing it without her.

He began looking for a file on one of his first cases in private practice, one from which he had learned a great deal, but also one he still felt guilty about losing. He'd been up against Dunlop & Schmidt, Les Cayhill more specifically. Cayhill had retained the Reliable Accounting Firm to represent his client in that case. Karansky looked at a book of pleadings, put it back, and pulled out an earlier one. There it was! The accounting study had concluded the private company in that case had been worthless. And the accountant who had prepared the report was…Scott Wendells!!

There is nothing wrong with an accountant representing a defendant in one case and a plaintiff in another. But there was something very wrong with an accountant purporting to represent one side while he was secretly working for the other. Karansky didn't know for sure that had happened. But he was suspicious. For one thing, the attorney in both cases was the same – Les Cayhill. What if Cayhill and Wendells had developed a relationship while both were working on the first matter, and they had decided to have Wendells become something like a

Trojan horse where he'd be hired by plaintiffs in Cayhill's cases, and then prepare studies that in fact were slanted in favor of the defendants?

Karansky didn't trust the discovery process, at least when it came to Dunlop & Schmidt. They had a way of making it very expensive and very time consuming to get even the most basic information. He decided to go on line, and searched for Wendells' name in the Superior Court records of all townships in New Jersey. He immediately got a list of thirteen cases. In all but the first of these, the case in which he had testified for the defendant against Karansky, Wendells had represented the plaintiff. He wasn't certain the list was exhaustive; it probably wasn't, because it only included those cases in which the accountant's testimony had been mentioned in a published opinion. There were more cases that were decided without a written opinion, so he guessed he was looking at a small percentage of the total cases.

He looked closer at the decisions, looking next for the results of the cases. Three of the cases had been settled following the decision and thus no results were given. The terms of settlement would be private, so these cases would yield no clues. Of the ten remaining, six of the cases had resulted in only nominal awards for the plaintiff, three had resulted in substantial awards, and one was still pending.

Next he looked at counsel. He started to get excited as he found Cayhill's name appear as counsel, or his firm appear as counsel, in three, then four cases. Of these, three had resulted in awards to plaintiff, but in amounts so low as to be clear wins for the defendant. The fourth case had a sizeable award. He wondered how many forensic accountants were active in the area and whether it was significant Cayhill and Wendells were involved in the same cases four times.

As he thought about this Karansky heard the soft but clear click of the front door lock being put back in place. Someone had entered through the front door. He tried but couldn't remember if Pam had scheduled any appointments for him that afternoon. Karansky logged off quickly, and yelled, "I'll be there in a second," so that the visitor wouldn't think no one was there. He stood up, and began walking out of his office into the reception area when he heard the same soft click. Whoever had come into the office had just left! He looked around, and saw nothing out of the ordinary. This was Pam's domain. She kept it neat, at least compared to his space. The only clutter on her desk was a pile of documents that he had asked her to stamp with a Bates stamp, a mechanical stamp that numbered documents sequentially. Then he saw the drawer to her desk open. He knew that was where she kept the petty cash for the office. She kept the drawer unlocked at his insistence, since he could never find his key but frequently needed cash after hours when she was not there. Pam never would have left the drawer open like it was now. He opened the drawer completely and took out the little metal box in which the cash was held. It was empty.

Even though he'd just given her a thousand dollars to put into petty cash, he was relieved this was all the damage the intruder had done. Satisfied he'd made real progress on the computer search and satisfied too that the intruder had been costly but no big deal, he decided to go downstairs to his bank, get another thousand dollars and replace the petty cash. There was no need to worry Pam about it.

Because Karansky had assumed the intruder had entered for the purpose of taking something away, he neither searched for, nor found, the document that had been added to the pile of paper on Pam's desk. The intruder, for his part, was doubly satisfied with the events of the day; not only had he been richly paid for the simple task of leaving behind a document in the lawyer's office, but he'd also found and taken the five hundred dollars he had found in the desk. He was relatively honest as thieves go, and told the man who had paid him to leave the document behind that he had found and taken some money, though he'd reduced the sum in his report to two hundred dollars. The man had laughed and told him to keep it as a tip for a job well done.

It was an afternoon where almost everyone involved was satisfied with the way the day had gone. The intruder for obvious reasons thought he had done well; Lester Cayhill, who had paid the thief to leave the document in Karansky's office, was pleased that not only had it been done as he had asked, but that the man, by taking the money, had covered his tracks; Laura was satisfied with the fact that she'd presented her neighbor's case so forcefully; and Karansky was satisfied that he was going to uncover a scheme by which a major accounting firm was selling its services to plaintiffs while secretly working for the defendants. Only Pam, whose nervous nature had made her take half of the petty cash from her desk as she left for lunch, felt a vague disquiet that she couldn't understand.

Chapter 18

Karansky walked into his conference room, and extended his hand first to Chapman's widow, and then to her stepson. "I'm sorry to intrude, but I felt we needed to talk again," he began.

The stepson rolled his eyes theatrically, interrupting with, "I thought we'd decided last time that we'd make a decision on settlement after receiving their response to all your questions and document requests." He looked at the widow who clearly was uncomfortable with the conflict between advisor and stepson, and demanded of her, "Well, mother," almost demeaning her title with his tone, "Isn't that what we decided for the umpteenth time last time?"

"Yes," she answered quietly. "Mr. Karansky, has something changed?"

He answered back, looking only at her, "I'm afraid so. The judge granted defendant's request for more time to provide us with their documents, which means they're not obligated to give us anything until after the time on their settlement offer runs out."

"That's just great," the stepson grumbled, as if the court order was many times worse than it was. He continued, "You just seem to keep getting outflanked by these guys."

"Mrs. Chapman," Karansky said, ignoring him, "maybe we would have found something and maybe we wouldn't. It doesn't really matter now.

Vampires

Defendant has offered ten million dollars. That's a lot of money. You need to decide whether to take it."

"What would you do, Mr. Karansky?" she asked.

"I can't decide for you," he replied, hoping she would make the decision without him.

"I know that. I am asking you what you would do if you were me," she said.

He sighed deeply. "Mrs. Chapman, please understand I have a vested interest in this matter that may not coincide with yours." She looked confused and admitted as much. Her helpful stepson interrupted, saying, "What he means, ma, is that if he can talk you into settling the case cheaply, he still gets a huge payout."

Karansky bristled. "Young man, I say what I mean and need no translation services from you." He turned, once again making eye contact with the widow. "Your stepson is right that ordinarily an attorney operating on contingent fee gets a windfall if the case settles, which is why you must take everything I say with a grain of salt. It's also true that ten million dollars is a lot of money. It is possible that we could get more; but we could get less, maybe much less. If I were making the decision I think I would take the offer. We're up against very tough opponents and I think it's a fair offer."

The stepson snorted and started to speak. But this time the widow cut him off, "That's enough Will. I have made my decision. Mr. Karansky, you've been fair to me and I want to thank you. I will take your recommendation. It's time to bring my husband's life to a close. In some way I suppose the lawsuit was a way of delaying that, but I want peace. Please settle this as soon as possible."

Chapter 19

The man who had entered Karansky's office had made it to Atlantic City, where he'd quickly lost the five hundred dollars he had taken, as well as a thousand dollars of his own. The casino personnel spotted him, bought him a fancy dinner with an expensive bottle of wine, and offered him his choice of an advance of ten thousand dollars or a woman for the night. He took the cash, thinking that if he did well enough he could always get a girl later. Not surprisingly, however, he did not do so well. In fact, he almost set a record for how fast one could lose ten thousand dollars playing blackjack at the one hundred dollar table.

The same helpful personnel now inquired how he was going to pay the ten thousand dollars. He called the emergency number Cayhill had given him, and then hung up. Cayhill called back on a cell phone registered to a Haitian company, and said simply, "Yes?"

"Mr. C.," said the man, "I want to change the payment arrangements. I sort of need the money wired tonight."

"I have made no such arrangements," Cayhill said.

"But you could," protested the man.

"Yes, but that was not the deal. Making such arrangements would be expensive."

"Mr. C.," the man said, "I need the full amount. Perhaps there's some other small job I could do for you?"

"Great minds think alike," Cayhill said. "How are your computer skills? Can you find financial information about somebody?"

"I'm the best," the man asserted, "Just give me his social security number and I'll get you his life story."

Cayhill had copied Karansky's social security number from the latter's annual certification to the state bar association, attesting that Karansky had met his requirement for continuing legal education. Cayhill had joined the otherwise thankless bar committee overseeing the standards just so he could gain access to the information on bar members the forms contained. He now provided Karansky's social security number to the man, saying, "Listen, the man who owns this number has been spreading money around. I'd like to find out where he is getting it. Can you do that?"

"I can," the man answered. "When can I get my money?"

"I'll set up the wire now. I will have it ready in an hour. It goes immediately upon my receipt of the information."

About an hour and a half later, after the second transaction had been completed, Cayhill was looking at the printout in wonder. "Damn, Karansky has balls!" he muttered to himself. The idea of selling the settlement value before it had been received was clever, but very risky. It also meant that Karansky was stretched financially. He smiled to himself. Time to make the chickens come home to roost.

The following day was the last day the settlement offer remained open. Karansky, his client now on board, had scheduled a meeting with

Cayhill at ten in the morning, and entered five minutes before that. He thought that this would be an educational experience for Laura and had brought her as well. When she walked in, Cayhill did a double take, recognizing but not quite placing her.

"You interviewed me," she told him. "I didn't get the job."

"Ah, my mistake. Nice work," he said, holding up the motion to compel. "I know when I've made too hasty a judgment. Let me know if you ever want to change the name on, and the amount of, your paycheck."

Laura nodded politely as she sat down next to Karansky, opposite Cayhill. She was surprised that Cayhill was alone, with none of the many attorneys he had working on the case in attendance. She didn't have the time to dwell on it, as the meeting began in earnest.

"Thank you for seeing us," Karansky said.

"Always willing to talk," Cayhill responded. "Let's see, this is about American Auto, isn't it?" he said as he pulled a file from a stack on the table and opened it. "Ah yes, we had an open offer to settle the case for ten million dollars." He looked up at Karansky.

"Which my client would like to accept," Karansky said.

"Yes, no doubt she would," Cayhill said. "The problem we have is that my client has instructed me to pull that offer off the table."

Karansky was seldom taken completely by surprise. He was now. He stared at Cayhill who added, "Look, it doesn't mean that they're not interested in settling. But the offer has been reduced from ten million to five."

Vampires

Karansky felt the blood drain from his face. Forcing his voice to remain calm, he said, "May I ask why?"

Cayhill looked at him for a minute and then said, "Well, I don't see the harm in telling you. Rumor has it that you're in possession of a doctor's report, stating that the plaintiff died nearly instantaneously, from a heart attack."

Laura didn't understand the significance of the claimed report, and looked at Karansky. "Such a report, if it existed, would cut off damages for pain and suffering," Karansky explained. "We never tried to split damages for wrongful death from pain and suffering, but I'd guess defendant's new offer is based on research about the value of a human life, without pain and suffering." He looked at Cayhill, whose smile confirmed he was correct. "The only problem with this theory is that such a report does not exist," Karansky finished, reasonably satisfied that what he said was true.

"Well now, it's not for me to say whether it does or it doesn't. I will say that we believe it does exist, and are prepared to try the case if you do not like the revised settlement proposal," Cayhill said, and stood up. The meeting was over.

Chapter 20

Preston Dunlop was going out to a luncheon engagement where he was speaking on Ethics, when he saw Cayhill leaving the men's room near the firm's library. "Ah, Les," he said, "I understand you had a meeting this morning with plaintiff's counsel in the American Auto case. How'd it go? Is it settled?"

"Not yet," Cayhill replied. As he talked he made a mental note to fire his secretary and get a new one. She must have let Dunlop know about the meeting, an unforgivable indiscretion. Even if he had found out some other way, Cayhill thought, he hated looking at her stocky legs and pudgy face.

"I will settle it as I told you," Cayhill continued. "But I have information indicating plaintiff's counsel is financially over-extended, and may need to settle the case or lose his home. So I'm playing it a bit first." He saw Dunlop start to protest, and added, "Listen, I know you want to settle this and I will. But you have got to appreciate that the world of trial lawyers has its own set of rules, and those rules go beyond any one case. If I give up ten million dollars without even putting up a fight, this firm will develop the reputation for being a bunch of pussies. The plaintiff's trial lawyers will no longer fear us, as believe me they do now, and American Auto and every other client we have will face more lawsuits than they do now. If on the other hand, I take this lawyer's house, put him through the wringer, and then pay him some money, our reputation remains intact. Preston, I told you I would get rid of the case and I will. But it has to be done right, and that's what I am doing."

Vampires

Dunlop felt his anger rising, as he listened to Cayhill try to explain why he was violating Dunlop's clear request to settle the case. "Les," he said, "I don't need the lecture about the firm's reputation as a tough outfit. And I don't accept the bullshit about one case making us look weak across the board. I'll give you a very little bit of rope here. But watch that you don't hang yourself. Give me a time period. I want to know how long it's going to take to settle the case if we do it your way."

Cayhill glared back at Dunlop, displaying his professional smile, the same sort of smile he gave younger attorneys whose names he forgot, and said, "One week."

"One week, then," Dunlop repeated. "And not a day more." He turned on his heel, and walked away, glad to be done with the conversation. He knew, however, that he now had to brief his Chinese counterpart, who likely would not be pleased.

Dunlop called the man he had negotiated with, to let him know it was taking longer than expected to settle the case against American. The man from the Ministry listened quietly, and then said, "We will make do with the new deadline. But I want you to understand very clearly that meeting the new date is important to us. It would be disappointing to miss it again."

Chapter 21

Karansky and Laura rode back to his office in a taxi, not saying a word. When they arrived, they got out, he paid the taxi, and spoke for the first time. "I don't think Cayhill is totally bluffing. We've got to find that report. Chapman's co-worker, though he was drunk and did nothing to help, stated in his deposition that he heard screams. You don't scream if you're already dead."

"Mr. Karansky," Laura said, "I guess this is a really bad time," she said and paused.

"For what?" he inquired, not remembering.

"I had scheduled my friend Cecelia to come see you this morning. She's probably already waiting." Cecelia was in fact already in the unusually crowded waiting room. There were two men in the room as well. As Karansky entered, Pam tried to get up to explain who they were, but the strangers were used to taking charge and did so. "Mr. Karansky?" one of them asked.

"Yes, I am Steven Karansky," he said.

"It is our understanding that the settlement offer on which the loan was based has been withdrawn. Under the terms of the loan agreement, that places you in default. You are hereby served with a notice of default, and an attachment of your house. You may of course request a hearing, but if you do so, under the terms of your agreement, you're also responsible for paying the attorney's fees for our prosecution of the foreclosure. You have 24 hours from now," and here the man pushed a timer on his watch, "either to request the hearing or move out."

The men left, and Laura said, "Oh Steven, I am so sorry." It was the first time she had called him by his first name, but the situation seemed to call for it.

Cecelia got up, feeling very awkward, and started to say, "Perhaps another time…"

But Karansky seemed unflappable. He almost seemed jovial. "Come, Ms. …" he let it hang in the air, and the woman answered, interjecting "van Horn. Cecilia van Horn."

"Well, Ms. van Horn. Please don't be concerned by the antics of our friends. They've taken their best shot, and we're still standing. Now it's time to open the second front. That's you Ms. Van Horn, you are the second front. Come in, come in, I have something to show you I believe you'll find interesting."

He shared his data with her and also shared his suspicion about the accounting firm she'd used and its connection to Dunhill & Schmidt. Cecelia listened with rapt attention until he had finished, and then said, "You're probably right. But what does it matter at this point? I simply don't have the money to fight them. And judging from the looks of things, neither do you."

Karansky laughed. "I've told Laura before that looks are deceiving. Whoever sent those men made a mistake today. They showed their hand. They also thought to intimidate me by taking the house. Well, they can have the house. It's not a great price but at a time I need the cash they essentially obliged, paying me two million for it. Now I intend to use their money to beat them. So, what do you say? Are you in?"

Laura was staring at him with a big smile now, and it gave him what little encouragement he needed to continue. Turning to Cecelia, he said, "I'm not sure what will happen, but I do know one thing. Cayhill doesn't like surprises, and he'll fall out of his chair when he reads the complaint we file tomorrow alleging federal racketeering and conspiracy claims, naming him and his firm as defendants. If the price tag for that much fun is to help you pay an old bill or two, I'd say it's a bargain, an absolute bargain. What do you say?"

Cecilia had long past stopped trying to look serious. The man was nuts, but smart and tough and on her side! She laughed, threw her arms around him, and said, "It has to be a loan. Win, lose, or draw, I will pay you back."

"If you insist," he said enjoying the hug, though he began to feel uncomfortable as she didn't seem ready to disengage. He gently moved her hands back to her sides, saying, 'Now then, you've a job to do, if you're willing. Someone has to get in touch with the women in those other cases and see what happened in the other divorces where the same accountant testified. There are only two of us dealing with the day-to-day legal fighting over this and another case. Very frankly, we could use some arms and legs helping with the investigation. You think you can do that?"

"Just point me. You'll see," she said.

"Good girl," Karansky responded. "As a first pass, look for any papers the women may have from the accounting firm, their legal bills, any recollections or reactions to the job Wendells had done. Then, depending

Vampires

on their answers, we may want you to circle back with a more detailed list of questions Laura will put together for you."

Cecilia warmed to the task. She shook her head to make her hair form a halo and winked at him with a wink that he knew had been used before, and said, "let me at 'em, boss." She took the list of names Pam had typed up, and headed for the door to get started. As she did so, Karansky couldn't help but stare at her bottom, which swayed invitingly as she walked. He then turned towards Laura, who had been watching him watch Cecilia. "What?" he said, but she said nothing as she turned and walked away.

Chapter 22

Pam had been doing calculations and had come in to share the good news: they were within two thousand dollars of being able to pay back the loan and save his house. But a look at Karansky's face made her stop short. He was smiling, an act which she thought to be strangely inappropriate given the circumstances. "Well, you'll do what is right, I'm sure," she said. "The only thing I can't quite figure out is how the five hundred dollars I left in the cash box turned into a thousand. I guess if we could get it to do that a few more times our problems would be over."

Karansky had given her a thousand dollars for petty cash and, not realizing she'd taken five hundred dollars to the lunch, had replaced the full amount when he found the box empty. He now confessed, telling them about the intruder, explaining his silence on the matter by saying he hadn't wanted them to worry. "Has it occurred to you," Laura asked, "that the real motive for the break-in might have been to leave something behind, not to take our mountains of cash?"

"Not at first," he responded. "But I began to wonder after Cayhill talked so assuredly about a document he claimed I have that I've never seen."

"Exactly," she replied. "I went through our inventory of documents and compared it to the documents that had been Bates stamped and are ready for production. Sure enough, there was a discrepancy."

"Let me guess," he said. "The discrepancy was a report from a doctor, concluding that the decedent, one Larry Chapman, died instantaneously, without any real discomfort, from …" He let this last piece hang in the air, waiting for Laura to fill in the blank.

She did so, saying "…a heart attack." She smiled ruefully. "Yes, the good Dr. Fong appears to have materialized at the scene of the accident within minutes of it happening. He just as mysteriously seems to have disappeared once again. The letter refers to the fact that he is returning to China, where he'll be working with lepers and will be out of touch for the next several months."

"Oh please!" said Karansky. "This is too much even for Cayhill. Are you certain his name isn't Saint Fong?" He thought for a moment. Then, "Laura, I don't remember any of the eyewitness accounts mentioning a doctor. Have you checked?"

"Not yet. Assuming they don't, what do you think? Is the document a fake?" Laura asked.

"Of course it's a fake," he said. "And Cayhill knows we know it. But he used it anyway to scuttle the settlement. What's his game?"

"What do you mean 'what's his game?' Laura asked. "He's withdrawn his offer and then let the bank know so that they'd take your house!"

"You're missing the point," he responded. "Look, Cayhill is smart. He has goals that he would hurt me to achieve, but hurting me is not one of his goals. So again, why is he doing this?"

"Because he is a cynical and dishonest son-of-a-bitch?" Laura guessed.

"He is of course, but that's not why. He's got to assume the doctor's report is eventually going to be revealed not to be legit. Don't you see? This is a short-term game, not a long-term one," Karansky said. He thought a minute, then his features lit up. "He wants to settle; he probably needs to settle. He's trying to save his client some money at the same time he puts pressure on us. But I guarantee it; he's hiding something and this is all a smoke screen to get us to focus attention on our short-term problems. This is," and he looked at Laura, "all a response to the motion to compel."

After he said this, he stared off in space for a minute. He said out loud, but with no intended audience, "Well, it can't be helped." He then picked up the phone and called the widow. The stepson answered the phone, and when Karansky asked to speak to the widow, the stepson said, "I first want to know whether it settled."

"And I first want to speak to my client, someone you are not and, if there is a God, you will never be," Karansky responded. He heard the phone being put down, and the stepson shout, "Hey, ma, that asshole attorney wants to speak to you. Grab the phone up there and I'll listen down here."

Ordinarily he would have insisted the stepson get off the phone prior to proceeding, but he was so fed up with the self-important little shit that he decided it wouldn't hurt to let him listen. "Mrs. Chapman, we did not settle. We waited too long, and in the meantime they have discovered a document that they believe helps them – a document that indicates that your husband may have died instantly." Her reaction was one of hope, asking did he really believe that could be. Her hopes focused on the possibility that her husband had not suffered so much, without a thought about the impact it might have on her case. "Shit," the stepson's exclaimed. "How much less does that mean?"

Vampires

Karansky was about to blow, when the usually quiet widow took charge. "That's enough, Will," she said sharply into the phone. "That's enough!" she said again, with an air of finality. "You couldn't make it any clearer that the only thing you care about, in fact the only thing you've ever cared about, is money. I want you to pack your things and go. And don't come back."

The stepson tried to convince her she had misunderstood what he had said, had misheard, and finally, was under the mind control of this attorney who has done a terrible job and was now doing everything in his power to drive away the family who loved her. Eventually he hung up the phone. Karansky heard more yelling, banging, and finally the sound of a door slamming. Then was quiet, interrupted only by the sound of the widow's deep sigh.

"So, Mr. Karansky, what now?" she asked.

"Now, Mrs. Chapman we try the case," he answered. "We try the case and ram it right up their…" he stopped short of finishing his thought. She finished it for him, "Up their asses, Mr. Karansky, you shove this goddamned case up their goddamned asses."

Chapter 23

The following day, Pam asked Karansky where he was going to sleep that night. "The twenty-four hours expires this afternoon, and judging by the seventy-three thousand dollar check you wrote yesterday to Dunlop and Schmidt on behalf of our new client, I don't imagine you're working on a plan to pay them back. Which tells me that you are going to need a place to stay."

"He can stay with me," Laura blurted out, and then blushed as they both looked at her, surprised. "Hey, I rented a huge apartment. I got a great deal because the previous tenant died of a heart attack in the place. Apparently, most people don't like living where other people died."

Pam almost reflexively said, "Ughhhh! I can't believe you're living there."

"Died or was killed?" Karansky asked. "I seem to remember a story about someone being murdered around here? Could it have been in your place?"

It was Laura's turn to moan, "Oooh! I hope you're joking."

Karansky smiled, as he said, "Relax, I was just testing you, although I don't understand why you'd be okay with one and not the other."

"A huge difference," Laura said, without explanation. "Anyway, there's plenty of room, just no furniture. You'd need a sofa bed. If you want to take a look, it's only about a five minute walk from here."

The three of them walked over to see Laura's apartment. It was as billed. It had only one full bath, but there was a bedroom and a second room, completely empty for now, that could house a bed (or sofa) with room to spare. It also had wireless broadband access, the first thing Laura said she had set up. It was near perfect.

Karansky walked up to Laura. "I love it," he said. But are you sure you feel comfortable with me staying here?"

"We're talking about you staying for a short time as a guest until you find something more permanent, right?" she asked. He shook his head yes. "And we're also talking about grown-ups who won't confuse an invitation to stay in my place with an invitation to climb into my bed, right?" Again he nodded his assent. "Then yes, I'm okay with it. You have to bring whatever furniture you need. And be out in a reasonable time."

Pam had been walking around and rejoined them in time to hear this last part. "You're going to have to buy something new," Pam said. "Did you ever read that contract you signed for the loan?" she demanded. He shrugged. "Well, there's fine print that says something about furnishings. Apparently, they have a lien against the contents of the house, including specifically your furniture, as well."

"That's fine," Karansky said, beginning to smile all over again. Thinking of the worn sofa in his waiting room, he deadpanned, "All the good furniture is at the office anyway." He elicited smiles, not the laughs he had hoped for. "Pam, how quickly can we have a sofa bed delivered?"

He turned to Laura and asked her, "And what kind of furniture would match the rest of your stuff?"

Laura laughed then, "There is no rest of my stuff. I have a matching bed and dresser, a kitchen table and two chairs. The rest was going to come in time."

"Well then, that's easy. Pam, get something that goes with "empty." Can we get something delivered today?" he asked.

She looked at her watch. "If you're very lucky, and are willing to buy a floor sample, just maybe. Provided you don't come and help," she added.

"On your way then," he said. "If it costs more than what we have in petty cash…" he began.

"If it costs more and it will, I'll charge it to my personal credit card, and you will write me a check to cover it. I am not going to risk embarrassment again by trying to charge it to yours," she responded.

When Pam left, Laura took the opportunity to solidify the rules that would apply. "Mr. Karansky…" she began somewhat stiffly.

He interrupted. "Listen, if you are about to tell me once again that this is just an arrangement to help me out and don't get any ideas, the least you could do is temper the blow by using my name. It's Steven."

"Well, Steven," she laughed, "I'm glad you get the picture."

"Absolutely," he said. "You don't need to worry. I make it a practice never to sleep with the associates who work for me. It makes it difficult, no it makes it impossible, to fairly assess their work in comparison to that of their peers."

She was puzzled by his response, and couldn't resist asking, "Just how many other associates do you have?"

His smile resumed as he responded, "Well, none actually. You're the first. That's a very good point. There really isn't a problem with you sleeping with me so long as I don't hire any more associates."

She laughed once more, and he decided he had better be very careful. He thought that she was pretty when she laughed. He therefore returned the conversation back to work. "Okay, you numba one associate. Tell me numba one, what do we do with this document written by the illustrious, mysterious and probably fictitious Dr. Fong?"

"Ah, man-too-old, I think we should give it to the defendant unless man-too-old rikes the young and strong men in the big house," she replied, not missing a beat.

He whistled. "You're quick. I feel for the man you marry. He'd better not give you any sass. By the way, I agree that we must give it to them. The question is when."

She didn't understand and said so.

"Look," he said, "there are two reasons I want to buy time. The first is one of focus. If Cayhill is hiding something, and we know he is, his modus operandi is to wait, wait, wait and then to give it, along with a hundred thousand superfluous pages, the day before trial. He's done that to me before."

"But that violates the court order," she protested.

"Yes it does. So what? Few courts will enforce such procedural orders in any meaningful way. They don't want to be bothered. Trust me, he'll do it and get away with it."

"So what does withholding this document have to do with his maneuvering?" she asked.

"Elementary," he said, sucking on a pretend pipe. "To get this document he must file a motion to compel. It puts light on the issue of missing documents. We then swoop in on his motion, remind the court that we've had one pending for longer than his, and suggest that the two motions be heard together. We give up our document and hopefully force a production by him of whatever he is hiding much sooner than we would otherwise receive it."

"Very clever," she said. "What is your second reason?"

"I need more time. As I mentioned before, I think the document is a fake. I need time to prove it. This guy Fong is just too convenient. He comes from nowhere, destroys our damages case, and then returns to nowhere. The document also is not on our register of documents and I am not so senile yet that I could have reviewed it, put it in the stack of documents to be numbered and then forgotten it existed."

"So where did it come from?" she asked.

We had a most unusual intruder, I think," he replied. "If I could only prove it, the hearing on the motions to compel, assuming he files one and both motions are considered at the same time, busts him wide open. I prove his document is a fraud; and we get whatever he's hiding."

Karansky looked heart Laura as he finished the explanation. He thought, just for a moment, that she was looking at him with admiration. He

Vampires

told himself angrily to get a grip; he didn't have the luxury of screwing things up with romantic fantasies.

Chapter 24

As Karansky worked on the accounting complaint and dug deeper, he knew he was on to something. A few of the women who had hired the accounting firm still had the reports that had been prepared and had been willing to give copies to Cecilia. One, a forty year old with an interest in a company that specialized in honey production, had been given a report asserting the threat of African "killer bees" had made the company a non-viable business. The business was assigned a nominal value of a half million dollars on the theory that maybe, if one were lucky, the company could make this much in income before being shut down. The company had made thirty-six million dollars in the year and a half since the report had been issued.

Karansky knew that expert reports were often subjective and that colorable arguments could be made in favor of the report. But, at best the report made every assumption, and answered every unknown question, in a manner highly favorable to the husband. He could have understood why the report was written the way it was if it had been prepared for the husband by an accountant willing to reach extreme conclusions to favor the party paying for its preparation. But it made no sense at all that an expert would make every subjective judgment contrary to the interests of the party that employed him.

The woman's name was Shirley Wangell, and the report was so suspicious Karansky didn't understand how it stuck. "You don't understand," she had explained, "it cost me nearly everything I had to get the report done in the first place. Then, the attorneys took over, fighting about every issue you could imagine. I spent my last dollar for a not-very-significant exchange of letters about how much support I should receive on an interim basis pending a final order. Altogether I paid nearly two hundred thousand dollars in legal bills before running out of funds. I then had judgment entered against me for default, meaning I got nothing, because my attorneys refused to continue working on the case, even temporarily, once I could no longer pay. No one even looked at the report."

Many of the other cases exhibited similar patterns. The clients would be run around in circles with legal motions being filed over meaningless issues, all at high hourly rates. Then came the expert report, which suggested there was little value to the case, followed by more legal skirmishing sapping the client's funds, followed by either a settlement for virtually nothing, or as in the Wangell case, an outright default for non-prosecution of the case.

"Goddamned bloodsuckers," swore Karansky, getting angrier as he read. "They suck the client dry chasing their tails, and then when the money is gone, they dump them! They're vampires in business suits," he ranted, making himself feel a little better by affixing a pejorative label to the less ethical members of his chosen profession.

He hadn't figured out the entire scheme yet, but didn't have the luxury of time. He needed to get this case filed quickly to put pressure on Cayhill. Karansky began drafting around six o'clock, and was totally consumed by it when Laura knocked on his door at eight. "How about at least moving the place at which you are working," she suggested. "I really need to go home. I'm beat, and I'd like to show you your new home, get you set up in the bathroom, and make certain the sofa has been delivered before it gets too late."

He apologized and quickly threw his laptop and his notes into an old leather carryall. He took that in one hand and a small duffel bag filled with clothing and toiletries in the other, looked at her and said, "Don't worry. Pam rescued more clothes, even my two best court suits. They should be in your apartment, along with the sofa."

The clothes were there when they arrived; the sofa was not. In its place was a note from Pam, explaining she'd had to go to visit her ailing sister, but stating the store where she had bought the sofa had given her concrete assurances the sofa would be delivered between 7 and 8 p.m. She also provided the store manager's home and cell phone numbers should there be a problem, which according to the manager, couldn't and wouldn't happen.

A few phone calls and the mystery was solved. No one had been home when the delivery team arrived. Pam had left a note on the door in English explaining that those delivering the sofa should get the key from the super. The note had been a mystery to the delivery team who only understood Spanish. However, they had found a very nice Spanish-speaking neighbor who was home two floors below Laura's fourth floor walk-up that Laura had rented, who had graciously agreed to accept delivery. If they would only knock on the neighbor's door then the neighbor would no doubt help them carry it up. Or they could wait until the morning and call him back and he would be even happier to have the delivery team return and finish the job.

As Karansky relayed to her what he had learned from the manager, Laura developed a case of the giggles, the kind that starts slowly with some silly piece of information and then makes you laugh at just about everything that happens. He tried to remain serious, and observed that she didn't seem to have anything else that he could sleep on in sight (small giggles), and that he really should try to get a hotel room (louder giggle). He called the one hotel close to them and was told it were fully booked (full scale giggle), and finally asked whether she would mind if they did disturb her downstairs neighbor and see if they could move the thing (total guffaw). She explained to him that her neighbor, Mrs. Arcos, was a 78 year-old lady who, while very nice, would do herself serious harm should they really involve her in moving the sofa up the two flights of stairs.

He looked at his watch, and asked her to call him a cab. "And where should I say this cab is going to take you?" she asked.

"I'll find some hotel," he said. "Maybe the cabbie will know of one."

"Stop playing the gallant hero," she replied. "Steven, I have a King-sized bed. It's huge! There is no reason why you couldn't sleep in it as well without ever touching me. Do I have your word?"

Relief flowed into his face, softening his features. "I'd promise anything to avoid getting kicked out at this time of night," he replied. "Yes, you have my word. No touching."

"Good," she said. You get the right side. And you take the second shower. Clear?"

"Clear," he replied, then raised his hand.

"For God's sake, Steven, don't raise your hand when you want to ask something. Just ask."

"Sorry, he said. "I just wanted to clarify whether I should touch you if you start choking on a chicken bone."

She gave him a sideways look but didn't otherwise respond. "Okay, I'm exhausted. I'm going to go get ready and then get in bed. Please wait at least ten minutes before you do the same."

"Take your time," he replied. "I'm going to stay up for awhile. I want to finish a draft of the audit scandal complaint. I would appreciate it if you'd review it first thing tomorrow to keep me honest. Then we file it by the end of the day."

"You want me to review your work?" she asked, surprised.

"Of course, it's not every day one can have one's work reviewed by someone who finished top in her class."

"Second," she said. "I didn't attend a single class since I started working for you. My international tax teacher knocked off some points for absence of class participation. Not a lot, but enough to slip me into second place."

"Sorry about that," he said and meant it.

"No big deal," she responded, beginning to yawn. "I'm going to turn in." She added a good night, approaching him and giving him an absent-minded peck on the cheek. She turned away, and then realized what she had done. "Oh my God, I didn't mean..."

"Not to worry. It registered as the sort of kiss a child would give her father," he said, not wanting it to be true.

"Good night, daddy," she said smiling, walked into the bedroom and closed the door.

Vampires

Chapter 25

Karansky finally crawled into bed close to three a.m. There was enough moonlight coming in from the window so that he could make out Laura's face as she slept facing the center of the bed. He realized she was far prettier without her glasses, and thought to himself that he'd love to be younger, at least young enough to attract a woman like this. He guessed she was in her late twenties; he was forty-one. He undressed down to his boxers as quietly as he could and slipped into bed, facing her, but staying as close to the edge of the bed as possible.

He clearly stayed on his side of the line, so what happened during the night can't really be blamed on him. Somehow Laura encroached on Karansky's side of the bed, initially facing him, but then backing into him with her posterior leading the way. Though asleep, he didn't give ground easily, and they ended up tightly coupled, both facing the same way, with his arm naturally falling around her. She, treating the arm as a pillow, mashed it into her breasts and he, without knowing it and certainly without enjoying it consciously, cupped one of those lovely orbs in his hand. So they slept until she woke, first with a smile, for the body is much more satisfied with the warmth and comfort of another body than without, but then as she realized the situation she was in, she roughly pushed his hand away and jumped out of bed.

This woke him up, and he stared at her, sleepy eyed but still able to appreciate the muscle tone of her youth, obscured only slightly by her undergarments. Perhaps he stared too long; perhaps she realized that he'd stayed on his half of the bed, making lengthy accusations problematic. In any event, she contented herself by saying, "Pig!" and then ran into the bathroom and slammed the door.

Laura cooled down by the time she exited the bathroom, wearing a robe. She decided to apologize for calling him a pig, and started to say, "Steven, I…" when she realized he wasn't in bed, and that she'd been about to apologize to a pillow. She walked out of the bedroom and did not see him. On the kitchen counter, she found a note apologizing for any offense he might have caused, requesting she read the draft complaint, and meet him at the office at ten. "What a strange man," she said out loud. The next thought she didn't articulate, because it came to her in bits and pieces throughout the morning. Steven Karansky reminded her a little of her father – not so much physically, for in that respect she found Karansky handsome in ways that she had never thought about her father. There also was something similar about them that she was able finally to identify: his voice had that same deep resonance as her father's voice had had, reflecting a calmness even in the midst of crisis, evidencing a deep comfort with himself.

After a moment or two of enjoyable daydreaming, she made a pot of coffee. Then, pouring herself a cup, she sat down to read.

Chapter 26

Cayhill had developed the habit of talking to judges hearing his cases, not about substantive matters the judge would be called on to decide – that would be wrong – but about procedural matters that would affect the way in which the case would proceed. That was also wrong, but less obviously so, and most judges would tolerate such discussion. Cayhill decided the time was ripe for such a discussion, and called Judge Hernandez who had been assigned the American Auto case.

"Judge," Cayhill began, "You know I don't ordinarily like to burden your docket with all sorts of procedural skirmishing." Judge Hernandez didn't know anything of the sort; in fact the statement wasn't true, but it was said so reasonably the judge didn't doubt it. "Well, your Honor, I am very sorry but I am filing today a motion to compel, and I am asking that it be given expedited treatment."

"I see," said the judge, not seeing at all. "Mr. Cayhill, what's all this about?"

"It's about a horrible and tragic death of an employee in American Automobile's Linden factory, your honor. He was pulled right into a machine. We've made what we believe is a generous offer of settlement, which I have to admit, your Honor, we reduced from ten million dollars to five million dollars just yesterday."

The judge found these discussions informative in ways that pleadings filed with the court rarely were. He was disciplined though and didn't reveal his substantive thinking. "Now why, Mr. Cayhill, would you do that?"

"Your Honor, we have reason to believe that Plaintiff has medical documents indicating that the decedent died of a heart attack without the horrible pain and suffering alleged in their complaint. Our motion to compel is designed to get this issue out in the open."

"You mean Plaintiff hasn't produced it yet? Who the hell is your opposing counsel?"

"Steven Karansky, your Honor, a fine attorney," Cayhill responded.

"He's going to be a fined attorney if he doesn't cut the crap," the judge said, and then chuckled at his play on words. "Thank you for calling this to my attention."

"Not at all, judge. In all fairness, I should mention that Plaintiff also has filed a motion to compel, Cayhill said.

"Okay, we can hear both motions together," the judge said.

"That would be fine, your Honor, only in that case we would respectfully ask you not schedule it for awhile."

"I don't understand," said the judge. "If I were in your shoes, I would want to see that medical report ASAP. And I mean ASAP."

"I do as well, your Honor. It could help settle the case if we could see it," Cayhill replied. "But the plaintiff, who has few documents of his own, had asked very broad requests of American Auto, requiring a massive search and production of what we believe are largely useless and irrelevant documents. Even though the factory has been great at supplying us the manpower, it is going to take us at least another week to do the file searches and make copies of all the responsive documents. Why, we've already copied about a hundred thousand pages."

"That's ridiculous," the judge said, becoming seriously annoyed at Plaintiff's counsel. "I can't stand gamesmanship, and I will tell you right now not to try any."

"No, your Honor," Cayhill said.

"Let me tell you what I'm going to do," the judge said. "I'm going to separate the two motions, since you tell me he only has a few documents. He, unlike you, has no excuse to delay. So I am going to hear your motion first, Cayhill. And this guy Karansky had better have a good reason for not turning over his documents."

"Gotcha!" Cayhill thought to himself. Out loud he said, "I will let Mr. Karansky speak for himself, your Honor. Just tell me when to show up, and I'll be there."

Vampires

Chapter 27

"Racketeering?" Laura asked. "Isn't that a little strong?" She was in Karansky's office, as he had requested, holding in her hand a copy of the complaint he had written the night before. She looked as if she'd slept well, as she had. Laura also had taken more care than usual with her appearance. She'd put on a pale peach shade of lipstick, and faint eyeliner. The amounts were so slight as to be difficult to notice; yet they set off her features in a way he found disconcerting.

He, on the other hand, was a mess. He'd slept just over three hours, and was troubled by what had happened that morning. He didn't want to be asked to leave, partly because he didn't have a very attractive alternative, and partly because he realized how excited he'd been to share a bed with Laura, even innocently. He wanted the day to pass and to find some way to do it again.

Laura said something, but he'd been daydreaming and had not caught it. "I'm sorry?" he asked.

"I asked why you want to file this under RICO?" she repeated. RICO was the Racketeering and Corrupt Influences Act. Passed by Congress to help fight organized crime, the language of the statute was so expansive it enabled any "conspiracy" that involved two related criminal acts in interstate commerce to be attacked as a RICO violation. Because criminal acts in interstate commerce included acts of fraud using the telephone or the mail, it was not difficult to put together allegations sufficient to withstand motions to dismiss. That meant one could get to the discovery phase of a trial, where one could force defendants to appear for depositions, where they had to answer questions under oath, and to divulge all documents that might be relevant to the case.

Karansky, however, had more than surviving a motion to dismiss in mind. "RICO gets us three things, Laura," he explained. First, look at the statute: if we win, we get three times the damages awarded by the jury, and we get our attorneys fees paid by Defendant. It doesn't get better than that. Second, it's pretty easy to get into federal court if you are concerned about the quality of the state judges. In many places the quality of the state judges is absolutely appalling, especially when they are elected by the voters."

"Then why would you ever file in state court even if you could?" she asked.

"Time," he answered. "The federal courts are often so clogged with a back-log of cases that you can wait months or sometimes even years for a chance at justice. Sometimes circumstances won't permit that kind of time."

"And the third reason for using RICO?" she asked.

"Publicity," he answered. "The very name of the statute is a huge help in convincing defendants to settle. There are not too many defendants who relish the publicity they get for being sued, as you put it, for racketeering."

"So what's wrong with RICO?" she asked after thinking a moment. "What would someone with more experience than I have say about this as a cause of action?"

"Damned if I know," he answered. "For the life of me, I can't understand why it isn't used more. When does Cecelia think she will be able to obtain a copy of the accounting report from her divorce case?"

"It should already have happened. She was going to go settle the bill first thing this morning, and request it," Laura answered.

"Get in touch with her and tell her to bring the report here as soon as she has it," he ordered. Assuming it confirms my suspicions, we file," he said, beginning to rise. "Now if you will excuse me, I'm going to run back to our love nest and shower."

Laura felt her face flush despite her best efforts to control her emotions. Everything seemed to happen at incredible speed around him. Lawsuits that normally took months to prepare got done in a day; he made decisions about his life on the fly; and he laughed when those decisions went bad. He was incredible, she thought, certainly one of the most incredible men she had ever met. But his reference to her apartment as their "love nest" had to be addressed.

"Steven, about what happened..." she began.

He interrupted. "Laura, what happened last night was an accident. But I enjoyed waking up with you this morning, more than I had thought possible. I want to do it again, this time with my eyes wide open and with full intent to do what we are doing."

She stared at him quietly for a moment. Then, "Steven, I think it would be a very bad idea."

He didn't understand. "But why?" he asked.

"Because I work for you. If we have a fight or break up, you lose a lover. I lose a lover and a job," she said.

"I can't deny the risk. No matter what I say, it might happen," he said. "But I can't get you out of my head. I keep thinking of being in bed with you, with my hand on your breast." She reddened. "You have to admit," he said, "it felt right. Didn't it?"

There was a rebellious part of her that wanted to scream, "Yes, of course it did!" But she suppressed it and said, "I'm sorry, Steven. Whether it did or didn't is not the issue. I can't afford to get involved with you because you are my boss. I'm sorry but that's the way it has to be." She paused and then continued, "I also think that you should move out – under the circumstances, I don't think that it's a good idea for you to stay with me."

"I can move out today," he said, every fiber of himself not wanting to, and hoping the offer would be rejected.

"I'm not throwing you out into the street," she said. "Find a place first. Could you do that in a day or two?"

"I'm sure I could," Karansky answered, not sure of anything other than he wanted this woman.

Laura walked back to her office and called her friend Cecilia on her cell to find out how she had done. She also needed to talk to someone who would understand what was going on and advise her on what she should do. Cecilia was jubilant – she had managed to deal with an associate who tried to impress her, and therefore did not check with anyone more senior than himself. The notation on her file was to hold it pending payment. He charged her extra for the copying costs, but gave her a copy of the accountant's report. She was just then entering the office building housing Karansky's office and was about to come up, when Laura had called.

"Do you have time to get a drink?" Laura asked.

"Is everything okay, sweetie?" Cecelia asked, picking up something in Laura's voice.

"I'll tell you when I see you," Laura said, still on the phone. "I'll be right down." Moments later, she stepped off the elevator and waved to her friend.

"I think I may have messed up," Laura added after exchanging a brief hug with Cecelia.

Cecelia said, "Don't look so serious. You're way too young to have messed up anything that you can't 'un-mess'. Here. Let's go in that one," she said, pointing to a bar across the street. "The bartender is a friend and I sometimes can get a free drink or two."

Cecelia's eyes sparkled mischievously as she answered Laura's question about why both of their drinks were on the house. "The bartender may be your friend but he doesn't even know me."

"Sometimes I think you should wear your hair in pigtails and go around saying, "Toto, I don't think we are in Kansas anymore," Cecelia said, laughing. "You wonder why a bartender with an eye for the ladies gives you a free drink? Even if he doesn't get a chance to take you to bed himself, honey, you're good for business."

Almost on cue, two men came over and tried to strike up a conversation. One sat down next to Cecelia, and leaned over and whispered something to her. She looked at him, asked "Really?" and when he shook his head "yes," she calmly took the glass of water and poured it in his lap. "I think the fire is out now," she said. The man stood up angrily and likely would have started something, except that the bartender, bat in hand, said, "I think it is time for you two assholes to leave." Any indecision they may have felt was settled by one of the burly bouncers who came over, and said, "Don't even think of it," and graciously opened the door for them.

When the men were gone, Cecelia returned to their conversation, saying, "Okay, Laura, what have you messed up?"

"My boss is now staying with me, because he lost his house, as you know. Last night, we slept together, but it was only supposed to be sleeping in the same bed. This morning I wake up with his hand on my breasts. Cecelia, it felt so good but I called him a pig. And…"

"Whoa, whoa!" interrupted Cecelia. "Just stop a moment. You're covering a lot of ground, and I'm having trouble following. Now slow down and tell me again." Laura explained their circumstances more slowly, and Cecelia listened. When Laura finished her explanation, Cecelia asked what was wrong.

"Don't you see?" Laura asked. "He's my boss! If we become lovers and we then break up, I'm out of a job!"

"Do you love him?" Cecelia asked.

"I don't know!" Laura nearly shouted. Cecelia said nothing for a moment, just staring and waiting for Laura to say more. At length Laura said, "Yes, yes I do. At least I think I do! But I don't know how he feels. He just stopped seeing someone else, and for all I know he's simply on the hunt now for his next 'piece of ass.' I don't want to be only that to him."

Cecelia put her hand on Laura's, which was resting on the table in front of her. "I understand the concern, Laura, but based on what you know of him, is he the type who just wants you as a sexual conquest?"

"No," Laura admitted.

"Then stop worrying about it," Cecelia said. "Life is too short," she added, "and the possibility of meeting someone like him doesn't happen every day. So what if you might lose your job if this doesn't work out; you might find love if it does. The reward seems greater than the risk. But there's something else. I saw how he looked at you at our meeting the other day. He is head over heels in lust for you! That and a little magic," and Cecelia pretended to sprinkle something on Laura's head," is a sure-fire recipe for love."

"Lust? Really?" Laura asked. "How can you tell?"

"By the way he looks at you mostly," and then Cecelia giggled.

"What?" Laura asked. "What aren't you telling me?"

"I don't think you're old enough to know all my secrets..." Cecelia said.

Laura was smiling broadly now as well, and repeated, "What? Cecelia, tell me!"

"Well," Cecelia said, "you may not remember but you put your hand on his arm at one point during the conversation."

"So?" Laura asked.

"Well, I stood up just after that, and as I expected he acted the gentleman and stood up as well. And," Cecelia smiled as she finished, "he was already standing up when he stood up!"

"Cecelia!" Laura exclaimed, surprised at her friend. Then she started smiling and said, "Really? How big was it?" They both started laughing.

Cecelia spoke first after the laughs had run their course, "Look, Laura, there are no guarantees. But you have a chance at something really special. Life is way too short to pass that up."

Laura gave her friend another hug, and repeated in heartfelt tones a final, "Thank you."

Cecelia said, "Not at all. Just promise me that if you decide not to give it a shot, let me know. I wouldn't mind seeing him without his clothes on…"

Chapter 28

Matt Thomson III, the hapless associate at Dunlop & Schmidt, had finished in the top three percent of his class at Yale, but had yet to impress the partners at the firm. It was he who had been raked over the coals about the document in the American Auto case. He entered the room for the weekly litigation section review eager to share his news. Cayhill presided over the review, moving quickly from associate to associate. Attorneys learned quickly that Cayhill expected every attorney to be able to communicate the core of what they were doing, together with any issues, in less than a minute.

Cayhill went quickly and efficiently, occasionally asking a pointed question. He came to Matt, who cleared his throat and said, "This isn't a huge success, but I was able to collect seventy-three thousand dollars that the accounting guys had just about written off simply by providing a copy of an old document in a case that the party had a right to anyway."

Cayhill was surgical. "That is a lot of money, isn't it?" he asked.

"Well, like I said it's not huge but it is a lot, I guess, under the circumstances," Thompson responded, a little nervous.

"Mr. Thomson, can you guess why someone whose debt we had nearly written off, meaning I assume that we were not actively trying to collect what they owed, would come and pay a lot of money in exchange for some old document?"

"No sir," the associate said, his voice beginning to quiver.

"Before we conclude that the person had an irrational urge to simply throw money at us, would you mind telling us what unimportant document he or she 'purchased' for seventy-three thousand dollars?" Cayhill had already guessed what the document was and was sufficiently irritated by that so that he felt little mercy for this boneheaded associate.

The associate, his hands shaking now, checked his notes to make certain he had it right, and then said in a voice that matched the tremble in his hands, "It was the accounting report prepared by…"

"Reliable Accounting," interrupted Cayhill. "Am I right?"

Totally convinced he had screwed up in ways that would not be forgiven, the ashen-faced attorney mumbled "yes, you are right."

"Never assume that the other side is made up of fools," Cayhill admonished, almost in a gentle teaching voice. Looking away from Thomson, he addressed the other attendees. "If someone is willing to pay seventy-three thousand dollars that we are not trying to collect, do not assume that person is an idiot. To the contrary, you must assume that they think what they are buying is going to be worth more than seventy-three thousand dollars. They may be wrong but that is their purpose."

"The problem with this particular situation is that the only people I can think of who might extract value from an old expert's report are the people involved in the case itself – either plaintiff's counsel, this firm, which represented defendant, or the accounting firm itself. Let us hope that whoever bought it overpaid."

Having finished what was for him a long speech, he concluded, "That's enough fun for one afternoon, kids. C'mon, there are clients out there with money just waiting to complain about your billed hours. Go make me rich!"

His closing drew a few nervous laughs. He spotted Thomson trying to exit, and said in a loud enough voice so all could hear, "Mr. Thomson, a word?"

Thomson returned and came to face Cayhill, who said, "Wait right here. I won't be a moment." He was technically right; he took about ten minutes during which time Thomson practiced various apologies and promises of improved performance. When Cayhill returned, the associate opened his mouth to speak but didn't have the chance.

"Spare me the speeches, Mr. Thomson, you are fired." He then handed him an envelope, continuing, "I stopped by payroll. There is a check inside with your pay calculated to 4 p.m. today. Congratulations, you get two hours pay for doing nothing. Your personal effects are in a box by the elevator. There is no reason for you to return to your office. Please leave." As he said this, he looked over the associate's shoulder and gave a sign to the two security personnel, who entered the room politely, but with a sense of purpose. One of them asked Thomson if he was ready. Cayhill answered for him, saying, "Yes he is ready. Please show him every courtesy as he leaves. "Goodbye, Matt. this may seem somewhat harsh but I assure you this is for the best. Get a clean start somewhere else. These lapses of judgment would mean you would never make partner here. I am saving you working eight years in the wrong place."

Vampires

The young attorney didn't feel particularly lucky. He felt ill, but he had no choice but to leave. He did gather enough courage to turn and ask Cayhill, "Didn't you ever make a mistake?" If he expected this to gain him a reprieve, he was wrong. Cayhill thought a moment, and said simply, "No." Then he walked back to his office to begin thinking through what this development meant.

He didn't have long to wait before the meaning became apparent. A process server showed up just before five p.m., and asked to see him. His secretary signed for him and then brought the papers to him. His poker face held, but barely so, as he read the complaint. It was for Racketeering and named him personally, his firm, Reliable Accounting and Scott Wendells. Worse still, it was in federal court before a judge with whom Cayhill had no relationship.

 Cayhill quickly skipped to the back of the complaint to see who was behind this and was startled to see Karansky's name on the pleading. "Why that son-of-a-bitch!" he thought to himself. Then, warming to the challenge, he muttered to himself, "This is war. One of us isn't going to come out of this in one piece. You picked on the wrong target, Karansky. I'm going to take you down."

Chapter 29

The lawsuit, Cecilia van Horn vs. Lester Cayhill, et al., was filed on a Thursday afternoon, at about four o'clock, in federal court. Karansky didn't hold a news conference, but the media very much affected his thinking on when to file. He wanted the law firm and the accounting firm to feel the heat, both because this might drive them to settle, but more critically because people under pressure make mistakes. He needed them to make mistakes, because he knew he didn't yet have enough facts to win. He had enough to file, and enough to withstand a motion to dismiss, but not to win.

Press coverage would give him the heat he wanted. That meant rushing to get it filed on Thursday, or waiting another three days to file on Monday. Friday was out because that was the day of the week to do something that you didn't wanted to see in a newspaper. Many newspapers cut back on their activities during the weekend, using canned material instead. The public too had been conditioned not to expect major developments on Saturday or Sunday mornings.

Thursday on the other hand was a great day to do something. The easy stories had been done earlier in the week and the papers were scrounging for newsworthy items. Give them a real story, such as a prestigious law firm and a prestigious accounting firm alleged to be engaged in a criminal conspiracy, and you had a real shot at page one.

The story made page two in the Star Ledger and was mentioned on the first page of the business section of the New York Times. Karansky had leaked the story to a friend of his at the Ledger five minutes after the complaint was filed, but then refused to give comments until nearly eight o'clock. Reporters were willing to work only so late for a story that did not involve life or death. They would grumble but write a story if it meant staying until nine o'clock, so coverage of his interview would be included in the initial stories. That would give Cayhill virtually no time to react and respond, and few reporters at that time of night would give him extra time to issue a response. That meant either responding on the fly, which seemed unlikely, or waiting until the following day to respond. That in turn meant that the initial coverage would cover the allegations without a meaningful response. At least that was the strategy.

It worked. Cayhill and his partners read the headlines the next morning, "Major Law and Accounting Firms Accused of Racketeering," and didn't like them one bit. Jonathan Schmidt, one of the very senior partners, made a rare appearance at the office, in order to complain to Cayhill that he did not appreciate having to explain to his child-bride, a buxom beauty whose twenty-six years were too few to warrant sharing a bed with her seventy-six year old husband, that he was neither a criminal nor a tennis player. Many of the other partners spent the better part of the day answering questions they weren't accustomed to answering, and they didn't like it.

Preston Dunlop especially didn't like it. His firm was alleged to be a party to this scurrilous activity. He also knew that the lawsuit put him at risk; the law firm was structured legally as a partnership, and a partnership could be found liable for the misdeeds of one of the partners. He had called Cayhill as soon as he had seen the allegations and was told by a new secretary that her boss was "unavailable." He became livid and walked down to see Cayhill but found his office door locked. He knocked but got no answer.

Dunlop called his secretary and asked her to get a quorum of the partners, excluding Cayhill, assembled in his conference room in twenty minutes. "If Cayhill wanted to play tough guy, so be it," he said to himself. He then stormed back to his office to make some notes. He not only was angry; he was concerned. Dunlop had seen from the newspaper that the attorney who had filed the RICO case was the same attorney Cayhill had met with on the American Auto case. That meant that the settlement of the American Auto case was about to get more complicated if Cayhill remained in charge of it. Add that risk to the risk that these allegations had some truth to them, and Cayhill started to look like a liability.

Cayhill's problem was that he didn't have a one-line response to make the RICO allegations go away. He laughed off the allegations, and told the newspapers there wasn't a shred of real evidence supporting this mass of sour grapes. Karansky, however, had done a good job of arraying the data to make troubling trends quite visible. For instance, Wendell's valuations averaged nearly 65% less when Cayhill was involved in the case. This appeared to have nothing to do with Cayhill's legal prowess; this was the initial expert report, before Cayhill had done anything in the case. Nor was it because the companies in these cases were less profitable; the data Karansky had included showed that for those companies for which information was publicly available, those companies in the "Cayhill was involved pile" actually were more profitable than those where he had not been involved, making the accounting estimates in such cases all the more difficult to understand.

The difficulty for Cayhill, of course, was that the allegations were true. This was not fatal to his defense; it just made it more complicated. He no longer was interested in the question of what was true. What did interest him, in fact the only thing that mattered to him, was what could be proved. And he did not think the allegations in the complaint could be proved.

Vampires

Cayhill knew Dunlop was looking for him. He would tend to those fences in good time. His immediate concern was the accountant, Scott Wendells, his "partner in crime." Wendells was a brilliant accountant but Cayhill had seen him get rattled on the stand. He wondered, somewhat pessimistically, whether the accountant would keep his cool here if things got very, very hot. Up till now, it had been relatively easy, but this current mess promised to be more of a challenge. He called the accountant on his private number.

"Jesus," Wendells started talking as soon as he answered. "How the hell did he figure it out? I thought you said that ..."

Cayhill interrupted, "He hasn't figured it out yet. He's guessing. As soon as he starts trying to put a case together you'll see. There isn't an accountant in the world that will testify that you made clear errors. That's the beauty of it; everything is within the realm of your reasonable expert judgment – shade the risk factors or depresses the sales projections and you're there. All we did was take some of the randomness out of the equation, creating great results for select clients. But he can't prove anything because of our introduction of anomalies into the mix."

It was genius, Cayhill thought, and not unfairly. He had established two levels from which the clients could choose: for five million dollars they got a guaranteed win, defined as the valuation coming in between zero and one million dollars. This he called gold service. Ironically, some clients opted for gold service even though the price they paid was greater than the savings they achieved in the case. Cayhill learned not to argue; to some, the thought of depriving their former spouse of anything they could was far more important than simply saving money. Ah, the power of hate.

For a mere one million dollars, a client could opt for silver service. In this category the clients would still win in two of three cases. But in the third case, which would be selected by purely random methods, Wendells would make judgments more sympathetic to plaintiffs and awards would be realistic, even generous. Gold service is where they made their money; silver service was offered in order to destroy any pattern in the results. "Just hang tight," Cayhill concluded, "He's tried to create a case by using only the cases which fit his desired pattern. Once we introduce the rest, his case becomes pure speculation." Cayhill said this last part in a soothing voice, before asking, "Now, are we okay?"

"Yeah," the accountant answered. "We're okay." In truth, however, Wendells was far from being okay. He was nervous and didn't like it.

Chapter 30

Dunlop had just started the meeting with other partners, when Cayhill walked in. The conversations in the room quickly dried up as the partners looked at him. One of the junior real estate partners broke the quiet by asking in a loud voice, "Hey Les, what's going on?"

"That's what I'd like to know," Cayhill responded, looking at Dunlop as he spoke.

Dunlop didn't shy away from a fight. "I brought the meeting together," he said, "to consider how to deal with the allegations against you and against this firm."

"Funny thing," Cayhill said. "Someone forgot to invite me."

"No one forgot," Dunlop responded. "You weren't invited. And you aren't invited now."

Cayhill sized his adversary up. He had never given the man any serious thought before, assuming Dunlop was like most of the other attorneys in the corporate section – nice enough people but not the sharpest minds in the firm. Since his run-in with Dunlop several days previously, he had decided he needed to build a dossier about him. Again using the man's social security number taken from his submissions to the NJ Bar Association, he had used the same private detective he had previously employed. Cayhill's first inquiry was for the man to find out Dunlop's spending habits, to determine whether Dunlop was indiscreet in his spending habits. He was.

Dunlop spent large sums of money using credit cards. Among the items that caught Cayhill's attention were a number of purchases at an expensive jewelry store. The store was close to their offices, and was quite expensive. As he looked more closely, the purchases all seemed to be on Thursdays in late morning, suggesting that it would be worth investigating what the man did with his Thursday afternoons and evenings.

That hadn't taken long to find out, since the following day had been a Thursday. Not thinking he was being watched, Dunlop did little to camouflage his intentions. He met Penny, one of the firm's secretaries at a hotel bar just after lunch. After a drink at the bar, they went upstairs.

Ordinarily, Cayhill would have applauded Dunlop's actions. Why not screw a good-looking secretary if she were available? Now, though, his partner's appetite for pretty girls made him fair game.

Cayhill gave a thin smile, and responded, "Of course, Preston, I will leave you and your fellow kangaroos to your court. But would you at least do me the courtesy of having a word with me in private before you hang me in absentia? I promise it will only take a moment." It was difficult to reject this seemingly reasonable request, made in front of the partners.

"Very well. Five minutes. No more," Dunlop said, and he walked out of the conference room, with Cayhill following.

Dunlop walked into an empty office, and Cayhill again followed. Dunlop tried to assert control, saying, "Les, spare me the denials…"

Cayhill interrupted, saying, "My five minutes, Preston. And I'm not going to waste time denying anything. I did the things alleged in the complaint, though they can't prove it. Do you remember you personally approved setting up an account in the firm's name last spring for what I called some irregular investments? Well, there's fifteen million dollars sitting in that account. Want to guess where it came from?

"You son of a bitch," Dunlop said. "I want no part of it…"

"Uh-huh," Cayhill interrupted. "Your denials of involvement will be very believable, especially since you signed a check making a charitable contribution for a million dollars, drawn on this account. My only question is how you sequence that denial with the others."

"Others?" Dunlop said, feeling less and less confident.

"Yes, the other denials. Like the denial that you and Penny Olmstead were having sex last Thursday," and here he put a picture of the two of them as they were going up to the room, holding hands, and a picture of them as they left. "You really have to know what to look for," he added, "but if you do you notice things when she left she is wearing a beautiful necklace that she wasn't wearing when she arrived. But, wait a second, she isn't wearing the earrings that she wore when she went in. She must have forgotten them. But don't worry; for a generous tip, I was able to get them back, along with a signed affidavit, from the maid who changed your dirty sheets."

Dunlop said nothing, so Cayhill concluded. "And finally, I wonder whether you deny your affair before or after you deny your request to me to withhold a clearly relevant document in the American Auto case, for fear that it would give a black eye to your client at a time when it was negotiating a deal with the Chinese commies."

Vampires

"That's your word against mine," Dunlop said.

"True," Cayhill replied. "But I can solve that credibility issue by simply producing the document in question."

"You wouldn't," Dunlop croaked.

"Oh but I would," Cayhill replied. "In fact, I am going to comply with all outstanding discovery requests in the American Auto case in the next ten minutes. I wouldn't want a potential change of counsel, in case you're thinking of it, to frustrate justice."

"What is it you want?" Dunlop said, knowing that he had lost this round.

"A statement of support would be nice. You know, something like, 'I know Les Cayhill and I am confident that he would not do the things alleged in the complaint.' And of course, a total stop to the nonsense in the other room."

"And if I agree?" Dunlop asked.

"Then for the moment you remain happily married, happily the respected senior partner of a prestigious law firm, and I can get about the business of taking apart this lawyer who has frightened you," Cayhill answered. Dunlop stared at him, trying to mask the hatred he felt. He finally nodded his assent, and walked to the other room to pull down the meeting.

Chapter 31

Karansky was livid. He had just received word from the judge's law clerk that the hearing on Defendant's motion to compel, a motion that had just been filed, had been scheduled for tomorrow morning at nine a.m. He called and asked whether there was some mistake – his comparable motion had been filed a week ago and was still pending. The clerk, courteous at first, said he would check. However, his tone when he returned to the phone after talking to the judge told Karansky that he was in trouble. The clerk was aloof, telling him nothing other than the time that he should be there. Finally, in response to Karansky's prodding, the clerk, fed up, said, "Look, if you really want to know what the judge said, he said, "Tell that asshole he had better show up and he'd better bring every damn document he's been hiding." With that, the clerk hung up.

"This is not good," Karansky said.

Laura looked up from the computer screen where she was doing some research. "You'll think of something, Steven," she said sweetly. Then she studied his face and became more serious. "Is it the motion to compel?"

"Yes," he answered. "That bastard has somehow convinced the judge to hear his motion and not ours. Goddamnit!"

"Wait a second? Cayhill can't just engage in ex parte conversations with the judge," she said, and then thought about it. "Silly me," she added.

"No, silly me," he said. "I just should have given him the damn document."

"Can't you do it now?" she asked.

"Not without looking like I'm really playing games with the court. Imagine how it would look to the judge – I hold out until the judge gets involved and then I produce it. I'd look guilty as hell," he moped.

"How are you coming with the work to prove the document is a fake?" she asked.

"I guess this is a good time to start," he said. "Do you know anyone at Homeland Security?"

"Sorry," she said.

"Damn. I thought you would have friends in important places. That's the only reason I hired you."

She laughed. "That and the fact that no one else was willing to work for what you pay," she said.

At that moment, Pam walked in. "Pam, how about you?" he asked. "Do you know anyone at Home Security? That I could talk to today?"

"Why in the world do you want to talk to someone in that organization?" she asked.

"Because they have records of everyone who comes in and goes out of the country. I am willing to bet that the mysterious Dr. Fong, who we are told went back to China, didn't go back because he doesn't exist."

"Well…," Pam thought a minute and said, "No promises, but I may know somebody."

"Give it your best shot, please. If there is a Plan B, I've got to figure out what the heck it is."

Chapter 32

Later that afternoon, while Karansky was occupied reviewing the case files to get ready for the hearing, and Laura was doing the legal research she said she wanted to do, Pam knocked on his door.

"It's open, Pam," he said. "What is it?"

"Line 1," she whispered. "It's Preston Dunlop."

"I don't know any…" He caught himself as he said this, and asked, "Preston Dunlop wouldn't be the Dunlop of Dunlop & Schmidt, would he?"

Pam shook her head excitedly, as she answered, "That's the one."

Karansky muttered, "How very odd." Then he picked up the telephone, and said, "Karansky here."

Dunlop wasted no time on introductory pleasantries. "Mr. Karansky, you don't know me," he began. "I am Preston Dunlop, one of the founding partners of Dunlop & Schmidt."

"How are you, sir?" Karansky replied, not knowing what else to say.

"I've been better," Dunlop said. "Before I begin, I just want to make certain I am talking to the right person. Are you the Steven Karansky that is counsel of record for the plaintiff in Chapman v. American Auto?"

"The same," Karansky replied.

"Well, Mr. Karansky, I want to tell you that Mr. Cayhill's action earlier of reducing our settlement offer was not authorized by American Auto. I wanted to reach out to you myself and let you know that the ten million dollars is still on the table through the end of the day," Dunlop said.

Karansky was shocked and said nothing in reply. Dunlop then made the mistake of speaking again, "Mr. Karansky, I know you feel like you've been jerked around, and in light of that the company has authorized me to go to eleven million dollars."

Karansky smelled panic. Nor did he believe for a minute that American Auto had authorized a settlement number only a million dollars higher. Large corporations had a habit of thinking in more than million dollars increments. He guessed that if they had increased the settlement authority, they probably had gone up at least a five million dollars. He began enjoying himself as he said, "Well, Mr. Dunlop, my client had been extremely reluctant to settle for ten million dollars, and was so incensed by your boy Cayhill's reneging on the offer that I am not going to take any offer back to her for less that fifteen million dollars..."

Dunlop made another mistake, interrupting to say that he understood, giving Karansky encouragement to continue, which he did, concluding, "or recommend a settlement for less than twenty."

Dunlop made a choking sound, and said, "Now just a minute here..."

But Karansky smelled blood in the water. Dunlop had given fifteen million way too easily, meaning there was more there. The next multiple of five million was twenty, and he guessed that Dunlop had the authority but hadn't thought he would need to use it. Still, it was worth the gambit to see. He again interrupted Dunlop, saying, "Look Mr. Dunlop, I don't mean to put you on the spot. We both need to check with our clients – you to see how much they will pay, and me to determine the minimum she will accept. Why don't we each take twenty-four hours and see whether we can't find some common ground here."

Dunlop was in a rush, wanting to tie the settlement down before Cayhill knew what was going on. He tried one last time, saying, "Please understand, Mr. Karansky that American Auto wants to settle quickly to avoid adverse publicity. As time goes on, especially if any of the details of the case are reported in the press, the case becomes less valuable, not more."

"I fully understand that. It's only twenty-four hours, during which I will be the picture of discretion. Why, I won't even share our little conversation with Mr. Cayhill."

Dunlop conceded the issue, thanking Karansky for the discretion and concluding with the remark, "So be it. I will talk to you, and he looked at his watch, at 4:30 tomorrow afternoon."

Chapter 33

"This is getting weird," Karansky said as he hung up the phone. He stuck his head into Laura's office. "I'm pretty sure that Preston Dunlop, of Dunlop and Schmidt, just called and offered me fifteen million, maybe more, to settle the American Auto case!"

"Didn't he know we said we'd settle for ten million dollars this morning?" Laura asked.

"Apparently not," he answered. "And I don't think Cayhill knows anything about what Dunlop is doing now."

"So?" she asked, the excitement starting to grow. "What happened? Did you accept?"

"Not yet," Karansky said. "I told him I'd give him an answer tomorrow afternoon. C'mon, come get a coffee with me and help me think it through."

Laura didn't feel at ease with Karansky at the moment. Her discussion with Cecelia had her thinking in terms she hadn't thought possible; but right now, she was undecided about what to do, and as a result didn't know how to act towards him. "Not right now!" she wanted to scream, but didn't. Didn't he understand she needed time to sort things out? "Can you wait a bit?" she answered. "I'm right in the middle of some research that I wanted to complete before the hearing tomorrow."

Karansky walked up to her and closed the computer screen she had been reading. "C'mon," he said with a touch of humor in his voice, "I'm the boss around here and I need to go over our response to Dunlop. For the moment, that trumps the legal research."

Karansky pulled Laura gently to her feet, and still holding her hand, started for the door. "All right, all right," she said. "Stop pulling and let me get my purse."

They walked to the coffee shop, falling into their pattern of waiting to get coffee before talking. "Okay," she began when they had seated themselves with steaming cups of coffee in front of them, "this morning we were going to accept an offer of ten million. Why on earth wouldn't we accept an offer of fifteen?"

"It sounds pretty compelling, doesn't it?" Karansky asked. "But doesn't it make you wonder what makes them want to get rid of the case so badly? The ten million dollars really was a fair offer; to offer another five million dollars means that they must be afraid of having the case proceed."

"Any ideas?" she asked.

"If I had to guess, it must have something to do with the joint venture that was announced between American Auto and the Chinese government. That certainly is big enough to justify the extra money if there were something about this case that might jeopardize the deal. And if my logic is correct, then I'd also say what he is afraid of isn't the potential liability in the case, which even if generous would be no more than a footnote to their financials; it's got to be something that they're afraid will come out if they try the case. That's where I run out of guesses; I have no idea what the real reason is, but it does make me curious."

"What are you going to do?" she asked.

"I don't know," Karansky replied. "But I have until tomorrow to figure it out. Maybe if I sleep on it, the answer will come to me." His choice of words reminded him of their last conversation about sleeping arrangements. "Are you sure it's okay that I don't move out today?" he asked.

"Yes, I'm sure," Laura responded. She didn't want to talk about it further now before she'd decided what she wanted. She sipped the last of her coffee, "Are you ready?" she asked.

"Go ahead," he replied. "I will be up in a minute."

She paused for a moment, and then asked, "Steven, is everything all right?"

"Yes. Absolutely," he said, with a cheerfulness he didn't feel. "I just want to finish my coffee. I'll be up in a minute."

That evening, Laura left work early and went to a shop that specialized in fine Italian lingerie. She'd decided to take Cecelia's advice, and though the pretty black La Perla camisole she bought seemed exorbitantly priced, she knew it made her look stunning. It was made of Italian lace, and barely covered her. It accentuated the movement of her breasts when she moved, drawing the eye to them with a plunging neckline. Wearing panties with it was optional; she decided not to. She admired herself in the mirror. She looked very sexy, and she knew it. Having made her preparations, she sat on Karansky's sofa (which had been delivered that morning) to wait.

She eventually fell asleep, waking only when she heard him noisily trying to unlock the door. He had played basketball, then gone to a bar. Karansky had drank way too much. He stumbled as he entered the apartment. Laura grabbed him to prevent him from falling, and they both fell onto the sofa's welcoming cushions. She extricated herself and took off his shoes, swinging his legs onto the sofa. Karansky stretched like a cat, with his eyes closed. Then, as she placed a cushion under his head, Laura heard him begin to snore. She stood up, looked at him, and with affection not apparent from the words themselves, said, "You dumb son of a bitch." Then she went into her bedroom and crawled into bed.

Karansky woke up in the middle of the night, dying of thirst. It took him a minute to figure out where he was. He went into the kitchen, poured water from the sink into a glass and took a deep drink. Then he took two aspirin, and drank more water. As he stood in the dark room, a memory pushed itself into his consciousness. He remembered seeing Laura in a black negligee and wishing he had not had so much to drink. Karansky looked at his watch by the light of the refrigerator; it was 3:30 a.m.

He walked to the bedroom door and tried the handle. It was unlocked. He opened the door and walked over to the bed. There was a half-moon, and there was just enough light for him to see that Laura was still wearing the camisole. She was sleeping with one leg under the sheet; the other above. He sat on the edge of the bed, took off his clothes, and got into bed with her. She stirred a bit, and the last thing he remembered before he fell back asleep was thinking that she had dressed this way for him, and he had been too big a jerk to realize it.

Later that morning Karansky woke with his arms around Laura, but this time she didn't jump. Instead she stretched, with her arms extending above her head and her toes pointed as part of the effort of stretching her feet in the opposite direction. As she stretched, he rolled on top of her.

"Good morning," she said. "C'mon Romeo, get off me. You missed your opportunity last night. There's no time now; we have a court date this morning, remember?"

He looked at his watch, and was considering the options when the phone rang. "No," he whined. "They can call back." She pushed him off her and looked at the phone.

"Steven, it's Pam," she said. "It could be important."

He sighed but got out of bed, still aroused, picked up the phone and said "Yes?" Laura got up out of bed, took off what she had slept in, and draped it on him on her way to the shower.

"Steven, are you listening?" Pam asked, wondering at Karansky's lack of reaction to what she had just said.

"Sorry," he said, "I dropped the phone." He had decided under the circumstances that a lie was easier on all concerned than the truth. "Could you repeat what you just said?"

"I said I found you a body," she said, her excitement evident in her voice. "He's a Director of Airport Security at Homeland Security."

Karansky was flabbergasted, and didn't try to conceal it. "Pam this sounds too good to be true. How in the world did you find this guy? And how did you get him to help?"

"You aren't the only one with a social life," she said. "I've been going out with him for two years."

"Pam, you never said a word," Karansky said. "Why didn't you say something yesterday?"

"I couldn't just announce this without checking with him," she responded. "And he had to check with his supervisor about whether it would be okay for him to help."

"They're willing to let him?" he asked.

"They are," she answered. "It is part of their public relations campaign. They think it helps with their public acceptance when they can strut their stuff."

"Last question," he asked. "Can you get him to court by 9:00 a.m.?"

"We're already here," she said. "At least we're at the coffee shop across from the court house. Where are you?"

"Pam, I swear you are a wonder. I'll be there in twenty minutes," he said. "Make that thirty," he corrected himself, as Laura walked back into the room with only a towel around her.

About thirty-five minutes later, or five minutes to nine, Karansky walked into the courtroom. Cayhill was already there, sitting at Defendant's table. "Good morning, counselor," he said. "It seems like we are going to get to know each other very well."

Karansky mumbled a response, something like, "I guess we will." He didn't know how men like Cayhill could do what they did, going for the jugular one minute, and being gracious the next. He wanted to hate the man, but found his smile and demeanor charming.

He stared at Cayhill for a moment, and thought of starting a more serious conversation, but the entrance of Judge Hernandez interrupted such thoughts. The judge, who had been appointed by the governor almost eight years ago, was used to having absolute power within his court. This causes a certain view of the world. Within his domain, he could be just or unjust. He defined those words, and woe to the attorney who didn't understand that.

Both attorneys rose as he entered the court room. Both started to sit as the Judge sat. Before Karansky felt the chair beneath him, the judge began, "Mr. Karansky, if it isn't too much trouble, would you mind standing a bit longer." Karansky rose again. "Good, thank you," the judge said. "Let's get right to the point. Do you have any document or documents, Mr. Karansky, that are responsive to Defendant's request for production that you have not turned over?"

"Your honor, it's not that simple…" Karansky began.

"Oh, but I'm afraid that it is," the judge responded. "It's a yes or no answer. Think carefully about the question, but don't you dare say anything else other than one of those two words."

Karansky sighed. "Yes," he said. "Now may I explain?" Karansky noticed as he said this that Laura had entered the back of the court room with Pam and the man from Homeland Security. He assumed that the witness was prepared and ready to go. He gathered himself and attempted to begin making the argument he had prepared with Laura that morning. The judge interrupted him before he could begin. "I'll ask the questions," the judge said. "When you get a courtroom and become a judge you can make the rules. Now I do." Judge Hernandez resumed his interrogation. "Was the document subject to a claim of privilege?"

"No, it was not," Karansky said, thinking he was having an out of body morning.

"Was it exempt under some specific rule, and let me warn you here that a lie here and I promise you I'll have your license to practice law."

"No," said Karansky.

"Did you bring the document or documents with you, and are you prepared to produce them at this time?" the judge demanded.

"I did not bring the document with me. And yes, I will produce anything your honor orders me to produce."

"It's a little late for gestures of obedience, counselor. You are hereby directed to produce such document immediately and to pay all attorneys' fees as may have been incurred by Defendant in seeking its production, said request for fees to be submitted by tomorrow." Here the judge looked at Cayhill, who signaled it would be done. The judge continued, "And you shall be fined one thousand dollars per hour, or any fraction of an hour, until you do produce said document. Do you understand? That means you already owe the court one thousand dollars."

The judge looked at Karansky, who said nothing. The judge started gathering his papers, and asked almost absentmindedly whether there were any questions.

"Yes your honor," Laura said, walking up from the back of the court to stand next to Karansky.

"And who might you be?" the judge asked.

"My name is Laura Simon, and with the court's permission, I am co-counsel to Mr. Karansky in this matter.

The judge looked bemused. "Young lady," he said, "you don't need my consent to appear as co-counsel before me, though I do appreciate the consideration."

"Actually, I do your honor. You see, though I graduated law school, I don't take the bar examination for another two weeks, and am not yet an attorney."

"Well, you have my permission, little lady," the judge was smiling now. Do you have a question about what happened?"

"Yes, your honor, I do," she replied.

Karansky leaned over and whispered, "Do you know what you're doing?"

She whispered back, "Trust me. This is what I had been researching." Then out loud, she said, "The imposition of a fine is akin to criminal contempt," she began.

The judge interrupted, "You're part right. Though it isn't really kin to criminal contempt," the judge was visibly having fun with this, "it is criminal contempt."

Laura paused and looked to make certain the court reporter had taken down every word. He had. "Well then, my question is this. How can you impose criminal contempt sanctions without an opportunity for a hearing?" Laura asked, and then cited two court cases from higher courts that said you could not. "The answer, if I may, is that you can't.

It would be like sentencing someone to jail without an opportunity to be heard."

The judge squirmed a bit, but wasn't about to give in to this woman who wasn't even an attorney yet. "That may be true if there is any issue to be heard, counselor," the judge said. But you heard your co-counsel. He admitted he had the document, that it was neither privileged nor was it exempt from any disclosure pursuant to any rule. What possible facts could the hearing elicit? I've got to tell you I can't think of a damn thing," the judge paused here and turning to the reporter, said, "please type that as 'can't think of a thing." Judge Hernandez felt the need to explain to this pretty, almost-an-attorney neophyte, "Don't get me wrong, young lady. I mean I'm into due process and all. But I am not going to sit here and waste my time if there are no facts under which your co-counsel's actions could be justified."

Laura glanced at Karansky; then took the plunge. "Your honor," she stated, "we would produce facts that will show the document is a fake."

The judge interrupted, saying, "That still wouldn't affect your duty to produce it."

Laura continued, "And that Mr. Cayhill was not only aware of this document, but already had a copy of it. Under such circumstances…"

Cayhill was back on his feet, "Your honor this is the most preposterous web of lies. Ms. Simon is casting wild accusations without a shred of evidence to back them up. I would ask that she be admonished by the court."

The judge stared first at Cayhill, then at Laura and asked, exasperated, "What the hell…" and he nodded at the court reporter again, and said, "heck" "…is going on here? Ms. Simon, is this bullshit," and here he said, "nonsense" to the reporter, "or do you have evidence?"

"Your honor," Laura began, "We have reason to believe that Doctor Fong, the alleged author of the document, does not exist. We also…"

Both Cayhill and the judge interrupted her. Cayhill shouted over her that the accusations were absurd, and that he had, in fact, had himself driven the doctor back to the airport." The judge yelled even louder at Cayhill to shut up, and then said to Laura, "I don't give a hoot about your beliefs, young lady. I asked whether you had any hard evidence. Now you do or you don't. Which is it?"

She looked at Cayhill, who assumed she was bluffing and began smirking. She looked directly at him, as she said in a clear voice, "We do your honor."

"Well, I'm waiting," the judge said. "Let's hear it."

"Your honor," I do this with great respect, but part of the evidence is known only by Mr. Cayhill himself. There is no one else who has been willing to attest to the existence of the supposed author of the document, Dr. Fong. If you want this matter cleared up, I would need to ask him a few questions."

"Ask away," the judge said. "Cayhill, get your butt in the witness chair."

"Your honor! This is very prejudicial," Cayhill objected. "I can't be expected to participate both as an attorney and as a witness."

The judge, whose wrath was doled out fairly, meaning to everyone, said, "Very well. Since you must be the witness, use a different lawyer.

I see Mr. Hooper, who I recognize from a former case, sitting behind you. Mr. Hooper, how would you like to be your boss's attorney?"

Mr. Hooper looked decidedly uncomfortable, but moved into place as Cayhill walked up and sat in the witness box. The clerk swore him in. Laura looked at the judge who had begun enjoying himself again. "He's all yours," he said.

Thank you, your Honor," Laura said. "I have only a few questions, Mr. Cayhill. First, you stated earlier that you had taken Dr. Fong to the airport, is that right?"

"Yes," Cayhill answered.

"Do you remember what day or date that was?" she asked.

"It was the week after the accident," he said. "I don't remember the exact date."

"Last question. Did you create the Fong report, or direct that it be created?" This last question, asked very calmly, caused a volcanic eruption. Cayhill came out of his chair, then thought better of it, and sat back down, replying, "I won't dignify that with an answer."

"I don't give a rat's ass whether the question has any dignity," Judge Hernandez snapped, waving generally at the reporter who signaled that the judge's language would be less colorful in the record. "You will answer the question, please."

Cayhill simmered for a second. "Of course not," He answered tersely.

Judge Hernandez nearly laughed. "Whoa, little lady. I thought you had him in a corner there," he said, chuckling, "but he escaped."

"Your honor, I wanted to give him the opportunity to tell the truth. I would now like to call Anthony Tomas," she said.

"Miss Simon, I haven't heard anything I'd call evidence yet. I will give this matter fifteen more minutes. If there's a point, I suggest you get to it quickly," the judge said.

Once the clerk had sworn Tomas in, Laura wasted no time. After asking him to state his name and address, she asked him to explain whether he was employed.

"I am the Director of Airport Security for the Office of Homeland Security," he answered.

"What does that job entail?" she asked. He looked at her, not understanding the question, so she tried again. "What are your job responsibilities?"

"I'm responsible for airport security," he replied.

"As part of your responsibilities, do you track everyone that comes through airports?" she asked.

"Yes," he said. Those listening had started to realize where this was going.

"Mr. Tomas, is it possible to enter or leave the country without your agency knowing about it?" she asked.

Vampires

"I won't say it is impossible for someone like James Bond to evade our controls. But for law abiding citizens and anyone short of super sleuths, we keep computerized records of everyone who comes and goes."

"Mr. Tomas, did you have occasion to check whether anyone with the name Fong left this country, headed for China, during the week of August 7?"

The judge interrupted, "For Christ's sake!" he exclaimed. "Just tell us whether anyone named Fong passed through a U.S. airport that week."

"There were two people with the name "Fong" that did leave that week," Tomas said, turning to face the judge. "The first was a manager at a governmental ministry who left for China out of Atlanta. Doesn't fit the profile here."

"Yes, yes," the judge said. "What about the second?"

"The second was a medical doctor who left out of New York," Tomas said. "I inquired further and it turns out the good doctor is a woman. I inquired further to see if perhaps she could be mistaken for a man."

"Well?" prodded the judge.

"I looked at the file myself, your honor," Tomas said, smiling. "There is no way Dr. Fong could ever be mistaken for a man."

"So what you're saying is the guy who signed that letter…" the judge paused…"

Tomas finished the judge's sentence: "hasn't gone back to China. He's still in this country. Or there is one other possibility."

"And what is that?" Judge Hernandez asked.

"That he didn't leave and he didn't stay," Tomas said. "That he never existed…"

At the end of Tomas' testimony, Laura asked the judge to vacate his previous order finding Karansky in contempt. Cayhill objected stating that all of these issues went to the weight that should be given the document and not a party's obligation to produce it. The judge held up his hand, saying, "Enough!" He looked pointedly at Cayhill and Karansky and said, "One of you deserves to be thrown in jail for your behavior during discovery. The only problem is I can't figure out right now which one of you that should be. The prior order is vacated, but I warn both of you that as soon as I figure this out, one of you is getting a long vacation up the river!"

"Now," Judge Hernandez finished, beginning to stand. "you all have a lovely evening. Court resumes at one tomorrow."

Vampires

Chapter 34

Karansky wanted to kiss everyone. He settled for kissing Pam, for coming up with the witness, Tomas for being such a brilliant witness; Laura for being such a brilliant attorney, and the waitress at the Time To Eat Diner for being such a brilliant waitress. "This day hit the skids around nine o'clock," he said, "but thanks to all of you I can't remember a day in court that started so badly ending so well!" They had a typical diner meal, with giant portions of comfort food at a reasonable price.

As the waitress was clearing their plates, Pam cleared her throat, and looked as if she were going to say something. She didn't, at least at first. Then, clearing her throat a second time, she managed, "Steven, I have something to tell you that you may not like." Then not happy with that preview, she added, "But you should."

"Okay," Steven responded cautiously, wondering where this was going.

"I haven't had a real vacation in so long, and now I want to go. Wait, wait," she added as Karansky was about to say something. "This isn't really a vacation. Tony asked me to marry him, and this will be our honeymoon…"

Laura gave a happy scream, threw her arms around Pam and gave her a hug. Karansky, who was not an overly demonstrative man, gave her a hug next, after asking her if she was happy and getting an "Oh yes!"

in response. For the next half hour or so, they forgot all else and heard about the happy couple's plans. Then, Pam asked for the rest of the day off so that they could go pack. She had truly waited until the last minute to share her news; they were leaving tomorrow.

Apparently, it takes much longer to arrange a wedding than it does a romantic trip, so they were reversing the order of things and taking a honeymoon trip together to Bermuda before rather than after they were married. This elicited further expressions of affection, along with statements of benign jealousy from Laura. Eventually, the two of them departed, leaving Laura and Steven alone. Laura sighed deeply, loaded with possibilities. Steven didn't pick up the invitation to explore what she was thinking and the conversation eventually drifted back to the safer topic of work.

"What do you think Cayhill will do now?" Laura asked. "He looked shaken."

"He was," Karansky said, happy to be back in a discussion where he felt comfortable. "But I don't think he's out of tricks. Besides, we don't really know if there's anything in his files. But I am supposed to call Dunlop back in about two hours, and I've got to decide whether it is worth the extra ten million dollars to see whatever it is they are hiding. I am troubled by the defense that could be mustered against our claim. You know, how American Auto really did try to do the right thing, and the result of lawsuits like this will be to punish it for trying to keep manufacturing jobs in this country. After all, if this accident had happened in most third world countries, there wouldn't have been a lawsuit."

"You sound like you believe that yourself," Laura said.

"Don't you?" Karansky asked, admitting his own feelings. "No, I think that if there is nothing in their files, then ten million dollars is a good settlement. And even if there is, I can't imagine any document generating more than another five or ten million dollars. I keep coming back to the fact that the smart thing here is to accept Dunlop's offer."

"So, that's it then?"

"It is if I am convinced that it's best for the client," he said. "But here is where it gets very delicate…" he added.

"What gets delicate?" she asked.

"The agreement under which I sold my interest in any settlement provides that if they take the collateral, which was my house and which they did take, and then monetize the collateral in an amount sufficient to satisfy their claims, then the participation in the settlement reverts to me."

"You have totally lost me," Laura admitted.

"It's a bit complicated," he admitted. "I borrowed two million dollars, in exchange for which I gave up my share in a settlement of the case. At the time, it looked like that share would be worth about three and a third million. But when that deal fell through, they seized the collateral, the house, instead. The house goes up for auction next Monday. If they receive as proceeds from the sale the amount of the original loan plus interest and expenses, then the interest in the settlement reverts to me. Now, the interest in the settlement at fifteen million dollars is worth five million dollars, significantly more than the two million I received. Thus, waiting for the house to sell is far better for me, for us, assuming that it does sell."

Vampires

She immediately saw the dilemma and volunteered, "But you can't wait until Monday if you're convinced that settlement is in the best interest of the client and that waiting poses a risk to that settlement. To do so would violate your ethical responsibilities to the client." She sat back a minute, before simply concluding, "Wow. That hurts."

"Yes, it does. But at this point I don't see an alternative to accepting the offer. I've thought about all the arguments I could make for waiting. At ten million they are colorable; at fifteen million they are not."

"So, what now?" she asked.

"I call this afternoon, which closes that case. That means we have one less case to work on. I'd say that calls for a celebration," Karansky said. "I think we go back, get cleaned up and go out for a really nice dinner."

She laughed. "Define 'cleaned up' before I agree."

"I thought I'd get in the bath, and you'd wash my back," he responded.

She smiled at him. "That's what I thought. I will think about it," she said, and they walked back to their car, thinking that if all was not right with the world, it still wasn't such a bad place to live.

Laura's cell phone rang, and she picked up after looking at her display and seeing Cecilia's name pop up. She had barely begun to say hello, when Cecilia, speaking in a panicky voice, whispered, "Where are you?"

"What do you mean?" Laura asked. "Where are you? And what's wrong?"

"I'm scared, I'm so scared," Cecilia said, sobbing softly.

"Cecilia, we are on our way. Just tell me where you are, and we'll be there as soon as we can."

"I came to your office," she said. "Everything was locked up, and I think I was being followed. I am hiding in one of the stalls in the women's room right outside the office."

"Okay, don't move. We'll be there in ten minutes."

"Hurry," Cecilia said, and hung up to choke off a sob. Karansky, never a great driver, drove like a maniac, weaving around cars as he sped towards their office. A few minutes from their destination, a police-man in a patrol car pulled behind them with his lights flashing, and signaled for him to pull over.

Karansky didn't stop, instead telling Laura to call 911 on her cell phone. She did and reached it right away, and told the dispatcher that they were in a 2004 Ford Mustang, and that they were being chased by a police car on Interstate 287 heading towards Morristown. She told the dispatcher that they were in a life or death situation, that someone had just called who was hiding in a bathroom and that they had to keep going.

The dispatcher tried calming her down first, saying "Ma'am, ma'am. Can you describe the car pursuing you? Laura had turned the cell phone on speakerphone so that Karansky could listen. He now yelled, "It looks like Bernards township colors."

"Okay, I'll be right back with you." As they waited, the cop pulled alongside of them, signaling angrily for them to pull over. Karansky also saw another police vehicle pulling onto the highway. The second car pulled in front of them and started to slow down, giving Karansky no choice but to slow down as well. He banged on his steering wheel in frustration, adding a "Fuck!" for good measure, when the second police car suddenly sped up and pulled into the other lane. As Karansky sped up again he pulled even with the police car. This time the cop gave them the thumbs up sign. Karansky checked his speedometer. It read ninety miles an hour. They got off at an exit before they hit the town, and Karansky drove as fast as he could, which seemed very slow, to their office near Headquarters Plaza.

Karansky pulled into a no-parking zone in front of their building, and jumped out of the car. He began running towards the building entrance, Laura close behind. As he reached the outside door to the building, he saw the police cars pull up and the two cops jump out. He started to punch in the electronic code to unlock the door, when Laura pulled on the door and it opened. She looked at him, and he didn't say what he was thinking, that it was not a good omen for what they would find. The short delay at the door gave the police time to reach them. One of them pulled his revolver, and said to let them go first.

"She called from a third floor bathroom, a lady's room in the hall. I can lead you there faster than you'll find it," Karansky said.

"Okay," the cop said, "go, but when we get there let us go in first." The deal was struck and Karansky literally bounded up the stairs. Laura was in far better shape, but was so apprehensive that she hung back, reaching the landing last.

"There," Karansky said, pointing at the door to the bathroom. The other policeman had pulled his revolver as well, and had called for backup on his phone. Looking at each other, they both went in quickly. There was no shooting and no sound at all for what seemed like forever, but was probably only a minute or two. Then Karansky heard what sounded like the sounds of one of them retching. He looked at Laura, and said that he was going to go in.

"Then I will too," she said.

"No, let me go in first," he said.

"Don't leave me," she pleaded.

"All right," he said.

The cops emerged, both looking as if they hadn't any color in their faces. "I'm sorry," one of them said. "She's dead."

Laura burst into tears and buried her face in Karansky's shoulder. The cop who had spoken said, "I'm very sorry, but we need one of you to go in and identify the body."

"I'll do it," said Karansky. He tried to disengage himself from Laura.

"No," she said. "I've got to see her too."

"Lady…," the cop started to say, but she cut him off.

"I know what you're going to say. But do you really think it is worse than my imagination?" Laura sobbed.

The cop shrugged. "Suit yourself," he replied. "Just be careful. I don't want either one of you touching anything." He stepped aside, and Karansky took Laura by the hand and led the way into the bathroom. He had expected blood. There was none, except around Cecelia's neck where the wire used to strangle her had cut into her skin. It was her

Vampires

eyes that were so disturbing, filled with horror and pain. No, not pain. Agony.

She was still in the stall, with her head by the toilet. Her hair was wet and matted. It looked as if her killer had pushed her head put into the toilet prior to strangling her. Karansky's wondered who would do such a thing?

The cop asked if they knew her, and Karansky said "Yes. Her name is Cecilia van Horn."

Karansky and Laura were then asked to wait outside. Homicide detectives were on their way. Karansky said they would wait in his offices, which were right next door. When they entered, Laura sat on the sofa in the waiting area, sobbing. His eyes were tearing as well, but he was also as angry as he'd ever been. While he had seen drugs spread around the body, he put no stock in their presence. Karansky was certain that Cecelia had been killed because of the lawsuit. The horrible way she had been killed had been intended as a message to others.

Karansky decided not to wait. It was late afternoon. Most hard working lawyers would still be at it. He wanted to know, he had to know whether Cayhill was involved. He knew that once the detectives were in charge of the investigation, they would not permit him to do what he wanted to do. He picked up the phone and dialed. Then, identifying himself to the voice on the other end, he asked for Lester Cayhill. Laura became quiet and stared at him.

Cayhill answered. "Calling to gloat?" he asked.

"You son-of-a-bitch, you know why I am calling," Karansky responded.

"I haven't a clue, but I don't have to listen to this…" Cayhill snapped, and was starting to hang up when he heard Karansky raise his voice, "Wait!"

"Mr. Karansky, I have nothing to say to you." Cayhill said, once again trying to end the conversation.

Either Cayhill really didn't know what had happened, or he was an exceptional actor. Karansky decided to test it. "I just wanted to let you know that we'll be filing a voluntary dismissal of the RICO case in the morning."

There was silence at the other end. Finally, Cayhill said, "I don't suppose it is because you believe me now. So to what do I owe my good fortune?"

"You're saying you don't know?" Karansky asked.

"Know what?" Cayhill asked.

"Cecilia van Horn was murdered in a restroom right outside my office," Karansky said.

"My God!" exclaimed Cayhill. "When?"

"Less than an hour ago. What I believe," responded Karansky, "is that she was killed because of the lawsuit. I'm not saying that you did it or had it done. But like it or not, you are involved and I suspect you know the killers."

"Has it occurred to you that I would be the primary suspect for her murder?" Cayhill protested. "Has it occurred to you that someone

might have wanted you to jump to the very conclusion you are jumping to? There's only one problem with your assumption: I didn't do it!"
Cayhill shouted into the phone, and then hung up.

Chapter 35

Cayhill sat quietly for a few moments before calling Wendells on his cell phone. When Wendells answered, Cayhill lashed into him, wasting no time on banalities. "I thought I told you to sit tight, and not do anything stupid!" he exclaimed.

Wendells responded, his tone angry and defensive, "What the fuck are you talking about? I did sit tight."

"Are you saying that you didn't have Cecilia van Horn killed?" Cayhill asked skeptically.

Wendells was shocked. "Do you mean the plaintiff in the Racketeering case?" he asked.

"Yes," said Cayhill.

"Jesus, I wouldn't do that," Wendells said. "The suspicion would come right back at us."

"No shit," Cayhill said. "It already has. Now think hard. Does anyone know about our relationship? Did you say anything to anyone?"

"Not a chance," Wendells responded. "The clients we've helped obviously know, but I can't imagine any of them spilling the beans. They'd take themselves down at the same time as they took us down. Why would they do it?"

Cayhill thought a minute, and then asked, "Scott, how about our present clients? Are there any that could have done it?"

Wendells laughed. "Donny Bruno could have. I'm never quite sure about that guy, if you know what I mean. But, I mean, why would he?"

"I don't know. If he hates women enough, and his wife in particular, he might not have taken kindly to van Horn threatening his scheme to screw his ex out of her equitable distribution. Or, he might just have wanted to kill the project, so to speak," Cayhill said. "Maybe he figured that if she blabbed and everything became public, then his effort to nail his wife would come out."

"Well, Bruno is definitely a possibility," Wendells said. "But whoever did it, they did us a favor, didn't they?"

"Gee, do you think so?" Cayhill asked his voice dripping with sarcasm. "Sure, the civil case goes away. In its place, if I'm not mistaken, will be a criminal investigation that will uncover our little operation, if we're not careful. And if that happens, you can bet that a criminal prosecution for murder one will not be far behind."

"So what do we do?" Wendells asked?

"We can do one of two things," Cayhill said. "We can admit what we did. We'll both be ruined professionally, and there's a good chance that we will be prosecuted criminally."

"Not to mention that Bruno won't be the only client wanting us dead," Wendells added. That option sucks. What's the other one?"

"That we tough it out and deny everything," Cayhill said. "That may require us to invoke the Fifth Amendment's right to refuse to testify to a grand jury in order to avoid incriminating ourselves."

"And what happens if we do that?" Wendells asked.

I don't know," Cayhill answered.

"Well, that's easy. The unknown beats door number one," Wendells said. "We've got to stick together," he said out loud. Privately, he started toying with the possibility of cutting a deal with the district attorney, essentially blaming Cayhill for being the mastermind of the entire deal and most likely being the murderer.

"I agree totally," concluded Cayhill. Cayhill didn't trust the man he had been talking to, and decided not to reveal his real strategy to Wendells. He was convinced that Wendells would try to double-cross him at the first opportunity. Unless Cayhill struck first.

Chapter 36

Neither Laura nor Karansky even attempted to sleep. The first several hours Laura spent sitting on the bed, rocking back and forth, saying things like "Oh God, it's my fault isn't it?" Gradually, the need to apologize to Cecilia was replaced by a slow and steady sobbing.

Karansky tried to comfort her, but the truth is he wasn't doing so well either. He had concluded his use of RICO likely contributed to the woman's death. He had prodded the bad guys and they hadn't liked it.

It was around two in the morning when Laura was finally composed enough to ask "Why?"

Steven shook his head. "I'm not sure. I think we're supposed to believe it was to kill the litigation. Without a plaintiff there isn't a lawsuit. The brutality of the attack looks like it would deter anyone else from wanting to take her place. My first thought was that it was Cayhill, or someone in league with him. But now I'm not so sure."

"Why?" Laura asked, not yet seeing.

"Because all this does for him is to trade a civil lawsuit against a poorly financed rival for a criminal lawsuit brought by the state where money is not an issue. A grand jury investigation has got to be Cayhill's worst nightmare, and he is smart enough to know it."

"So if he isn't involved then who did it?" she asked.

"I don't know," Karansky said. "What about her ex-husband? Is he capable of this kind of violence?"

"I've never met him," Laura replied. "But Cecilia never mentioned any violence. It's possible but I'd have thought she would have said something to me if he beat her, or was the type to scare her."

"How about boyfriends?" he suggested, as he went down the mental checklist in his head.

"She said something about going out with some guy named Larry she met recently. He's a ball player. But again, she never mentioned anything about him hitting her or doing anything that made her scared of him," Laura said.

"You know, Cayhill said something interesting," Karansky observed. "He asked whether it had occurred to me that someone might want us to think that he'd committed the murder. It becomes very interesting when one considers it from that angle. Who would benefit from the litigation coming to a close, and would also gain from Cayhill being charged with Cecelia's murder?"

She thought a moment and then realized she thought she knew the answer. "What about Preston Dunlop?" she asked. "Had the lawsuit continued, the reputation of his law firm gets tarnished, and he and the rest of the partners are put at risk because one partner is legally responsible for the acts of other partners."

"Right," he agreed. "Plus you have to assume that there's bad blood between the two men for Dunlop to try to settle a case Cayhill was handling behind Cayhill's back. This would be a way to get at Cayhill without leaving fingerprints."

"It fits!" she said, "Do you really think he did it?"

"It's possible; I don't know the man beyond a phone call. Which reminds me," he said, "with all that's going on, I forgot to call Dunlop back and give him an answer on the American Auto case. Come to think of it, I didn't hear from him either."

"Maybe he was busy?" She was facing away at the moment she said this. He went up and stood close to her, putting his arms around her. She leaned her head back and let it rest on his shoulder. He kissed her on her ear and said, "This horrible tragedy has prevented me from telling you that you're the best thing that has ever happened to me," he said.

"You're not too bad yourself," she said and paused before adding, "sweetheart." She hadn't before used terms of endearment with him, and wasn't certain if he'd like it.

He did, responding, "Aw, I'm crazy about you," he said in response. Then, he smiled and added "muffin."

The joke, though, was on him. She not only made him tell her over and over that he could not imagine his life without her, but also made him promise her a raise, given how indispensable she'd become. Once he'd agreed, she thanked him for bringing her pay to almost a quarter of what she would have made had she gone to work at Cayhill's firm.

"Can you imagine," she mused, "if Cayhill had offered me a job? Everything would be so different. I would have been working there, and if we'd met at all, it would have been in a situation where we were opposing counsel."

Vampires

"Do you think he's handsome?" Karansky asked, suddenly feeling it was important that she like him more, much more, than Cayhill.

"God, no!" She looked at him. "Don't go developing some male insecurity complex," she teased. "He's not my type. Besides, I haven't seen his wounded puppy look. Yours is great." She was smiling again. It felt good.

Shortly afterward he looked over and saw her sleeping in her chair. He gently carried her to the bed, and got in next to her. A moment later he too was asleep.

Chapter 37

Despite the lateness of the hour they fell asleep, Karansky woke up relatively early – at 6:15 a.m. He got up quietly and went into the bathroom to shave and shower, both of which he did while Laura slept. He then got dressed quickly, kissed her softly on the forehead, and let himself out the door. He walked the short distance to work, took the stairs up to his office, and tried to think.

It was only a few minutes after seven, normally a time when the phone was quiet and the ideal time for him to sort things through. Karansky started with the question uppermost in his mind: who killed Cecelia? There were three choices: Les Cayhill; Preston Dunlop; and some-one else. The third category he included for the sake of completeness, though he had a strong feeling it was one of the first two. Karansky tried to understand his conviction that it was one of the first two, but couldn't articulate a reason. He had learned to trust his instincts, and they were telling him that one of them, even if they hadn't personally killed her, was involved in Cecelia's death.

He first thought through Cayhill. It didn't make any sense for the reason Cayhill himself had angrily raised when Karansky had called him. Cayhill was the natural suspect, and was bound to be put under a microscope by the district attorney. If the RICO allegations were factual, and Karansky believed that they were, then Cecelia's murder increased the risk to Cayhill that a methodical investigation, which the DA could do far better than Karansky, would unearth the truth.

That would likely mean jail time, and almost certainly end Cayhill's career. Why would Cayhill risk that?

Dunlop, on the other hand, would be an unlikely target for the DA. Not only was his connection to the victim more remote, but Dunlop was such a powerful political force in this part of New Jersey that he would be just about the last person the DA would want to tangle with. Yet he was a clear beneficiary of the RICO case's demise, and if he truly did want to cause harm to Cayhill, this would do it. But a lot of the reasoning that made Dunlop a plausible suspect depended on the relations between the two men, a relationship about which Karansky was only guessing at this point.

As he was beginning a mental inventory of what he knew about the relationship between the two men, his phone rang. It was Dunlop. "I was going to leave you a voicemail," Dunlop said, sounding surprised. "I didn't know you'd be in this early."

"But I am," Karansky said. "So we can get this done. What's the offer?"

"Eleven million dollars," Dunlop said. Kransky's intake of breath upon hearing the offer gave away his disappointment. The number was less than the offer Dunlop seemingly had put on the table during their last discussion. Dunlop hurriedly continued, "Now, before you become disappointed about the number, let me explain. "First, I became aware yesterday that you were prepared to accept ten million dollars," Dunlop began.

"That is no longer the case," Karansky said. "For one thing,…"

Dunlop interrupted. "I understand. Please allow me to finish explaining the offer, before you object to what it is."

Karansky was contrite. "I'm sorry. Please continue. I will wait to react until I hear it all."

"Thank you," Dunlop said. "The agreement will be signed next Tuesday," he said, stressing the timing. "Of course, I am aware of the timing on the auction of your house, and the fact that you would lose your share of the settlement if this settles before your house sells.

"What does my house have to do with the settlement?" Karansky asked, not liking the direction Dunlop seemed to be going.

"Well, in addition to the eleven million American Auto will pay to settle the case next Tuesday, I commit to you separately that I will bid no less than two and one half million dollars for your house on Monday, an amount if you study the agreement as I have, you will see covers the necessary fees and returns the interest in the lawsuit to you. That means, of course, that you will get to keep your original interest in the settlement. If I'm not mistaken, you'll get a third of eleven million dollars, or more than three and a half million dollars, rather than the two you would get if we did the deal today."

Karansky did his best to maintain a poker face, though it was clear he had underestimated this man. Karansky had no idea how Dunlop even knew about the private terms of his arrangement with his client. "I can see that you have been talking to Cayhill. Does he know about this offer?"

Dunlop was silent a moment and then answered, "No, he does not. You are talking to me, not him. I speak for the client, not him. If I didn't tell you before, I'm telling you now: if any of what I offered leaks to him, then the deal is off. Now, what is your response?"

"My answer is no," Karansky said. "I can't possibly take a deal where I profit separately from my client, as you ought to know. If you want to settle this, then take the money you are using to buy the house, and include it in the amount of money given to plaintiff. But the way it is structured is a blatant ethical violation."

Dunlop frowned. "Fortunately, you don't need to worry because another of my partners sits on the Ethics panel and he told me privately that should this matter ever come to him, he would find it not to be an ethics violation. And no, I don't want to pay the extra two and a half million to the widow. The difference is that in my formulation I get the house."

"You're amazing," Karansky said.

Dunlop, who agreed with that assessment, saw in it no sarcasm, and replied simply, "Thank you."

"The answer is still no," Karansky said. "The deal stinks, in my opinion and it doesn't get any better because a crony of yours is ready to say it smells like a rose."

"I think you're making a terrible mistake," Dunlop said, his voice cold. "You have until tomorrow morning to reconsider. After that, it's out of my hands."

Karansky hung up the phone just as Laura walked into his office. Seeing him pale, she asked if everything were okay.

"I just talked to Dunlop," he answered.

"And?" she prompted.

"It didn't settle," he replied, explaining why briefly. "We've got to get ready to try the case against American Auto. Are you ready to handle witnesses?"

"And that, ladies and gentlemen, concludes today's entertainment. Yes, Mr. Karansky, I'm here to support you."

He shook his head. "What you've done is great. But I'm talking about taking witnesses, leading ours though direct and protecting them during cross, and cross-examining theirs."

"I'm not ready for that," she insisted. "Pleadings are familiar; we practiced writing those in law school. But I have never questioned a witness, not even in a deposition. I'm not ready for that."

"Well, I think you are. In any event," he said, "it would be nuts not to use you. The judge took a real liking to you. He doesn't think much of me. I'm telling you that makes it vital that you be seen taking an active role in the case. And that means taking witnesses."

Laura did not look well. "Steven, I would love to – if I could. But it won't help if I get up in front of this judge and fall on my face."

"You won't," Karansky said in his soothing voice. "Look, there are a few basic rules for questioning witnesses. Follow them and you'll look like a pro. Rule one: don't ask open-ended questions that enable the witness to make speeches. You ask the question, make the speech, and then turn to the witness, and say, "isn't that so?" The last thing in the world you want to do is to ask a question that begins with "why." It will permit the witness to run amok, giving speeches as to why he's good and you and your client are evil."

"Steven…" she tried to say.

Vampires

"Are you listening?" he asked. She nodded and tried to interrupt but he continued. "Next, rule number two, never ask a question that you don't know how the witness will answer. Keep one step ahead of him. Got it?"

She nodded. This time she didn't try to speak, letting him finish.

"Last rule. Make your point and sit down. Don't ask that extra question," he concluded. She looked puzzled at this one, so he explained. "Geez, didn't they teach you anything in law school? Well, this last rule is designed to prevent the witness, after you have made your point, from undermining it. The example my professor used was: 'Question: So you did not see my client bite off plaintiff's ear, is that right?' Answer: That is correct.' That is the time to sit down. The extra question would be: 'Question: Then you have no basis for claiming that he did in fact bite off his ear, do you?' And the witness answers, 'Well sir, I saw him spit it out.'"

Karansky got the expected chuckle from Laura, but she wasn't entirely convinced. "I'm sure you are a great teacher, but do you really think that little tutorial equips me to go head to head against Cayhill?"

"No, probably not," he answered. "He's very good. I'm not certain I can beat him either. Just remember that the judge likes you and that is huge. You'll find you win skirmishes you didn't deserve to win. Hell, you may find you win wars."s

Chapter 38

The next day was a swirl of activity. Karansky filed a notice in federal court dismissing the RICO case, since the case could not proceed without a plaintiff. Cecilia was dead, and he had no desire to see whether any of the other victims of the scam wanted to take her place. About an hour after that, the district attorney's office contacted him, asking him to come talk to them to fill them in on everything he knew about the murder. He told them he had already talked to the police, which they didn't seem to know and, frankly, that didn't dissuade them from their request. He sighed and agreed to meet with them that afternoon.

As he hung up from that call, the phone rang again. It was Cayhill, asking where he wanted slightly over a hundred thousand pages of documents delivered. It was, he said, full compliance by American Auto of all outstanding discovery requests. Cayhill further suggested that they agree to inform the judge that a hearing on Karansky's motion to compel would be unnecessary in light of the full compliance. The two men discussed the mechanics, and agreed that Karansky would review the documents in Cayhill's possession and indicate which ones he wanted copies of to avoid literally being buried in paper. They further agreed to cancel the hearing on the motion to compel; what could Karansky really complain about at this point?

The answer, of course, was that he could have complained about the fact that Cayhill had not produced in all the mounds of paper the single document most relevant to the case, the Mahoney report on the safety of the machinery in question. Cayhill was holding that in reserve, until he saw what happened. He certainly didn't intend to give it away simply because the rules said he should.

The truth is that experienced lawyers consistently violate the rules on discovery, because judges rarely impose any sort of meaningful sanctions for their violation. As a result, the rules are honored consistently only by the naïve or the inexperienced trial lawyer. Cayhill was neither.

Karansky brought Laura with him to meet the district attorney, who was attracted to the case because of the publicity it had already received. While they were thanked for their cooperation, the DA also told them that he had already impaneled a grand jury, and it didn't really make much difference in which way he got their files. Karansky also tried to engage the DA in discussion regarding his own theories of who the murderer might be, but got nowhere. The DA lacked interest in Karansky's theories. The reason why became apparent later that afternoon.

Karansky and Laura were back in a conference room at Cayhill's office, looking over the first batch of documents Cayhill had made available in the American Auto case. There were reams of irrelevant financial information, union grievances, pollution statistics and the like. Laura was the first to break, throwing down some of the documents she had been reviewing in disgust. "This is ridiculous," she said. "We have only a few days left before trial. We could spend every minute going through these boxes and still not finish by the time the trial starts."

"I know," he said. "But what he did is perfectly legal. It's an advantage that big litigants have over small ones. Don't read things that don't appear helpful. We're not after financial documents. Make your first pass incredibly quick, the purpose being only to discard documents in categories that we are going to assume are not helpful."

They were moving more quickly now but still laboring under the challenge when a white-faced Cayhill interrupted them. He entered the conference room where they were working and asked if he might have a word with Karansky privately. Karansky was about to protest, when Laura said that she needed a cup of coffee anyway and left the two of them alone. "You sir, have given us a lot of shit," Karansky said, "Are there any pearls to be found?"

"Not in there," Cayhill said. "But there is something that I may have forgotten to put in the document inventory that might be helpful, which I would be prepared to remember under the right circumstances."

"And those circumstances would be what?" Karansky asked.

"That you represent me in the criminal trial being brought against me for the murder of Cecilia van Horn," Cayhill said.

Karansky stared open-mouthed at Cayhill for what seemed to be years. "There are so many things wrong with your proposal, that I don't know where to begin," Karansky said finally.

"Start anywhere," Cayhill said.

"For one thing, I don't do criminal law," Karansky said.

"You could," Cayhill said. "It's not so difficult. Besides, you did handle a criminal matter last year that you were assigned by the court." It was true; as a member of the bar, Karansky had been assigned a case involving a bar-fight where the police had charged everyone involved with criminal mischief. It was not a capital offense, but it had been a criminal matter. Cayhill had done his homework.

Vampires

"And what about the conflicts? I mean, what am I supposed to do - run from one court room where I am fighting you into another where I am representing you?" Karansky asked.

"That isn't going to happen." Cayhill said. "My firm has suspended me from further activity where I would be acting in a partnership capacity. Mr. Dunlop let me know that at the same time he told me that I was about to be arrested. American Auto is not my client; it is his. I was merely handling their litigation. They have elected to stick with him rather than be represented by a murder suspect. I can't blame them under the circumstances. Effective..." and he looked at his watch, "in about one hour, American Auto will formally be represented by Mr. Hooper."

Karansky was stunned, and really didn't know what to say. "This is nuts," he finally managed. "I met with the district attorney this morning and it was pretty clear his investigation was just getting underway. What does he gain by arresting you and making a big splash now before learning all the facts? What if he is wrong and you are totally innocent?"

"Which I am," Cayhill said. "By the way, I'm curious. Do you believe me?"

Karansky smiled. "Yes, I believe you had nothing to do with her murder," he said. "Just as I believe that you are lying about everything else. About the accounting fraud. About the document production."

"Before I respond to that, I need to know who I am speaking to," Cayhill said. "Am I speaking to my attorney?

Karansky couldn't quite accept that mantle yet. "Cayhill, why me? Surely your own firm..."

Cayhill interrupted, "You don't get it, do you? Dunlop is not unhappy about the indictment; hell, I think he may be behind it. We have had our differences recently and this may be his way of solving our conflict. In any event, the firm wants nothing to do with me at the moment. They have politely declined to represent me or to otherwise become involved in what they are calling "these unfortunate circumstances.""

Karansky chose not to air his own speculation that Dunlop might have been involved in Cecelia's death. Instead, he asked, "You didn't answer the question about the accounting fraud. Were the allegations correct?"

"And you didn't answer the question about whether I am talking to my lawyer if I do tell you," Cayhill repeated. "I won't tell you if you're not my lawyer." They stared at each other for a minute, before Cayhill broke the silence. "Counselor, in about five minutes I am going to be arrested. It would be a real shame if I have no one to whom to make my one phone call."

It is difficult to describe the mix of thoughts and emotions that ran through Karansky's head. He was both intrigued and disgusted. In the end, curiosity and a sense of obligation to the profession won out. Everyone deserved representation. He had always believed that, which is why he had stayed away from criminal law. He had never wanted to represent people he knew had done what they were accused of; yet that is what a criminal lawyer is expected to do. Here, while he knew that Cayhill had done many reprehensible things, Karansky did not believe he had committed the crime of which he was being accused.

At long last, Karansky said, "Okay, I will represent you. I want a million dollars retainer up front, and I will charge you the same rate that you currently charge your clients. I also want whatever documents you have been hiding in the American Auto case." Laura walked back into the conference room just in time to hear Karansky say he would represent Cayhill. "I'm sorry, I seem to have wandered into the wrong room," she said. "I was trying to find my way back to planet earth."

Karansky started to explain, "Laura, I…" However, before he could get beyond this prelude the doors to the conference room were pushed roughly open and two detectives came into the space. Going up to Karansky, they asked, "Are you Lester Cayhill?"

Karansky was too well-trained as a lawyer to be helpful. He answered the question put to him, saying, "No, I am not."

The police looked at each other and then looked at Cayhill. "Are you Lester Cayhill?" they asked hopefully.

"Yes, I am," Cayhill replied.

"Mr. Cayhill, you are under arrest for the murder of Cecilia van Horn," the one detective said. He then starting reading him his rights, but was interrupted by Karansky. "He has a lawyer," Karansky said. "And I do not want him questioned in any manner without my being present." Karansky fished in his wallet and got out his last business card, a bit the worse for wear, and gave it to the cop.

"Now you know how to reach me," Karansky said. The cop put the card in his shirt pocket, and helped his partner put the cuffs on Cayhill. Cayhill wasn't resisting and his partner didn't really need the help. But the partner, in simply putting the cuffs on, was missing the opportunity to use the process to make a statement. The cop remedied this. Taking Cayhill by the arm, he pushed Cayhill's face into the wall. His partner said, "Hey Pete, I got him."

The second cop, Pete by name, said, "Yeah, no problem. I just wanted to show him not to try nothing." Then he looked over at Laura, who was staring at him with a mixture of horror and disgust. He didn't care for that and he walked up to her, getting very close, before saying, "You got a problem, hun?"

Karansky went over and stood in front of Laura, his face only inches from the second cop's face. In a voice that was totally calm, he answered the cop's question, saying, "She doesn't have a problem, but if you touch even a hair on her head, you will."

The cop looked around at his partner but found no support for any more fun. He laughed nervously and told Karansky that he was just having some fun with the lady. Then, the cop leaned close to Karansky, so close that no one else could hear what he was saying. "Man, I bet she sucks some mean cock," he said. "I mean look at those…"

It was at this point Karansky hit him. It wasn't an elegant punch, or one that did excessive damage. But it connected with the cop's nose, and caused a fair amount of blood to leak out of the man's head. Some splattered on his police tunic, some sprayed over the general vicinity, making the damage appear worse than it was.

Karansky, on the other hand, got a beating far worse than it looked. The cop, who was set upon in this "unprovoked attack" felt justified in knocking Karansky to the ground and delivering a series of kicks to kidneys, ribs, stomach, and groin, after which he put his knee into Karansky's back and cuffed him. As he was marched out of the office, Cayhill told Laura that the retainer agreement was with his secretary. Laura nodded, and then told the policemen that Karansky was represented by counsel and that they should neither interrogate nor beat him without her present.

Vampires

Chapter 39

Both men were arraigned the following morning before Judge Hernandez. Cayhill's case was called first, and he was escorted to the table for the defendant. The judge recognized him from the hearing in the American Auto case, and asked, "Mr. Cayhill, I don't see counsel with you. The docket sheet indicates you are represented. Are you or aren't you?"

"I am, your Honor," Cayhill responded.

"Then where is your counsel?" the judge asked.

Karansky tried to stand but was given such a menacing look by the bailiff that he elected to speak from a seated position. "I am here, your Honor," he said.

"Who said that?" the judge demanded, becoming irritable upon looking out at his courtroom and seeing no one standing.

Karansky stood. He looked like he had spent the night in a cell, which he had. In addition, he had a black left eye, was unshaved and unkempt. He said, "I am sorry your honor, but I spent the night in a cell, and was given nothing this morning to help make me more presentable. I am his lawyer."

"Name?" asked the judge, not recognizing him.

"Your honor, I am Steven Karansky," he responded.

The judge looked up as he heard the name. "Jesus, what happened to you?" he asked, and then paused. "And weren't the two of you fighting like cats and dogs in that discovery matter in the other case? How the hell are you going to represent him?"

Laura stood up. "Your honor, if I may. I represent Mr. Karansky."

"Ah, Miss Simon," the judge said, a smile appearing on his face for the first time. "Are you sure you want to get mixed up with these clowns?"

"Yes, your Honor," she replied. "I work for clown number two."

"Well, would you mind explaining what the hell is going on," the judge said.

"Well, your Honor," she replied. "I am not sure I know everything. Mr. Karansky and I were in Mr. Cayhill's conference room working on the other case, when I went to get coffee. When I come back, two policemen entered, and placed Mr. Cayhill under arrest. One of the policemen hit Mr. Cayhill, and then approached me in a menacing manner."

The judge interrupted, asking what the hell she meant by that. "I mean he came extremely close to me and asked, if I recall, "Do you have a problem, honey?"

He called you "Honey?" the judge asked.

"Or hon," Laura said.

"Okay," said the judge. "Then what?"

"Mr. Karansky came and stood between me and the officer," she continued. "The officer said something to him, and Mr. Karansky hit him. Then he, I mean Karansky, was beaten up and arrested."

The judge looked back at Karansky. "Sticks and stones, Mr. Karansky. Sticks and stones."

When Karansky didn't respond further, the judge asked, "All right, Mr. Karansky, please share with us what the officer said to you that provoked you to attack him."

"I'd rather not, your honor," Karansky responded.

"I don't care what you'd rather do," the judge exploded. "So help me, unless you want to be held without bail pending trial, you will tell me what he said."

"He asked me whether Ms. Simon gave good head," he said, but too softly for the judge to hear.

"I can't hear you," the judge answered.

Karansky shouted it this time, "He asked me whether Ms. Simon gave good head."

Laura's face reddened, as did Karansky's. It took a minute for the statement to sink in, and then the judge bellowed in a rage at the attorney from the district attorney's office. "Where the hell is the DA and where the hell is the arresting officer?"

The attorney from the district attorney's office, who appeared totally unprepared for what was happening, looked at the files he had been handed that morning. Arraignments were generally non-events, with the defendant's simply pleading guilty or not guilty and bail being set. He had been instructed to go listen to their pleas, oppose bail for Cayhill and argue for high bail for Karansky. He tried looking through the files in his hand for the name of the arresting officer, but instead dropped the file on the floor, the papers scattering as the binder popped open.

The judge, not a patient man under any circumstances, lost his temper. Judges are human, and have their likes and dislikes. Judge Hernandez had decided he liked this young attorney, Laura Simon, and the hapless performance of the district attorney's office, in the face of allegations that the arresting officer had misbehaved and then covered it up by arresting Karansky, was too much for the judge to stomach. Addressing the young attorney, the judge said, his temper white hot, "Don't bother trying to find whatever you are looking for. Let me tell you what you are going to do. I want you to go back and tell the DA what we just heard. You also will tell him to have his butt in my court at 3:30 this afternoon. And you will tell him that he will bring the arresting officer with him. If he does not do both things, then you should tell him that he should pack a toothbrush because he is going to spend the night, and maybe many more nights, in his own jail. Now do you think you can remember that?"

The youngster managed to croak a "yes" and then scurried from the courtroom, wondering what he had done to warrant such bad luck. As rough as the judge had been on him, he was reasonably certain that the DA would be even harder, blaming him for allowing the judge to require him to appear. He nearly ran back to their offices, which were not far from court in any event, and checked with the DA's secretary, hoping against hope nothing important would have to be moved on the big man's calendar. His heart sank when he saw what was scheduled from one p.m. through the end of the day: it was designated as "meeting with fundraiser." Everyone in the office knew what that meant, and that it had nothing to do with raising funds. It was, instead, how his secretary marked his calendar when he was going to spend time with his latest conquest.

The young attorney told the DA's secretary about the judges' order and asked her to get in touch with the DA, to which she replied, "I don't think so."

His luck was a little better with the arresting officer. He managed to get in touch with him. However, the cop too seemed unimpressed with the judge's order, replying to the request for his presence, "Man, if the DA ain't showing why should I? I've been on duty for 12 hours now, and I'm going off duty in twenty minutes. If the judge really needs to see me, leave me a message and I'll be over there first thing tomorrow morning."

The young attorney wasn't inordinately brave, but someone had to go back to court to explain to the judge why the others would not be there. Frustrated and cursing his luck, he went back to the courtroom that afternoon. The judge was hopping mad when he entered the court. Karansky and Cayhill were back, both still in cuffs, and Laura was seated at counsel table.

The judge wasted no time, addressing the attorney from the DA's office, "Mr. Pittman, your courage is commendable but I did not require you to come back. I didn't even want you to come back. I wanted the DA and I wanted the arresting officer."

"Yessir," said the young Mr. Pittman, "I know that sir. It's just, well, it's just that someone had to explain to you why the others would not be here."

"Tell me," the judge said. "I'm all ears."

Vampires

The attorney swallowed and then said very quickly, "The DA is at a fundraiser, and the policeman was going off duty, and asked if he could come in the morning."

"Where is this fundraiser if I might inquire?" the judge asked.

"I-I'm not really sure," the attorney said, looking more and more uncomfortable.

"Young man, I will give you one more chance, before I assume you are party to whatever your boss is up to. Now, where is this fundraiser?" the judge demanded.

The attorney looked almost relieved at the judge's threat. It gave him license to tell what he clearly was uncomfortable keeping as a secret. "I believe it is at a room in the Hyatt Hotel."

"Bailiff!" the judge yelled. "Get some police men in uniform. Then go to the Hyatt hotel, here, take this warrant with you, and please bring the DA to me."

"What if he doesn't want to come?" the bailiff asked.

"Then arrest him," the judge replied. "I feel pretty confident that he'll be convicted, following hearing of course, of contempt."

The judge had looked at Laura when he said that, and now asked, "Am I okay with that, counselor? So long as I give him a hearing, I can jail the son-of-a-bitch, right?"

She smiled at the deference being accorded her. "That's right, your honor," she replied. "Would your honor find it convenient to finish the arraignment of Messrs.'. Karansky and Cayhill while we wait?"

"Good idea," said the jurist. "Who's first?"

"Mr. Karansky, if you please, your honor," she replied. "That way, if your honor finds it acceptable to free him on bail, he can represent Mr. Cayhill."

The judge was a man who did not take long to make judgments, or once made, to act on them. "Mr. Karansky, please rise. Now, when you told me in court what the officer had said to you before you slugged him, you were not under oath." The judge then turned to his clerk and asked her to put him under oath, which he did. The judge then proceeded. "Mr. Karansky, you now are under oath. If I asked you what the officer said to you before you hit him, would your answer be the same?"

Karansky said yes.

The judge smacked down his gavel, making most in the court jump. "You know," he said smiling, "I have never gotten tired of doing that. Case dismissed. Let the record show that neither the DA nor the complaining witness showed up for the arraignment despite explicit orders from the court that they do so."

"Thank you, your honor," Karansky said. "May I have a minute to confer with my client before you call his case?"

"Why not?" the judge said. "I've got to take a leak anyway. Waving at the court reporter, he added, "Just put 'request granted;' there's no need for anyone reading this to learn that judges are human."

Vampires

Karansky sat next to Cayhill. "Have you been questioned or said any-thing to anyone about this case?" he asked.

"I was questioned. I said nothing, though," Cayhill responded.

"I told that weasel you were represented by counsel. I should have been notified," Karansky said.

Cayhill shrugged. "What do you expect? In any event, it was informa-tive…for me. The man questioning me, who was different than those who brought me in, volunteered that Scott Wendells was cooperating. I don't know if it's true or if he said that to try to get me to say some-thing. Knowing Scott, it's probably true."

They heard the clerk say "All rise," and Karansky asked Cayhill to confirm that he wanted to plead not guilty. Cayhill nodded yes, and Karansky dutifully entered the plea when asked.

"Thank you," said the judge. "Now as to bail, what are you proposing, Mr. Karansky?"

"I believe he should be let out without bond on his own recognizance, your honor," Karansky replied. He is an upstanding member of the community, he has substantial ties to the community, and he is…"

"…alleged to be a murderer," said the judge. "Bail is set at a million dollars." The judge banged the gavel down once more, and said, "If I'm not mistaken, I see you boys back in court this afternoon for a last status on that wrongful death case prior to trial. Is that right?"

"Your honor will see Mr. Karansky," Cayhill said. "Not me. I am no longer counsel to the defendant in that case."

The judge stared at him for a moment. Then, after giving all the benefits of his wisdom on that by saying, "Whatever," the judge retired to his chambers.

Vampires

Chapter 40

The next morning, as Karansky lay in bed watching Laura walk to the bathroom, he thought for some odd reason of the promised document from Cayhill, and the envelope that Cayhill had said contained the retainer. He chuckled to himself about his mental association of the mysterious document and seeing Laura, a sight he still thought semi-miraculous. She had a wonderful, youthful body, which he thought he would never tire of admiring. He then started thinking of how he looked to her.

Feeling self-conscious, he closed the bedroom door partway so that he could inspect himself in the mirror Laura had hung there. He had the beginning of a slight paunch unless he sucked in his gut. He heard the bathroom door squeak open and sucked in his stomach while attempting to otherwise look and act naturally. It didn't work. Laura took one look at him and began smiling, suppressing for only a moment a loud laugh.

"I'm sorry," she said, "but you don't have to stop breathing to impress me. I knew I was making certain sacrifices when I fell in love with an older man." She had meant to poke fun at him, but he didn't take it that way.

"You what?" he said.

"I what?" she answered, not knowing what he was talking about.

"You said you were in love with me!" he said, standing up and holding her.

"Well, duh!!' she said. "Do you think that I would be standing here like this with you if I weren't? What do you think has been going on? Do I need to worry that you feel differently?"

He hadn't thought of it in those terms. He did now, and realized how much she had come to mean to him in so short a time. "Yes, I love you too," he said, expecting a strongly positive reaction. What she focused on, however, was not his eventual answer but the time it took to provide it.

"Well," she said, a little in a huff, "I ought to get dressed." She pushed him out of the bathroom.

"I meant it," he said from the other side of the door. She pretended not to hear him though she had.

She changed the subject, still talking from the other side of the wall. "Oh, I forgot to tell you. In my briefcase, there's an envelope with your name written on it. Take a look."

He pulled out the envelope and opened it. Inside, he found a two-page memo from the Product Safety Commission, with what looked to be an email attached. He began reading, and became lost in the document, his worries about Laura momentarily forgotten. She came out and put her hand on his shoulder. He remembered then, looked up and told her, "I do love you. I just had never thought about it before. But I do."

"I know," she said. "Now finish reading."

"Almost done," he said, and then a minute later, "Now I am. What do you think?"

"They had this in the files, and weren't going to turn it over?" she asked, incredulously.

"Nothing you can make of that, though I agree. You can't tell a jury that the other side didn't play nice but that you now have what you need," he said. "The question for us now is how to use it."

"How about exhibit 1?" she suggested.

"Can't" he said. "It's hearsay. We can't introduce it as evidence," he said.

"But that's ridiculous. This is the most relevant document we've seen, and we can't use it?" she asked. "C'mon, there must be some lawyer tricks that you've learned. It would be absolutely crazy to keep this evidence out."

"Short of bringing the author to court, the answer is no, we can't introduce it as evidence. None of the exceptions to the rule against hearsay seem to fit. But that doesn't mean we can't get it in front of a jury using a 'lawyer trick or two," he replied.

"I know," she said. "We can use it to impeach."

"Right you are," he said. "American Auto is going to have to put a witness up to testify that the death didn't result from their own negligence."

She frowned. "They do, if we make some sort of showing that there was negligence. Otherwise, there will be nothing for them to rebut. So where do we get the evidence to make the prima facie showing?"

Vampires

"Don't forget that it's the American Automobile Company we're talking about," he said. "They are a big company and they act like one. They are going to have someone connected to the litigation in some way present in court from day one whose job it is to report back independently from the outside counsel. Whoever that is we call as our second witness."

"The widow being our first?" she asked.

"The widow being our first," he answered. "The witness that follows her is going to find a jury loaded for bear." He sat quietly for a minute, and then asked, "Was that all that was in the envelope? I thought Cayhill said it also contained his retainer."

"There was also this," she said, handing him a note, "together with a check, which I've already deposited. The note read: 'If you are reading this, you've agreed to become my attorney. Thank you. Enclosed is my guess at what your requested retainer would be, together with my last official act as counsel for American Auto. Enjoy!'"

"The check was for a half million dollars," she told him.

"He guessed low. Well, it doesn't matter," Karansky said. He thought about money, which led him to think about damages, which led him to realize that he had just thought of a way to get the Mahoney memo into evidence! Taking a yellow pad, he wrote on it, "Use document to prove that they knew!!" across the top in big letters.

Chapter 41

When the young attorney returned to the district attorney's office, he couldn't wait to share what had happened in court. There was a good deal of jocularity, most of it vulgar, about the DA. Apparently his dalliances with young woman and girls were widely known but ignored. However, he was a political appointee who, having fired a number of the professional employees for having the wrong political views, had caused hard feelings with many of the employees who worked in his office. It should not come as a surprise, therefore, that one disgruntled court employee tipped off the local papers.

What did come as a surprise to many was that the woman he was found with was not yet a woman, but a fifteen year-old cheerleader and friend of his daughter. The footage of him taken in cuffs from the hotel made the local news that evening. The events that took place in court did not, at least not as live video.

The judge would not permit cameras in his court, which perhaps contributed to the large numbers of press who attended. The large turnout, in turn, prompted Judge Hernandez to be more colorful than usual. The district attorney had done his best to groom himself on the way to court. Using as a pretext the need to empty his bladder, he ran into a restroom where he combed his hair and tucked in his shirt properly. Still, there was no hiding the look, the smell, the demeanor that declared he had just spent the afternoon in bed with a fresh young thing, and was sorry only that he had been caught.

"Well, Mr. Vanderweg, how good of you to join us. Might I inquire how the fund raiser went?" the judge asked, although he had a television in his chambers and already knew the answer.

"Your honor, I…" the DA began.

"Listen," Judge Hernandez said, interrupting, "I didn't ask whether you wanted to come to my court this afternoon; I ordered you to be here. Imagine my disappointment when I had to dismiss one of your cases because I couldn't get you to respond. And imagine my utter and complete disgust that you refused to honor a judicial order," and here the judge stopped talking and screamed the remainder, "because you wanted to fornicate with an underage girl instead! Does the term 'statutory rape' ring any bells, Mr. Vanderweg?"

The DA said nothing because there was nothing to say. He felt like saying, "And I'd do it again you old fart," but his survival instinct wouldn't let him. Instead, he did his best to appear contrite, while trying to think how he could convince his wife to stand beside him at a press conference to admit and apologize for what he had done…what he would do again in a flash. Press conferences at which one admitted the very worst of offenses, accompanied by one's family, were the modern equivalent of the confession: all was forgiven, provided the wife stood by you and said she forgave you.

The judge asked, "Do you want a hearing where we can explore whether you were doing what you were doing and were not here like I ordered you to be?"

The DA was grateful for a question he could answer. "No, your honor," he said.

"Are you sure?" the judge asked once more.

"Yes, your honor," the DA responded.

"Let the record reflect that Mr. Vanderweg waived his rights to a hearing," Judge Hernandez said, a note of triumph in his voice.

"Wha-a-a-?" the DA said, completely surprised.

"And having waived those rights, I hereby find you in criminal contempt and sentence you to ninety days in the county jail. Bailiff!"

Vanderweg was pissed, not just because he was going to be staying in county lock-up, but also because the sentence would cause him to be in jail during the Congressional election. He had a commanding lead in the polls prior to this and stood a great chance to be the new Congressman for the 14th district. Sure, this episode would hurt, but if he had sufficient time and if he could get his wife to appear with him as he confessed to lapses in judgment, he could make it all back.

"Your honor," he protested, "Ninety days will require me to spend the remaining weeks up to the Congressional election and even Election Day itself in jail. That is tampering with the electoral process and might even hand the election to my opponent."

"I sure as hell hope so," the judge said. Looking at the court reporter, he added, "You can leave that one in."

Vampires

Chapter 42

One of the people who got a kick out of the footage of the district attorney being escorted in handcuffs from the hotel room was Donald Bruno, Scott Wendells' current client. Wendells actually had been hired by Priscilla Bruno, who everyone called Prissy, to place a value on the family business, Bruno Sanitation. But it was her husband that Wendells really answered to. The evaluation had come back at roughly one million dollars, about the amount of profit the company made every two months. However, the report said, the business was fraught with peril, facing incursions by such national powerhouses in the garbage business as Waste Management. It also was in the midst of an inquiry by the District Attorney into the possible ties of the business to organized crime. In the face of such threats, the report read, "one thing is clear: the business of the past is gone; the business of the future is too frail and speculative to assign it more than nominal value."

Of course, Wendells, the report's author, failed to mention that Waste Management had decided to pull out of New Jersey after two of its trucks were set on fire, one with the driver still in it. The District Attorney's inquiry was business as usual; he wanted a piece of the profits for not looking into the truck burnings in any serious fashion, and the inquiry was merely a negotiating tactic while they hammered out whether the proper percentage for protection was closer to three or five percent.

Bruno was a "gold" client, meaning that he had paid the full five million dollars to make certain the report came out in his favor. He was, therefore, more than a little upset that the scheme might become public, costing him the five million dollars plus whatever that whore of an ex-wife might be able to get. Although Wendells nominally worked for Bruno's wife, and his report was done supposedly on her behalf, Bruno did not have the slightest compunction about summoning the accountant to his home as soon as he was told that van Horn's body had been found. And Wendells knew better than not to go.

"Listen, asshole, I told you once before that I don't like my name in the papers," Bruno began. The paper, in addition to covering the allegations that had appeared in the original RICO complaint, had also gone into the current clients for whom Wendells was working. Each story picked up the fact that the accountant was now working for Prissy Bruno, and mentioned in passing that Bruno had "alleged mob ties." Bruno didn't like it. "I don't care personally, but the missus," he said, meaning his new mistress, "she gets perturbed." He had a thick New Jersey accent and his pronunciation of the word "perturbed" almost caused Wendells to smile.

"You think it's funny?" Bruno asked. "You think this is ha-ha funny, my friend?" Bruno repeated, only this time taking a large pistol from his desk.

"Relax," Wendells replied. "I assure you I know it is completely serious and I will act accordingly."

"Oh good, you will 'ax accordionly'," Bruno mimicked, not knowing exactly what Wendells had meant, but not liking it. His face was starting to show his irritation, with his cheeks becoming slightly flushed. "So what the fuck are you gonna do to give me assurance that I get what I paid for?"

Wendells tried to sooth him, saying, "Listen, I have it under control. What you need is me as your accounting witness. You still have that. It would have been nice to have Cayhill as your lawyer, 'cause he's good. But you don't really need him. In fact, the safest thing for you to do is to fire him. After all, he can't focus on this case when he's being charged with murder himself."

"Jesus, you're cold," said Bruno. "I thought youse guys were partners."

"Business first, Mr.Bruno, business first," Wendells responded.

"So how is dumping him gonna fix things?" Bruno asked.

"It won't if the police believe that she was killed to put a lid on the allegations about my accounting testimony. But that is not what the police believe," Wendells said.

"And why don't the police believe that?" asked Bruno, thinking to himself that this was starting to get interesting.

"Because they found some of the girl's very sexy underwear that Cayhill had in his possession, and a video of the two of them having pretty wild sex. It's not bad; let me know if you want to see it." Wendells replied. "Anyway, it's gonna look like she jilted him, and he lost it and killed her."

"You cooperating with the police?" Bruno asked.

"Let's just say that I've talked to them and their investigation is not focused on me," Wendells answered. He had, in fact, begun talking to the district attorney even before Cayhill's arrest. The current District Attorney understood the basic elements of politics – money and the use of it to acquire power – and Wendells and the DA understood each other. There would be no investigation of any connection between the murder of the girl and the allegations of accounting fraud in her RICO complaint. Sometime in the future, after the litigation was over, Wendells would make a sizable campaign contribution to the DA.

He turned and faced Bruno. "You satisfied?" he asked.

"Shu-ah," said Bruno. But in Bruno's mind, he was not. He didn't trust anyone who would sell out his partner, like this jerk had done. Did the guy really think he would be impressed? As soon as the accountant had testified, he would no longer be necessary. And people who weren't necessary tend to be very accident-prone.

Chapter 43

Cayhill made bail, but didn't know what to do with himself when he regained his freedom. His adult life had been the law, not an admirable side of the law, but the law nonetheless. He'd personally been handling the defense of two major cases at the same time (the American Auto and the RICO cases), had been supervising a slew of others, had been continuing the accounting business, and had been Bruno's lawyer. Now his clients had fired him, and the RICO case had been dismissed. In its place was a case against him for murder, which he had hired Karansky to defend. Moreover, his suspension from the firm had deprived him of the supervisory responsibilities he had enjoyed as head of the litigation section of the firm. There was nothing for him to do and he could not stand it.

As soon as he was released, he went to Karansky's office. It was nearly six o'clock p.m., and Karansky was packing up, trying to leave at a decent hour so he could have dinner with Laura. Cayhill walked in, saw him preparing to leave, and protested, "Hey, I thought this party was just about to get started! Counselor, you have my life in your hands. I hoped we could work on the case tonight."

Laura was the one to decide. Kissing Karansky on the cheek, she told him to stay and work. "I'll see you afterwards," she promised.

He gave an inward groan, and after she left, turned to Cayhill, and said, "Okay, Cayhill. Let's get to work. What is it you think we ought to do tonight?"

Vampires

"Why you dirty dog! Boffing the young associate are we?" Cayhill said, finding amusement in the news.

"We're trying to, but something always seems to come up, you being the latest. So unless you have something we need to work on tonight, it sounds like a far preferable way of spending my evening than talking to you."

Cayhill became serious, "I don't know what you think of me," he said, "but the law is my life. I will not give that up in order to save my skin. Do you understand? I am not going to defend myself against murder charges by admitting I was doing what you had alleged in the RICO complaint."

"Were you? You are now talking to your attorney," Karansky said.

"If we reach a point where you truly need to know in order to defend me, I will tell you. Can you demonstrate a need to know, or is this idle curiosity?" Cayhill responded, answering a question with a question.

"Yes, I believe I need to know," Karansky said. "It goes to motive. If you were engaged in a plot such as I alleged, then you had a motive for the murder. If you weren't then you had no motive to cause her harm."

"Assume the DA has motive," Cayhill said, "This or something else. If Wendells is playing ball on their side, the DA will go elsewhere to find a motive. He will not want to allege any conspiracy with me because that would implicate himself as well. Wendells is about to testify for a guy named Bruno, or actually Bruno's wife, in their divorce. I represented Bruno until today. He fired me. Bruno's a dangerous man and he would not take kindly to information about any alleged scheme coming out. No, if Wendells is cooperating with them as I think, he is leading them away from anything and everything to do with the allegations you raised in the RICO complaint."

"Got any ideas where they'll go then?" Karansky asked.

"She was an attractive lady," Cayhill responded. "If I had to guess, that would be the angle I think they'll use."

"And…?" Karansky asked.

Cayhill didn't bite. "And what?" he responded.

"Were you involved with her?" Karansky pressed.

"No, I was not," Cayhill said. "If that is where they go with the case, I am prepared to testify, as is Bruce."

"Bruce?" Karansky asked, not yet understanding.

"I am gay," Cayhill replied. "So anything they would come up with that supposedly implicates me with that woman sexually would be a lie. Bruce Harrison and I have been partners for several years, and we are both prepared to reveal that if necessary."

Karansky sat back and stared at Cahill. He was impressed, and now understood Cayhill's strategy. If the district attorney with Wendells' help went down the path proffering the end of a sexual liaison as the motivation for murder, they would be shredded. The evidence that Cayhill killed Cecilia van Horn tied to a love affair between the two would blow up in their faces. It was a beautiful play.

Vampires

Karansky decided to push for a speedy trial to avoid having whoever was going to try the case begin questioning the veracity of their star witness. He told Cayhill that he'd push for immediate trial at the status conference the next morning. Cayhill was not surprised, and agreed with the logic, but was nervous all the same. "Are we ready?" he asked.

"Not really," Karansky answered. "But we don't have to be. The real question is whether the district attorney is ready. And the answer to that is no. We need to push him to proceed before he realizes that."

Chapter 44

"Your honor, it is unreasonable to compel us to begin tomorrow," the assistant district attorney told Judge Hernandez. "This is a complicated case, and we're still collecting evidence."

"Mr. DeSoto, is it?" the judge replied, his voice dripping with sarcasm, "Normally, I would expect the prosecutor to have reviewed the evidence before arresting someone and giving a press interview claiming this to be an open and shut case, supported by conclusive evidence."

"Your honor," the assistant DA looked positively pained, "my boss…"

The judge cut him off. "Careful counselor, if you're going to disparage your supervisor. Does Mr. Vanderweg still speak for the district attorney's office, or not?" Judge Hernandez demanded.

"He does," the assistant said, the only answer he could give.

"Good. Trial begins tomorrow morning at nine o'clock, right here," the judge said.

That evening, Karansky made steaks at Laura's after buying steaks, steak knives, plates, napkins, and a bottle of red wine. Laura had confessed to a lack of experience in the kitchen, so that her empty cupboard shouldn't have come as a complete surprise. Still, Karansky was taken aback when he opened the refrigerator to see what he could make with the steak, and found it not just barren of useful things for their dinner, but completely empty except for a half loaf of white bread, a quarter pound of salted butter, less about a third, and an artificial coffee creamer.

He held up his hand to silence her protest, "Hey I'm not complaining. I just didn't know that by "not much in the house" you meant that you didn't have anything other than a half eaten loaf of Wonder bread, a little bit of butter, and coffee creamer."

"You want me to eat? Then pay me more," she deadpanned back.

They had grilled steaks and drank the wine with it. As they were cleaning up, he began talking about the American Auto case. "Laura, you've been practicing law for nearly two weeks now. You're a veteran. It's time to try your first case."

Laura narrowed her eyes as she looked back at him. "What are you talking about?" she asked.

"You know what I'm talking about," Karansky replied. "I want you to try the case against American Auto."

"Steven!" she exclaimed. "I'm not ready. I'm not even officially a lawyer yet."

He walked to her and put his arms around her. "You're ready. Maybe not against a Cayhill who has tricks up his sleeves, but you're already better than any of his minions who might try the case in his place. Even against Cayhill, you're not too far away from being able to hold your own." He paused. "Besides, we don't have many other options. I need you to try the case because I can't, or at least I couldn't do it the way it should be done. I talked to Judge Hernandez's law clerk today regarding scheduling. The judge has blocked out the next two weeks on his calendar and plans to try the Cayhill criminal case in the mornings and the American Auto case in the afternoons. That means that I can't do both, or if I tried, I wouldn't really be able to prepare adequately for either."

"Couldn't we at least get a continuance so that I have more time?" she asked. "That way…"

He interrupted. "I tried," he said. "The judge was adamant. The trial starts tomorrow." He saw the reaction in her face, and cut her off. "Don't worry. I more or less had a trial plan. We'll spend a couple of hours going over it. You should be fine."

She looked at him, her exasperation apparent. "What makes you think the judge will even permit me to try the case?" she asked. "He's been tolerant till now in letting me appear before him, but trying a case is different."

"Judge Hernandez will let you," Karansky said. "He told me." Laura looked startled that he had talked to the judge. "Look," he explained, "when the clerk told me the schedule, I objected. The judge picked up the phone and asked me what the fuss was about. I told him that I couldn't realistically try two cases at the same time, and it was the judge who then said that he had every confidence that you could try the American Auto case. I almost think the schedule is like it is so that you will try the case. Laura, he likes you, and that is an invaluable tool for you to have in your arsenal."

She said nothing for a minute. After thinking about it and coming up with no alternatives, she said with a sigh, "Okay, let's go over the trial plan. If I am going to try this, I have a lot to get into my head, and not

much time to do it. I hope you're right about the judge, though. I am
going to need every edge I can get."

Chapter 45

"The people versus Lester Cayhill," the clerk called. Karansky and Cayhill went to the desk on the left, which for whatever reason was the one traditionally reserved for the defendant. Karansky was startled to see the district attorney himself approach the table to the right.

"Good morning counselor," the judge said looking at Karansky. Karansky nodded and responded, "Good morning, your Honor."

The judge then looked at the district attorney, his dislike poorly concealed. "Is the state ready, Mr. Vanderweg?" he asked.

"We are, your Honor," the district attorney replied. The DA felt equal or greater antipathy towards the judge but kept his feelings guarded. He didn't want the judge to ruin his plan for the morning. Vandeweg had posted bail pending an appeal of his sentence for criminal contempt, and was out of jail so that he could try this case. Vanderweg figured that if all went as planned and he obtained a conviction, he could return to jail and still win the election. A lot depended on bringing down Cayhill, and painting the lawyer as a major force of evil, tamed by the embattled district attorney. To give the case maximum exposure, he had tipped off the press that a major test of his administration was about to unfold, raising the stakes for a successful outcome.

He wasn't that concerned. He'd investigated the matter sufficiently to know that the allegations made in the civil RICO matter had been true. Recognizing his opportunity, he had called in the accountant, figuring correctly that he would be the easier of the two participants to manipulate. Threatening to bring a conspiracy charge and name Bruno, the reputed crime boss as a conspirator, Vanderweg had quickly forced the accountant to see the light. Staying a million miles away from the truth, Wendell's would implicate Cayhill in the woman's murder by sexually linking the attorney to Cecilia van Horn.

Vanderweg had demanded evidence; at the second meeting, Wendells had produced it: a pair of lady's panties they had confirmed belonged to the victim, as well as a tape showing Cayhill and the decedent having sex, both given by Cayhill to his pal Wendells for safe keeping. The district attorney didn't want to know more. As far as he was concerned, Cayhill was scum and the DA had him! The DA believed that Cayhill had murdered the girl; at the least, he was the brains behind the accounting conspiracy. Convicting him of murder, though, seemed both easier to do, and also more impressive fodder for his political campaign.

The DA knew he was playing high stakes poker now. Out on bail, he had to secure a conviction or face political embarrassment. He didn't intend to let anyone ruin his plans, including this judge.

"Very well," the judge said. Turning to the bailiff, he told him to go get the first batch of jurors. Jury selection can be half, or even more, of the battle. There are highly paid consultants who do broad sampling, using mock juries, so they can advise the sort of jurors more likely to acquit or convict. The government rarely avails itself of such consultants, because funding is not within the prosecutorial budgets. Cayhill almost always brought the consultants into his cases, but in the haste to bring his own case to trial, they had no time for it.

They were looking for eight jurors, six jurors to vote, and two alternates who would participate fully but would then not vote unless something happened to one of the first six. Twelve potential jurors, seven women and five men, walked into the room and were seated in the jury box. Judge Hernandez addressed them briefly, telling them this was a first-degree murder trial. He then asked if any of them would find it impossible to impose a death sentence, no matter what the facts showed. One of the women raised her hand and she was gone, replaced by a man who appeared winded with the exertion of walking from the jury room to the courtroom. The judge turned to the district attorney first, who got up, fastened his jacket, and began: "Ladies and Gentlemen, this is murder most foul. Defendant is accused of a crime so hideous…"

Karansky was on his feet, objecting, "Your Honor, I thought that we were here to ask the jury questions, not to try to prejudice their impartiality with…"

"That will be enough from both of you," the judge said. "Mr. Vanderweg," he said, addressing the DA, "keep the speeches short, and Mr. Karansky, you do the same with the objections, hmmm?"

The DA acted as if he had won the skirmish, smiling, and saying "thank you, your honor." Turning back to the jury, he asked one or two questions of various jurors, before focusing on Juror number 2, a black man, about 45-50 years old. The man looked distinguished. He was wearing a suit, and listening with rapt attention. "Have you ever been in trouble with the law?" the district attorney asked.

"No I have not," came the reply.

"Never stole anything?" the district attorney asked, looking at the other black person as he did. She was a young woman seated as juror number six.

Vampires

"No sir!" the reply, now spirited, came back.

"May we approach the bench, your Honor?" the district attorney asked.

"Very well," the judge responded. Both the district attorney and Karansky approached the judge's bench on the side away from the jury.

"Your honor," the district attorney began, I'd like to remove jurors number two and six for cause."

The judge interrupted, saying simply, "No."

The district attorney glared at the judge with hatred for a moment, then resumed his poker face, and said, "Well then, I will use two of my peremptory challenges." Each side in a criminal trial can excuse any number of potential jurors for cause, and a certain defined number of jurors for no reason at all. The district attorney, believing as do many in his position that blacks are generally more sympathetic to defendants than whites, since "they get in so much trouble themselves" as he had told a colleague, was attempting to cleanse the jury of any people of color. "The state objects to jurors two and six, and accepts the remaining jurors," he said as he walked back towards his desk.

"Mr. Karansky?" the judge asked, inviting him to question the jury. "

"No questions, your Honor. They are acceptable," Karansky said, giving a big smile to the jury as he did.

"Well, we're making good time," the judge remarked to the jury. "Jurors nine and ten, would you please take the seats of the two excused jurors. No, it doesn't matter. Take either chair."

Two more jurors took the empty seats. Both were white, and the district attorney, a satisfied look on his face, asked a few perfunctory questions and told the judge he was satisfied. He was done with the jury. Karansky now rose. Buttoning his suit coat as he approached them, he said good morning to the jury. Then, taking a deep breath, he asked, "If the facts introduced lead you to the conclusion that someone involved in this case is gay, and by that I mean homosexual, could you render your decisions without regard to any prejudice or bias?"

"Your honor, I don't like to object and disrupt Mr. Karansky's questions but I think I'm going to have to object" the district attorney began, not because he objected to the question but because he was totally blindsided by it and needed time to think.

The judge didn't give him any. "Overruled." Then to Karansky, he said. "You may proceed, counselor. I assume the question has some relevance to someone who will appear before the jury?"

"It does, your Honor," Karansky responded. None of the potential jurors volunteered anything, so Karansky professed himself satisfied with the jury, smiled at them once again, and sat down.

Judge Hernandez was delighted to wrap up jury selection so quickly, thanked both attorneys, and addressed the jury, admonishing them to do their duty as he spelled it out, and thanked them in advance for their attention. Then, smacking his gavel on the wooden block, he declared a fifteen-minute recess, after which he told the district attorney, he should be prepared to give an opening statement.

Vampires

Chapter 46

"Why did you tip him off to the issue about my being gay?" Cayhill demanded, as upset as Karansky remembered seeing him.

"Because he's locked into his theory of the case; he has nothing else to offer," Karansky explained. "And, because the jury is now waiting to hear who is gay, and is not going to leap to any wrong conclusions until they find out. And finally, because I am your attorney, and until you decide to replace me, I am going to try the case in the manner I see as best designed to get an acquittal."

Cayhill cooled off and smiled. "Okay, okay," he said. "Geesh, don't have a cow. I just was wondering what the DA would do now that he had notice that something was up."

"There's not much he can do," Karansky said. "He made his bet on Wendells. I think he now is concerned but has nowhere else he can lead the jury. My guess is that right now he is wishing he hadn't posted bail."

Karansky was mistaken. So sure was the district attorney of his view of the case that he had decided that Karansky's question was a bluff. Still, he gave Wendells a very hard time to make certain that he understood what his star witness was going to say. Satisfied that he understood, and that Wendells was still on board, he decided the best thing was to stay the course. Looking at his watch, he said to Wendells, "Come on, it's time. This is not a judge to keep waiting."

As they walked back into court, Judge Hernandez was just taking his seat. Wasting no time, he asked, "Is the State ready to make an opening statement?"

"Yes, your honor, I am." Venderweg cleared his throat and began, "Ladies and Gentlemen of the jury. Cecilia van Horn was only 42 years old when she was killed, savagely strangled in the stall of a woman's bathroom just outside his office." He pointed vaguely at defendant's table, forcing Karansky to object, "Excuse me, your Honor, but the jury should know that it happened outside my office, not the defendant's."

The district attorney continued without pause, "The evidence will also show that the victim tried to fight off her attacker, and to subdue her prior to strangling her, he pushed her head into a dirty public toilet more than once." Karansky looked at the jurors and saw several wince.

"You will hear evidence that the defendant was having a sexual relationship with the victim, and that the day before her death she had told him that she didn't want to see him anymore. You also will hear an eyewitness testify that he saw the defendant at the scene shortly after the murder was committed." The district attorney went on and on, but Karansky stopped listening long enough to write on a yellow pad, "You were there?" which he then shoved in front of Cayhill. Cayhill wrote "mistake" on the page and shoved it back.

Satisfied as he could be with the answer, Karansky listened to the remaining remarks of the district attorney. The district attorney also referred to the fact that the jurors would not need to rely on his or anyone else's statements that the two were lovers, but would get to see film of this with their own eyes. He then closed with a laundry list of forensic evidence that the victim was killed by someone right handed, that the defendant was right handed, that Ms. van Horn had written in her diary the day before her death that she was "Tired of L. – will tell him." And finally after again describing the condition that Cecelia's body had been in when found, Vanderweg closed with a general polemic about evil and the sacred duties of jurors to fight it.

It was Karansky's turn. He got up, looked at the jury, and began, "Ladies and gentlemen, it is indeed tragic that Cecilia van Horn was murdered. She was a client of mine, and a friend. In fact, my colleague and I found her body. Her tragic death deserves to be avenged. I will not take a back seat to anyone on that. But she deserves more than an abbreviated investigation, with a convenient villain targeted and prosecuted so the district attorney can generate the right sort of headlines in the middle of his campaign for a seat in Congress."

"Your honor," the district attorney began.

"Mr. Karansky, you know better," the judge instructed, but not too harshly. "Please contain yourself to describing what your evidence will show, and spare us all the details of your beliefs as to the reason why we are here."

"I'm sorry your honor," Karansky said, feeling anything but. He had planted the seed he wanted to plant, and while the judge had admonished him, he hadn't diminished the effect with an instruction to the jury. He continued, "I am instructed to inform you what the evidence will show. I really can't, because I don't know what the evidence will be. I do know what the evidence will not show: It will not show my client to have done what the district attorney claims he did. I can tell you this without knowing what the evidence will be because Lester Cayhill did not murder Cecilia van Horn. Any evidence that makes it seem like he did is a fabrication, and any witness that claims he did is lying. Thank you.”

The judge, again happy at the pace of the trial, decided to plow into the witness testimony, without slowing down to take a break. Turning back to the district attorney (who had expected a break), he said, “Let’s not lose the momentum. Call your first witness.”

The district attorney was surprised but looked forward to Wendell’s performance. Checking to make certain that both Wendells and the news reporters were in the courtroom, he said in a melodramatic voice, “The state calls Scott Wendells.”

Wendells walked up to the witness stand, oozing with self-importance. The look of hatred between Wendells and Cayhill was so intense that Karansky thought one of them would lose his cool and swing at the other. Neither did, but only because each thought he was about to hurt the other far more using the civilized weapons of the court.

The bailiff swore in Wendells, and the district attorney started immediately laying the groundwork for what he imagined to be a knock-out blow of the defense. Yes, he and Cayhill had worked together for a number of years; yes, he would say they were friends; and yes providing this testimony was breaking his heart, but he had no choice. No, he had not known Cayhill had been dating van Horn until her death when Cayhill had called him, very excited, and said his girlfriend had just been killed, asking if he would do Cayhill a big favor and keep a package for him.

“And did you do that?” the district attorney asked.

“Yes, I did,” Wendells replied.

"And did there come a time when you looked inside the package to see what was in it?"

"Yes, though not right away." Wendells answered. "After I read the newspaper stories about the murder, I decided I couldn't not look. I took the package to the district attorney's office and opened it for the first time in front of your assistant."

The district attorney interrupted. "Do you mean Mr. Warren?"

"Yes, I believe that was his name," Wendells responded.

"And when you opened the package, what did you find?" the district attorney asked, walking over to stand by the jury box so that Wendell's answer would be directed towards them as well.

"A-a lady's undergarment, and a video tape," Wendells answered.

"Was this the undergarment?" the district attorney asked, holding up the skimpiest of thongs, a small red triangle with a few red strings attached.

"Yes," Wendells answered.

"And was this the tape?" the district attorney asked, handing the videocassette to the witness.

"Let me see, yes, that's where I marked it, as Mr. Warren suggested," Wendells replied.

After the predictable wrangling over authenticity, both the thong and the tape were introduced into evidence. The jury watched the tape, at least for a few moments until the judge halted it. It showed Cecilia having sex with a man who for the most part was only visible from the back. Twice, however, one saw the man from a perspective that showed his face. The face was clearly that of the defendant, Lester Cayhill. After few more wrap-up questions, the district attorney finished the direct of the witness. With a look of triumph, he tendered him for cross-examination.

Karansky rose, and without even looking at Wendells began his cross. "Mr. Wendells, I have in my notes here that you were close friends, no I am sorry, good friends with the defendant. Is that correct?"

"Yes, I would say that," Wendells agreed.

"And how long would you say the two of you were friends?" Karansky asked.

"Seven, no eight years," Wendells answered. "At least I considered us to be friends. I think he did too."

"What made you think you were friends?" Karansky asked, becoming a bit combative for the first time. "Did you tell each other what was going on in your lives?"

"Well, not every little thing, but the important things, I'd guess," Wendells said.

"Please don't guess, Mr. Wendells," Karansky said. "Not in a murder trial. Either you discussed the important things or you didn't."

"Yes, I'd say we discussed the majority of important things going on in each other's life," Wendells said.

"Mr. Cayhill is single, is he not?" Karansky asked.

"Yes," said Wendells.

"Mr. Wendells, could you please identify the names of three women with whom he has had a relationship during the eight years you and he have been friends, telling each other about the important things going on in your lives?" Karansky looked at Wendells for the first time as he asked the question.

Wendells thought for a moment, and then said, "I'm sorry, I don't know of any. Listen, if your point is that we aren't as close as I assumed we were…"

"Mr. Wendells, I am not making any point, I was merely trying to ascertain whether someone who considered himself a close friend ever knew him to date a woman, and I take it the answer, before his alleged relationship with the decedent, was 'no.' Am I right?"

"Yes," said Wendells.

"I have no further questions at this time," Karansky said.

"Then we are adjourned until 9 a.m. tomorrow morning," the judge said, adding admonitions to the jury not to discuss the case with anyone, including other jurors.

Karansky leaned over and told Cayhill that he'd see him tomorrow at 8:30, adding a prediction that the district attorney would wrap up his part of the case as early as tomorrow.

"That's good, right?" Cayhill asked.

Vampires

"Yes," Karansky answered. "But it also means that we need your partner here, just in case we have the opportunity to begin presenting our case. What's his name again?"

"Bruce Harrison," Cayhill answered. "He's very nervous. Will you meet with him?"

"I suppose I ought to," Karansky said. He looked at his watch. "Tell you what: bring him by the office at five. I promised Laura I would sit in on your old case – Chapman versus American Auto. They start in a little over an hour."

Chapter 47

"No, please!" Sarah Chapman begged. "I couldn't bear to sit in court and have to talk about his death all over again." Tears rolled down her cheeks, as she listened to Laura explain why it was necessary. During the discussion, Karansky entered the witness room, a small private room adjacent to the court where Laura had been trying to prepare Mrs. Chapman to testify. Upon seeing him, the widow appealed to Karansky for help, hoping to get a different answer. She didn't get one.

"Now, Mrs. Chapman, I've told you from the beginning this would be necessary. We'll do our best to get you on and off as quickly as possible. But the jury has to see you, and understand what you've gone through," Karansky said. The widow searched his face for indecision, but finding none, finally burst into tears while waving one hand in the air as a sign that Karansky interpreted as "okay."

"Right," Karansky continued. "Let's get a jury and get her on."

Cayhill had hired jury consultants for this case early in the proceeding. They had conducted elaborate mock trials in front of juries of different ethnic and socio-economic backgrounds. The results from this work lay in reams of paper in front of Lawrence Hooper, who understood it but was too inexperienced in leading a trial team to employ it wisely. Rather than committing its few main lessons to memory (such as rich whites, or union members or politically liberal jurors were bad; blacks, poor non-union blue collar workers were good), he had the papers spread in front of him, and had an associate check the prospective juror answers against the profiles. It didn't take long for the people in the jury pool to realize that their participation was dependent on these computer spread sheets, which they resented.

On the other hand, the jurors saw that the other side was represented by a young woman, who split her time between trying to take notes on the answers to questions the jurors gave, and comforting the older woman sitting next to her. The jurors took to her immediately. She objected to one person for cause, because he owned a Ford dealership, but that the jurors could understand.

The jury was eventually selected after a long and tedious process. The judge, noting that it had taken most of the afternoon, asked Laura whether she wanted to wait till morning or give her opening then. She was about to gratefully accept the delay when Karansky slipped her a note. She looked at it quickly as she began to stand to address the court. It was a single word, "Now." Laura shot him a pained look, to which Karansky smiled in return.

"I will give my opening now, your Honor," she said, her voice shaking a bit. "Ladies and gentlemen of the jury," she began. She reached behind her as she said this for a stack of index cards on which she had scribbled notes for her opening. She encountered instead Karansky's hand, which lay on top of the cards. She looked at him in anger and panic, and tried to move his hand. He kept it where it was.

"No notes. Speak to them from your heart," he whispered. She stared at him long enough for her pause to be noticeable.

"Is everything all right?" Judge Hernandez asked.

"No," she said, and then, "I mean yes it is." She turned to the jury box and began. "This is a sad case. It is about the death of a man, her husband," she said, gesturing towards the widow. But more than death, it is about dying. Death can bring peace, as it probably did for Sam Chapman. But first you have to die, and dying can be hard, very hard.

"Sam Chapman was an experienced drill press operator. He had done that kind of work for more than thirty years. But on the last day of his life, his sleeve was caught in the machinery and he was pulled ever so slowly into the gears. First the fingers of his left hand were crushed. Witnesses tell us that he screamed in agony. Then more of his arm was pulled in and crushed. It is unclear how much of his body was crushed while he was alive, but it is clear that he lived long enough to experience pain and suffering more intensely than many of us can even imagine."

Laura looked at the widow, who was crying uncontrollably. She was biting her top lip with her bottom teeth in an effort to suppress her wailing, but one loud moan escaped her at this point. Some of the jurors were also in tears; all had their eyes on the widow. Laura resumed.

"Why did this happen? It happened because the machinery being used did not have an automatic shut off. Most machinery of this type will automatically shut down if something gets caught in it – much like an elevator will open if you put your fingers between the doors. But this drill press didn't have it. It was made in China and they eliminated the shut off safety feature to save money.

"This accident didn't come as a surprise to American Auto. They knew the machinery being used was dangerous. And they knew that the government warned against the use of the machinery, and told companies if they did have such machinery to have a second employee ready to turn it off.

Vampires

"American Auto did assign a second employee – someone with a chronic drinking problem. Unfortunately, on the day of the accident, he was too drunk to stand up and he was therefore unable to shut off the machine.

"What is it that we want? Why are we here? True, we want to recover for the value of a life, whatever that is. And we want compensation for his pain and suffering. But we want more than that. You will hear the American Auto defend its conduct here because it doesn't feel that it did anything wrong. In fact, the same conditions that led to the horrible death of Mr. Chapman continue to exist at its factory. There is a new worker doing what Sam used to do, using the same piece of machinery. Ladies and gentlemen, this is wrong. We are asking you to tell American Auto that Mr. Chapman's death is enough, is way more than enough, by awarding punitive damages against the company. Thank you."

Laura turned and walked back to counsel table. She saw Karansky smiling at her, the widow weeping quietly into a handkerchief. As she sat down, Karansky whispered to her, "Nice job."

"Go to hell," she replied, still fuming at the way he had forced her to untether herself from her preparation. "You had no right."

"But you were good!" he retorted.

She reflected, and couldn't keep the faint traces of a smile from undermining her indignation. "I was, wasn't I?" she asked, and then without waiting for an answer, finished, "But you still had no right." This time some of the anger was removed from the message.

Laura returned her focus to what was happening and listened as Mr. Hooper dug a deeper hole for himself with the jury. Unlike Laura, who had been forced to address the jury without notes, Hooper used a yellow pad with page after page of notes as he walked the jury methodically through the elements of proof. It was a very logical, well put together presentation. First, Hooper dealt with the concept of what kind of duty the company owed the decedent, because as he correctly pointed out to the jury, "Without a duty, and a breach of that duty, there can be no recovery." American Auto, he argued, did not owe the decedent a duty to have an injury-free workplace, but only one that was not unreasonably dangerous.

He then went over the "breach of duty" issue with equal logic, focusing on the fact that American Auto had tried to do everything right. There was no equipment now available with the shut off feature, and the company had asked another employee to do nothing other than observe the machine's operation. Yes, the man suffered from alcoholism but American Auto's hands were tied. They couldn't fire him because alcoholism was a disability under New Jersey law.

In the war of logic against emotion, emotion invariably wins. Most on the jury couldn't get Laura's closing question out of their minds – if the company had done nothing wrong that meant nothing would be changed and someone else was now running the same risk as the man who had been killed. It was a heavy responsibility for a juror to conclude that was okay. Although Hooper had laid out the defense with great logic, he at most made a few jurors waver. He had not won them as converts.

The wavering stopped when Sarah Chapman took the stand. It was late and the judge had indicated a readiness to conclude the day's proceedings when Laura requested with a great sense of urgency that he permit them to run just a bit longer, so that Mrs. Chapman could testify, and not have to think about testifying over night. The judge seemed to understand, and in any event agreed.

Vampires

Sarah Chapman was extremely nervous, and twirled the hair above her right ear over and over as she took the stand. Laura did her best to put her at ease, starting with gentle questions like how long had she and Sam been married (thirty-eight years), where they had lived (within thirty miles of Linden, New Jersey her entire life). Laura then asked her to describe a typical day before the accident. The widow became confused, saying "I'm sorry. I don't understand."

Laura prompted, "Well, for instance. What time did you get up and what did you do before your husband left for work?"

"Oh, I see," the widow replied, momentarily relieved because she could answer the question. "Well, Sam got up like clockwork every day at five a.m. so that he could read the paper and have breakfast before leaving for work."

"Did you have breakfast with him?" Laura asked.

Hooper rose at this question, objecting that their breakfast arrangements were not relevant.

"Overruled," Judge Hernandez replied. The judge then turned to the widow, smiled at her, and said, "You may answer Miss Simon's question."

"Okay, thank you, sir," the widow said, before catching herself and saying, "I mean your Honor. Well, you may think we were a bunch of big sillies, but breakfast was our special meal together. Sam ate a lunch I packed for him at work, and dinner was always hit or miss because we would never know how he would feel after a day at work. The factory was hard work and we were hoping he could retire when he turned 65. We were so looking forward to the time together…" She didn't so much stop talking as she faded into a reverie that was so soothing as to make her forget where she was. Laura gently reminded her.

"Mrs. Chapman, you were talking about breakfast?" Laura said.

"Yes. It was the time when we were together. Not just physically in the same room, but together. It's hard to describe. But I treasured that time. I would get up at 4:30 each morning so that I could make his lunch and squeeze him fresh orange juice. Sam loved that. He used to tell me that it made him feel like he was staying at the Ritz." She stayed quiet for a moment and then said, "You know, mornings are now the hardest time for me. I don't know what to do with myself, and I find myself not even wanting to get out of bed." Laura asked a few more questions but the point had been made. This was a warm and loving woman who had been deeply in love with a man who was now dead. It wasn't right that he had been killed.

Mr. Hooper was at least smart enough not to ask Mrs. Chapman any questions. Judge Hernandez looked at the clock, thanked the jurors for their patience and told them they would resume tomorrow afternoon. The day was over.

Laura was ecstatic. She had not only survived; she had done well. She wanted to throw her arms around someone. Karansky came towards her and presented himself as a would-be object of the hug. She hugged the widow instead, telling her she had done well. She then looked at Karansky, and told him again that he had had no right.

"I accept that," he said. "I threw you in deep water. But you swam!"

She tried looking at him sternly, before her smile broke through. "Oh, Steven, I did. It is an unbelievably exhilarating feeling!" she exclaimed as she nearly jumped on him, giving him a big hug. As they were

Vampires

celebrating the day, Karansky noticed out of the corner of his eye the man who had been sitting in the back of the courtroom during the trial had stared at them, shaking his head as he stuffed some notes he had been taking in his briefcase. As he started to leave, Karansky quickly disengaged from Laura, yelled at him, "Excuse me sir, might we have a word?" and ran towards the man.

"No, we may not," said the man. "I am from American Automobile and have no wish to speak to you."

"You are right," Karansky said. "If you are from American Auto, we should have no further conversation." The man smiled faintly, and started to step around Karansky. Karansky stepped forward and blocked the man once again. "But now that I know that you are from the company, I can give you this," Karansky continued. "It's a subpoena requiring your presence in court tomorrow. Would you mind telling me your name?"

The man responded, "Yes, I would mind. Now if you'll excuse me."

Karansky let him pass, and turned to face Laura. "Sorry about that, but I couldn't let him just leave."

"Who was it?" Laura asked.

"I don't know," he replied. "But he's from American Auto and he is going to be our second witness."

Chapter 48

Karansky was restless as he waited for the trial to resume. He had met the day before with Bruce Harrison as he had promised. The man seemed honest, though Karansky had a difficult time visualizing him and Cayhill as lovers. Cayhill was such a cold fish, and his lover was not only much younger, but also a very different personality. Karansky thought for a moment and decided that he would have described Bruce as "bubbly."

It was late when they broke up, and Karansky headed home. On the way, he became morose. He started out thinking of how funny a couple Cayhill and his lover were, and drifted into ruminations about Laura and himself. How were they any more appropriate a couple? The age difference was similar, and he was starting to believe that their personality differences were at least as great. Did people look at them and wonder what she saw in him?

He arrived at Laura's apartment late, needing reaffirmation. He didn't find it. Instead, he found the note Laura had taped a note to the door of her bedroom, stating, "Need sleep. Please use the sofa. Probably just for tonight. Love, L." Karansky stared at it for a long time. He understood everything except the word "probably," an ambiguous term that he spent hours trying to decipher. He fell asleep late, overslept, and would have been late for court if Laura hadn't shaken him by his shoulder gently, asking if he didn't need to get up. Now he was sitting, restless, next to Cayhill, thinking about Laura, and waiting for Judge Hernandez.

Vampires

Cayhill leaned over, and said quietly, "Rough night, counselor? I need you here today. Are you going to be okay?"

Karansky perked up, and said "yes," just as the judge appeared. Hernandez sat down before anyone had a chance to stand, and waved them not to stand. The judge looked at the district attorney, who was facing away from him, talking to a witness. The judge said good morning to the jury, and then, cleared his throat. The district attorney turned around at long last.

"We need a witness, sir," the judge said, "unless you plan on resting your case."

"No, your honor," the district attorney responded. He called the first of his three witnesses that morning, one of the officers who found the body. The officer reiterated the gruesome state van Horn's body had been in, corroborating that part of the government's case. He also testified that they had found her diary while searching her apartment for clues following her murder, and the woman's diary had an entry the day before her death, stating that she was "tired of L," and "planned to tell him."

On cross-examination, Karansky asked the officer how many men's names he could think of that began with the letter "L." He looked at the jury as the officer answered, and was pleased to see many of the jurors looking like they were performing the exercise independently of the officer. His follow-up question was to ask the officer to look at the diary entry about three weeks earlier, which read in part: "Larry stayed over for the first time…" Finally, he asked the officer whether Larry had confirmed his relationship with Cecilia when he had been questioned, to which the officer had said, "Sir, to my knowledge he has not been questioned." Karansky was shocked but no longer surprised at the level of incompetence exhibited by the district attorney's office

– they were proffering theories without even checking whether the evidence would support them.

Surprised at the loss of his "L is for Lester" theory, the district attorney called his second witness, the coroner, who went into graphic detail about the killing. Yes, the victim had fought back, yes, her attacker had subdued her not only by beating her but by nearly drowning her in the toilet, and yes, death had been caused by strangulation, a conclusion reached due to the contusions around her neck, the bulging eyes, and the grotesque position of the tongue. Finally, the coroner testified that she had been strangled by someone right handed, who was quite strong.

After the district attorney finished, Karansky was out of his chair quickly. "Doctor," he said, "was there evidence that the victim had had sex recently?"

"Yes," the doctor replied. "There were very mild abrasions, caused by what I would describe as consensual but still rough sexual intercourse. And there were trace remnants of semen in and around her vagina."

Karansky was surprised, because he remembered no mention of this in the pre-trial statement about the doctor's testimony. Either it was an elegant trap, or the district attorney once again had been horribly negligent. He normally would not have pursued the matter without knowing what the doctor would say, because the wrong response could damn his client. But here, he didn't care – if it were Cayhill's semen, then the man was lying to him, and Karansky could live with the result. If it was not, then the district attorney's case was in very bad shape. Knowing the high stakes involved, Karansky paused long enough to draw the attention of those in court to him. Then he asked very deliberately, "Doctor, I'm sure you compared the semen to my client's DNA. Was the semen his?"

Vampires

The doctor, just as deliberately, answered, "I did. And no, the semen was not his."

"Did you compare it to Larry's?" Karansky asked, to rub the point in.

"I did not. Until just now I had never heard of anyone named Larry involved in this case," the doctor replied.

There was a stir in the courtroom at the disclosure. Karansky thanked the doctor and returned to his seat. The district attorney quickly called his third witness, pretending that all was proceeding according to plan. The third witness was a maintenance man who claimed he had seen Cayhill leaving Karansky's office on the day of the murder. Karansky had a choice — to attack the identification itself, or to attack the witness's memory of when he had seen him.

The man was so certain that he had seen Cayhill that Karansky decided not to fight him. He would try one trick, and if it didn't work, he would leave the witness alone. "Mr. Stevenson, are you absolutely certain that it was Mr. Cayhill that you saw on Wednesday, November 17?" It was a cheap trick, one that rarely worked. He had misstated the date; the murder had actually occurred on Wednesday, the 16th. Karansky expected a screaming objection from the district attorney, whose job it was to protect his witnesses from such tactics.

To his surprise, the district attorney wasn't paying close attention and raised no objection to the question. The witness, who was focused on the question's challenge to his identification, also didn't pay close attention to the rest of the question. "Absolutely, there isn't a doubt in my mind!" the witness stated with emphasis.

Karansky decided not to spring the trap just yet. "How can you be so sure?" he asked. "Perhaps it was a different day; perhaps a different date?"

The witness grew exasperated at the questioning over and over of something he had already said. "Look here," he said, not trying to keep the emotion out of his voice, "I saw that man on Wednesday the17th! You got that? Now don't ask me again!"

"You made it very clear," Karansky said. "I only have one more question. You say you saw him on Wednesday the 17th. The question is this: since Wednesday was actually the 16th, which part of your answer that you are so sure about is incorrect – the date or the day?" And without even waiting for an answer, Karansky added "no further questions, your honor," and sat down.

The district attorney had no other witnesses to call. He rested his case on a sour note. The judge looked at Karansky and asked if he were ready to go or did he want a short break. "Five or ten minutes would be useful, your Honor," Karansky responded.

"So be it," said the judge. Feeling generous, he said, "Resume in fifteen minutes."

Karansky looked for an open witness room, and signaled Cayhill to follow him. As soon as they were both in the room, Karansky closed the door. Then, turning to face Cayhill, he said, "That went very well. You have a decision to make. We can do nothing, call no witnesses, and essentially take the position that the prosecution did not prove anything beyond a reasonable doubt. I think we will win. On the other hand, it's not a hundred percent certain, and this is your one chance to take the stand. If you don't, there's no going back for a do-over."

Vampires

Cayhill thought for a moment, and then asked, "What would you do if you were in my place?"

Karansky stared at Cayhill, as if he were still trying to fathom the man's innocence. "I would take the stand if I were innocent; I wouldn't risk it if I weren't."

Cayhill laughed. "If this is a test of my innocence then I pass. I want to testify."

"Good," Karansky replied. "You will be clean-up. I am going to call your friend Bruce first. If after his testimony, it wouldn't serve any purpose, I won't put you on. Fair?"

"Fair," Cayhill replied.

"Okay then. We're back in," Karansky said, standing up. They went back into the courtroom, and as they walked in, the judge was sitting down. "You presenting a case?" the judge asked Karansky.

"Yes, your honor. I call Bruce Harrison to the stand," Karansky said. Karansky led the witness through the preliminary questions concerning his name, address and occupation, which was interior design, and then got down to business. "Mr. Harrison," he began, "how long have you known the defendant?"

"Oh my," the witness said, "our fifth anniversary is next week already, isn't it?" He looked at Cayhill with some apprehension as he said this, checking to see if he had revealed something he shouldn't have. Cayhill smiled at him, and his confidence was restored.

"How well do you know Mr. Cayhill?" Karansky asked.

"Goodness," the witness replied, "I know him very well." He paused, and then added with a barely suppressed giggle, "Biblically."

"Are you and Mr. Cayhill lovers?" Karansky asked.

The witness looked at the judge when this was asked, and said to the judge, "Will I get in trouble if I answer that? I don't want to incriminate anybody, including me."

Judge Hernandez answered in a gentle voice, "No, you won't get into trouble. It is not illegal to be homosexual in New Jersey. Please answer the question."

"Well then, yes, we are lovers."

"And how long have the two of you been lovers?" Karansky asked.

The witness smiled as he answered this, saying, "Exactly three weeks less than we've known each other. Nearly five years."

"Now there was earlier testimony that Mr. Cayhill had a female lover. Does this surprise you?"

"The idea is preposterous," the witness said.

"How can you be so sure? How would you know if he were cheating on you?" Karansky pressed.

"Are you serious? How do you know you're loved and it's not just an act? Why it is in a million different ways – how he looks at you in moments of weakness; whether he still brings you little gifts or calls

Vampires

you even when he is so tired that he can barely stand. A man can tell these things," the witness said.

Karansky stole a peek at the jury as they listened to this testimony. One of the women was visibly nodding her head in agreement, and one of the men was fidgeting uncomfortably. He decided he would take it – it took a unanimous jury to convict. If he reached one or two, that was all he needed. He decided to keep the testimony narrow; the district attorney would be limited to cross examine the witness only on those things that he had discussed on direct. He wanted that to be only on Cayhill's sexual preferences. He asked one final series of questions. "Mr. Harrison, based on your five-year relationship with Mr. Cayhill, do you think it is possible that he had an affair with the victim?"

"No, I do not," the witness said.

"But we had a witness testify that Mr. Cayhill told him that he was having an affair with her," Karansky said, serving up the question like a slow pitch right over the plate. The witness hit a home run. "If you mean that shifty-eyed little sneak who testified first, I wouldn't give two cents for whatever he said. Can't you tell? The man's a liar." Karansky walked back to his chair, smiling despite trying not to. He checked his notes and then sat down as he said, "No more questions."

The district attorney was a successful politician, not a skilled trial lawyer. He got to his feet, slowly, not certain of where to take the cross, and then asked, "Mr. Harrison, where was Mr. Cayhill on the afternoon of November 16th?"

Karansky rose halfway through the question, and objected just as the district attorney was finishing. "Your Honor, I object. I did not produce this witness as an alibi witness, and he did not touch the subject of Mr. Cayhill's whereabouts during direct. The question is beyond the scope of the direct testimony and is improper."

"Sustained," Judge Hernandez said. The district attorney looked lost for a moment, and then asked as a way of covering his retreat, "So is it your testimony that Lester Cayhill couldn't have murdered a woman because he didn't like them?" The question was objectionable but Karansky didn't object, relying instead on the witness to dispose of the questioner. Harrison did not disappoint.

"No that was not my testimony," he said. "My testimony was and is that if Ms. Van Horn was killed by a jealous lover, it is highly unlikely that her murderer was Lester."

Once again, the district attorney had his tail between his legs as he finished a witness. He asked no more questions, and Karansky called his last witness. "I call Lester Cayhill to the stand."

There is always an undercurrent of noise in murder trials that one can hear when a witness is called. It is made up of the individual conversations whispered among those in attendance, commenting on the witness and whether it was a good move or bad move, based on that spectator's opinion. Here, the undercurrent of noise became very loud, partly because it was the defendant being called and partly because of the juicy testimony that people expected he would give. Karansky waited impatiently for him to be sworn, and after he was, he began his examination.

"Mr. Cayhill, are you a homosexual?" he asked.

"Yes," Cayhill replied.

"For how long have you been a homosexual?" Karansky asked.

Vampires

"As long as I can remember," Cayhill answered. "One is born that way; it isn't something one converts to at some later point."

"Have you ever made love to a woman?" Karansky asked.

"No, I have not," was Cayhill's response.

"Mr. Cayhill, you heard Mr. Wendells' testimony, did you not?" Karansky asked.

"Yes, I heard it," Cayhill responded, his voice dripping with disdain.

"He said you told him that you were having an affair with the decedent, that you made a tape showing you having wild sex with her. Is any of that true?" Karansky asked.

"Not a word," Cayhill replied coolly. "I like women, but not in that way. As for the tape, I have some experience with doctored tapes. Lighting is the Achilles heels of those who would insert new frames into existing tapes – it is nearly impossible to edit a tape and inset new footage taken with the exact same amount of ambient light as the original. I think you'll find that if you look at the tape carefully, the amount of light on my face comes close, but does not match precisely the amount of light on the woman's face. It's a very skillful fake."

Karansky was taken by surprise by the testimony because Cayhill had not discussed this before taking the stand. Neither had Karansky's question called for comment on the tapes; Cayhill had volunteered it. Still, if true, it strongly corroborated Cayhill's testimony. Hoping that Cayhill knew what he was talking about, he asked the court for permission to replay the tape. Judge Hernandez agreed, and moments later they came to the first spot where a facial profile appeared. Karansky didn't see it the first time, but two of the jurors did, and pointed excitedly at the screen. They stopped the tape, went back and this time, Karansky focused not on what the face looked like but rather the amount of light on the faces of the man and woman on the screen. It was there, a subtle but noticeable darkening occurred both times Cayhill's likeness appeared. It took three times but eventually every juror picked up the difference. Satisfied that each of the jurors had seen it, and that there could be no better place to stop, Karansky turned to the judge, and said, "Nothing further, your honor. The defense rests."

The jury returned a not guilty verdict in record time. They were charged with brief directions by Judge Hernandez about a quarter to twelve, and told that if they didn't reach a verdict by 12:30, they would have to come back tomorrow. They had decided the case by five minutes after twelve, finding Cayhill not guilty. The verdict triggered mild pandemonium as the members of the press ran to use pay-phones or to exit the court so that they could turn on laptops and cell phones. Karansky ushered Cayhill out of court, but not before the latter told the press that he was relieved, but more significantly how grateful he was to his lawyer, Steven Karansky, to whom he attributed his acquittal.

Neither Karansky nor Cayhill wanted the spotlight, but there was someone who did. The district attorney, always one to roll with the punches, announced that his office was not through with its efforts to find the killer, and would be investigating further the witness in the case, the accountant, who had attempted to trick the district attorney's office with doctored evidence. As for Wendells himself, he vanished shortly after the jury verdict. An eyewitness said he saw Wendells step willingly into a limousine that pulled up next to him as he walked from court.

He has not been seen since.

Vampires

Chapter 49

Exhausted and exhilarated, Karansky went looking for Laura. He found her sitting in one of the witness rooms near Judge Hernandez's courtroom, her face white. He said "Laura?" and got a limited response – she half turned her head to where his voice was coming from. As she did, she knocked a piece of paper onto the floor. He picked it up, while keeping his eyes on her face. Her eyes widened as he took hold of the paper, and again said, "Laura?"

"They're going to kill me," she said, so softly that he couldn't understand her until he had prompted her to repeat what she had said.

"No one is going to kill you," he said, his blood starting to boil at what he assumed was a very dirty trial trick by Cayhill or one of his associates.

Laura shook the idea off, gesturing towards the piece of paper he now held in his hands.

He unfolded the paper, which he subconsciously had wadded into a tight ball, and unraveled it. The message said, "Drop the case or your dead." On the back were some Chinese characters, but it was not clear whether they had anything to do with the message on other side. "Where did you get this?" he said, raising the piece of paper that he had just read.

"It was on the top of this pad," she indicated a short stack of pads, most of them with most of their sheets already used, in the conference room.

"So how do you know whether that message even was intended for you?" he asked. He began to smile as he realized this incident might not be as serious as he first thought. She too, allowed a trace of a smile to appear on her face, as relief that she may have not been threatened coursed through her. "Besides, he can't be a very smart killer in any event. Just look at the grammar ("your dead" instead of "You're dead), he remarked, trying to make her smile. She tried to relax, but was not yet able to be that relaxed.

A knock on the door interrupted them. Laura gave Karansky a wild look of panic. He started to say, "Just ignore…" but the door opened and he too stopped talking. It was Cayhill. Strangely, Steven felt a great sense of relief at seeing who it was, as if he were now a friend.

"Ah, I thought I'd find the two of you together. Listen, I just wanted both of you to know that thanks to your great work," and here he nodded to Karansky, "I am getting my life back. Dunlop called and explained that it was all a big misunderstanding. I am no longer suspended. But the real reason I wanted to find the two of you is that I am back on the American Auto case. I wanted to let you know so that you wouldn't have a heart attack when you see me at counsel table in five minutes or so." He started to leave, smiled, and said "Good luck." Then he closed the door and was gone.

"That son-of-a-bitch," Karansky said. "I should have let him twist in the breeze for a bit longer."

"No, it sounds like you played it exactly right. But now I need you here," Laura said. "I can't beat him alone. He's too slippery."

"Laura, you can. You don't know how good you are," he said. "But I won't fight you on this. Tell me what you want me to do and I'll do it."

Her face softened with relief. "How about taking the next witness, the mystery man from American Auto?" she said.

"Be happy to," he replied. "Speaking of which, we ought to get back into court. We don't want to tick off the judge." They walked back into court, too late to avoid getting an angry stare from Judge Hernandez. "I'm sorry, your Honor," Karansky said, "With your permission, I will be participating in the trial going forward on behalf of the plaintiff."

"And I for the defendant American Automobile, your Honor," Cayhill said.

The judge looked at them both for a moment, and thinking of no reason that he could use to prevent them from participating, contented himself by warning each of them that any attempts to turn his court into a three-ring-circus would be dealt with harshly. Then, Judge Hernandez looked at plaintiff's table and said to no one in particular, "Call your next witness."

"Thank you your Honor," Karansky said. "I call that man," pointing to the man sitting in the back of the courtroom to whom Karansky had given a subpoena the day before.

The judge, who had not been looking up, had not seen Karansky point. He looked up now. "Did you just call Batman to the stand, counselor?" the judge demanded.

"No sir. I called 'that man,' the one sitting in the next to last row of the court," Karansky replied.

Vampires

"You don't know the name of your own witness?" the judge asked, incredulous. "I warn you counselor, if this doesn't produce relevant testimony, you will be cut off at the knees. I have you on a very short leash!"

Karansky assured Judge Hernandez that he understood, and promised to make the testimony very relevant. As he spoke, he waved the man up. The witness looked lost, and stared at Cayhill for direction as he approached the witness chair. Cayhill shrugged as if to say there was nothing to be done about it now. The clerk swore him in.

Karansky went up and stood next to him. "Could you state your name for the record, please."

The witness replied, "James A. Crandall."

"Are you employed, Mr. Crandall?" Karansky asked.

"Yessir, I am. I work for the American Automobile Company," Crandall responded.

"In what capacity? In other words, what do you do for them?" Karansky asked.

"I am the Director for Quality Operations," Crandall said.

Bingo!! "What does that mean exactly?" Karansky asked.

"I focus on ensuring that the factory turns out cars having world class quality by focusing on our processes. If we make the processes all world class, the product quality follows inevitably," Crandall replied, his demeanor displaying some of the quality guru's religious zeal about process improvement.

"Does your responsibility extend to the manufacturing process?" Karansky asked, moving slowly to make certain he didn't permit the witness an easy escape.

"Of course," Crandall said.

"And as part of that manufacturing process, do you monitor the equipment used in that process?"

"Yes, I do," the witness said.

"In your opinion, is the manufacturing equipment utilized in the company's Linden Plant safe?" The question was so simple, and should have been expected. Yet, it paralyzed the witness. He couldn't answer either yes or no without getting himself in trouble. Afraid to say no, he tried "yes."

"So the piece of machinery that killed Mr. Chapman was safe?" Karansky asked.

"Well, every piece of manufacturing equipment poses some risk," the witness said. "That alone doesn't make it unsafe."

"I see," Karansky said. "Has every piece of machinery in the factory killed someone?"

"Well, no," the witness said, starting to not like the direction this was taking him. Didn't people understand that he cared more than anybody about safety and that was why he had lobbied so hard to have a

Vampires

second employee do nothing but sit by this machine, ready to intervene and turn the damned thing off if necessary. He heard Karansky say something and realized he had missed the last question. "I'm sorry," he said, "could you repeat that?"

"I asked whether you had any reason to believe that this piece of machinery was unusually dangerous," Karansky said.

"Well, we had received some warnings about the machinery from the U.S. Product Safety Commission, and had taken the steps they recommended to ameliorate the risks," Crandall said.

"Was that a 'yes'?" Karansky pressed.

"I'm sorry?" the witness responded.

"You didn't answer the question I asked. I asked whether you had any reason to believe that the equipment was unusually dangerous. Yes or no."

"Yes," the witness answered with a sigh.

"And what was the basis of that belief?"

"We had received a communication from the U.S Product Safety Commission, warning about this machine."

"Now this warning advised against using this machine, because of the absence of an automatic safety cut-off, isn't that right?"

"Yes, but we followed their recommendation and had another employee on hand to shut the equipment off in case of problems," the witness said.

"I thought their recommendation was not to use the equipment at all because, and I quote the memo they sent you, 'We know to a virtual certainty that a certain number of workers will not only be killed, but killed in the most ghastly manner, pulled slowly by an arm or sleeve into the machine…' Didn't they in fact recommend that manufacturers not use this equipment at all?"

"Yes, but they also recognized that there may not be substitute equipment available and told manufacturers to have another employee on hand to turn the equipment off should anything bad happen. That is what we did," Crandall said.

"It didn't work did it?" Karansky asked.

"No it did not," Crandall reluctantly agreed. "But we did try."

"What you did was to assign to this duty a man that his supervisor knew to be a drunk, isn't that right? A man who was too drunk to stand the day Mr. Chapman was slowly chewed up by the machine, just as the memo in your file stated would happen. Right?"

Crandall's once clear and strong voice was shaking now, as he again said "yes." But he added in the company's defense that they couldn't fire the man since alcoholism was a protected disability under New Jersey law.

Karansky had his teeth into the witness now and wouldn't let go. "Come Mr. Crandall," he said, "the fact that you weren't supposed to fire him didn't require that you put him a position where he might need to act decisively to save someone's life. Why not put him where he couldn't hurt anybody? Like in marketing, or sales?"

"Those are management jobs." The quality director paused, trying to figure out how to explain. "They are…"

Karansky saw the witness struggle to find the right words, and helpfully offered some of his own, "…too important to be filled by a drunk?"

"No," said Crandall, "I was going to say that they were different pay grades than the supervisor here."

Karansky wouldn't let up, asking, "Can you explain the differences, please."

"Sure. The supervisor was a salary grade 5, what we called an SG5. The marketing and sales personnel started at SG6, so the supervisor would have had to receive a promotion to transfer into that organization."

"So what? Why not transfer and promote the supervisor? Wouldn't it have been better than put him in the position of the last line of defense against fatalities – a job that he was demonstrably unsuited for?" Karansky asked.

"But he wasn't on our promotable list!" Crandall insisted. "He was an…" the witness stopped mid-answer, realizing he couldn't complete the sentence the way he had intended.

"A what, Mr. Crandall? You were going to say an alcoholic, weren't you?" Karansky asked.

Crandall remained silent, looking venomously at Karansky. "Your honor," Karansky said at length, "Could you instruct the witness to answer the question."

Judge Hernandez was about to do so, when Crandall said, "Yes, he was an alcoholic and the other groups would not take him."

"Thank you," Karansky said. "Your honor, I have nothing further for this witness. Picking up the Mahoney memo, however, he said, "At this time I would like to introduce the Mahoney memo into evidence."

Cahill was out of his chair, shouting, "The document is hearsay, your Honor, and can't be admitted."

Karansky had winked at Laura as Cayhill was making his objection. She looked at him, puzzled, and wondered where he was taking this. Karansky then revealed his hand, "Your honor, it's not hearsay because I am not seeking to admit the document in order to prove the truth of Mahoney's statement that the equipment is dangerous. I have independent evidence to support that, namely the fact that the machine killed plaintiff's husband. I'm seeking to admit the document instead because it provides evidence that American Auto knew about the problem and chose not to satisfactorily address the issue. That is part of our proof on the issue of "willfulness," an element of our case for punitive damages. Because we are using the document to prove that the company received a warning, and not for the separate issue of whether or not that warning was correct, the document is not hearsay."

Cayhill had been outflanked. Judge Hernandez let him speak, but then ruled against him, "I'm sorry Mr. Cayhill, but Mr. Karansky is correct here. So long as he does not seek to use the document as evidence for the truth of the statements contained in it, it is not hearsay. And he's got you because the fact that American Auto was warned and chose to ignore such warnings is clearly relevant on the issue of damages. Your objection is overruled."

After the witness was excused, Judge Hernandez looked at Karansky and said, "Counselor, how much more are you going to have?"

"Your Honor, we have at most one more witness, a medical doctor whose testimony I could probably dispense with if Mr. Cayhill agreed that I could introduce his report into evidence without requiring him to testify."

The judge turned to Cayhill, with an inquiring look, adding "Counselor?" Cayhill was surprised since normally plaintiffs wanted the doctors to testify. There must be something wrong with this one, but despite his suspicion, he had nothing solid and no reason to reject the offer and require the doctor to appear.

"No objection to the document being introduced into evidence without its author your Honor," Cayhill said. Karansky silently breathed a sigh of relief. He quickly read to the jury a few paragraphs of the report, which indicated that Chapman's death had not been instantaneous, but that it had been caused by the loss of blood, resulting from several arteries in his arms being severed by the machine.

It would have been better to have live testimony but the doctor had told Karansky at the last minute that he was going to the Caribbean and would be unavailable. Had Cayhill insisted on live testimony, it would have been a real problem for the widow's case: without the doctor there, or Cayhill's agreement, the doctor's report would have been inadmissible as hearsay, meaning Karansky would have had no medical testimony at all. The only alternative would've been for Karansky to subpoena his own witness, essentially forcing him to come against his will. That was a recipe for poor or worse testimony. Karansky breathed a sigh of relief.

"Good," the judge said after the reading. Turning to Karansky he asked," I assume you rest?" Karansky nodded his assent, and the judge then turned to Cayhill, saying, "I assume you move to dismiss." Cayhill smiled back to indicate that he had been planning to do so. The judge continued, saying "Fine. Consider the motion made, and denied."

Judge Hernandez next asked Cayhill whether he planned any rebuttal case, and Cayhill responded, "Your honor, I'm not sure at this point. I need to review the events of the day first. I will let you know tomorrow."

The judge frowned, but there was nothing he could do about it now. He turned to the jury, and said, "Ladies and gentlemen of the jury. Thank you for another day of dedication. We'll see you tomorrow at one p.m."

Chapter 50

Karansky and Laura headed from the court directly to her apartment. He was jubilant – now that the document was in evidence, the jury would consider it for all purposes, no matter how the judge tried to control its use with instructions. Also, this would mitigate any threat against Laura -- why do violence now that what you were afraid of was already out on the table? He therefore saw no reason that they could not freely pursue what they had run short of time to complete this morning. He wanted to make love to Laura.

Laura felt less secure that the threat was addressed by placing that one document into evidence. Karansky seemed so confident and strong, though, that her fears largely subsided. She went out during their mid-morning break and, visiting the same lingerie store where she had shopped before, had bought another La Perla creation. This one, a chemise made from black lace., was even more expensive and less substantive than the last. She had dispensed with the wrapping and tucked it neatly into one of the pockets of her current dress, where it fit with room to spare.

They were walking hand in hand, entertained by their thoughts as to what the evening would bring, when his cellular phone rang. The name that appeared on his screen as the party calling was … Cecelia van Horn! Someone was using her cell phone to call. Karansky picked up, and said, "hello?"

It was Cayhill, who said immediately, "Listen, I know what you are thinking. I'll explain it all later. For now, and I don't know why I am doing this, don't go to Laura's home. Do you hear? They're waiting for you there!"

"Who is?" Karansky demanded.

"Does it matter?" Cayhill countered. "Just don't go there tonight." Karansky heard a click as Cayhill ended the call. He turned towards Laura who had not heard the words, but had picked up Karansky's emotions and said, "C'mon, it's probably a false alarm but let's get a hotel room."

"Steven!" Laura exclaimed, alarmed.

He looked at her. There were tears of fear and frustration spilling onto her cheeks, as she searched his face for answers. He didn't know what to do, so he kissed her – so fully that it took both of their breaths away for a moment. Then he said, "I don't know what is going on, or why. But at this point, I don't want to ignore what Cayhill just told me, which was that we shouldn't go to your apartment. So come." After a momentary look of panic, Laura's face became more composed, and they turned and retraced their steps in the direction of the Hyatt. As they entered the hotel, Karansky leaned over and said, "Just play along, would you Mrs. Smith?"

They approached the front desk. "We'd like a room, preferably the honeymoon suite, please," he said.

"A regular room is one hundred and forty-nine dollars a night plus taxes," the desk clerk said in a bored voice, "and the honeymoon suite is four hundred and ninety-nine dollars a night, plus taxes, though you do get complimentary champagne and strawberries." The clerk paused, and then asked, "Now then, which would you like?" He had gone through this routine many times before, almost always finding the extra three hundred and fifty dollars for the honeymoon suite too pricey for most couples.

"The honeymoon suite sounds fine," Karansky responded, without hesitation. Then he leaned over so he could have a private conversation with the clerk, "Do me a favor. There are some people not happy with our marriage. Under no circumstances do you tell anyone, no matter what story they use, where we are. Got that?" Karansky slipped the clerk a hundred dollar bill he kept for emergencies, and winked at the clerk.

"Very well, Mr.….uh…?"

"Mr. Smith," Karansky said, and handed the clerk a driver's license that bore his likeness with that name.

"Do you need help with your luggage?" the clerk asked.

"No, but thanks," Karansky responded, taking the key and guiding Laura towards the elevator.

The room's purpose was unambiguous.. There was a heart shaped bed, with a large number of pillows, and a mirror on the ceiling above it. There was a night table without the usual alarm clock, which instead had two crystal champagne flutes. Karansky thought a minute, and realized that he'd forgotten to ask about the champagne when there was a knock at the door. It made each of them jump. He went to the door, and said, "Who is it?"

"Room service," a voice answered, "Your champagne."

"Just leave it there," he responded.

"Yessir," came the reply, disappointed at the absence of a tip.

Karansky read the tone, and feeling safe enough to answer the door, opened it quickly, gave the man a ten-dollar bill, and said "thanks," before closing it, and looking for Laura. She had gone into the bathroom. He walked up to the door and knocked, not knowing what to expect. Her answer, "A moment, please," delivered in a voice dripping with sexuality, made him smile. After so many false starts and misadventures, he wasn't in a patient mood, so at the risk of ruining whatever surprise she might have been preparing, he opened the door and went in. She was just putting on the chemise over her head when he entered. He went up to her, and put his hands on her breasts, as she slid the chemise down. He then moved his hands down her body, and lifted her gently and carried her to the bed. He fumbled with the buttons of his pants, but managed at length to free himself from his clothes, and to move what little she was wearing out of their way. A bit fumbling and awkward, they made love, first tentatively and as they got the hang of it, enthusiastically.

After, their shared euphoria eased, leaving each of them clinging to the other. For a long time, they did nothing else but enjoy the physical closeness of each other. Finally, Karansky felt Laura stir. She leaned over and gave him a kiss, then got out of bed and used the bathroom. As she walked back to bed, she asked, "So who was it that was going to harm us if we had gone home, how did Cayhill know about it, and why did he warn us? I don't think of him as our best friend."

I don't know," Karansky said. "Maybe it's his way of saying, 'thanks' for his acquittal yesterday. "At least we know where he will be today, and can ask him." He looked at his watch, and was surprised at how much of the night was gone. In a few hours it would be time to get

up and prepare for court again. Karansky fretted. He was more concerned than he had admitted to Laura, because he didn't know from
where the threat was coming. He looked at her; she was falling asleep.
He couldn't though he tried. When the clock hit seven, he got out of
bed, made a pot of coffee and called Cayhill. Karansky didn't really
expect to get him, and he didn't, but it made him feel that at least he
was getting a jump on the day.

Chapter 51

Cayhill in fact had been in his office when Karansky called. He might even have answered the call had it not been for a visitor who demanded his attention. Dunlop was steaming mad. "Our Chinese friends…." He had started, but Cayhill cut him off, no longer trying to hide the animosity between them, "You mean your Chinese friends," he retorted.

"I mean our Chinese clients…" Dunlop tried again.

Again, Cayhill cut him off. "No, they're not our clients until the deal is done, which requires government approval." Waving some documents in the air, Cayhill raised the stakes in their discussion, "You know, I couldn't quite figure out why your Chinese friends would be so interested in a factory accident case. Given the wealth of the Chinese government, even a huge verdict for the plaintiff wouldn't really concern them financially. It occurred to me there must be something else, some other reason they wanted the case to end."

Dunlop sat in his chair, waiting to hear how much Cayhill knew.

"I took the liberty of going through the boxes of documents we had withheld from plaintiff during discovery, and in particular, those where we asserted attorney–client privilege. I'll be damned if I didn't find documents containing no legal advice at all! One did contain contractual analysis about shifting all auto production from the United

States to China beginning in three years under the moronic agreement we signed, but that isn't legal advice subject to the privilege. I also found a buckslip, signed by one Preston Dunlop, attached to that document, arguing that for political and public relations reasons, early disclosures of such plans should be avoided "at all costs." Now, you know as well as I do, that you can't claim legal privilege for everything said by a lawyer; there has to be legal advice involved before one can invoke the privilege."

The back of Dunlop's neck had turned bright red. "For your information," he hissed at Cayhill, "I negotiated the agreement you reference (Cayhill interrupted with a caustic, "Now there's a surprise!"), and the clients at American Auto were delighted. It's hardly 'moronic.'"

Cayhill was having none of it. "Let me get this straight. What you're telling me is that the current management, whose total lack of judgment is responsible for that company's demise, loved a plan negotiated by you, under which they will get huge bonuses because it provides front-loaded benefits to American Auto! As I said before, what a surprise."

Dunlop looked daggers at him, saying, "Don't think you are immune from retribution should you defy the wishes of the Chinese."

"Is that a threat?" Cayhill asked.

"No," Dunlop stated, "merely an observation."

"Well, you and your observations are welcome to come sit in court today. In fact, I need that asshole Fong in court today. And tell him to come without his guns, brass knuckles and whatever else Chinese thugs carry these days. He's got to go through security, and he's got to look like the doctor that he'll never be."

Judge Hernandez opened the court session the next day by announcing that due to a backlog of criminal sentencing, he could only devote an hour to the case that day. "That means we either have a final witness if you have one, or closing arguments if you don't. But I don't have time to hear both. Now, Mr. Cayhill, any witnesses?"

"One," your Honor," Cayhill replied.

"Very well," said the judge. Then we will finish the witness testimony today, and do closing arguments tomorrow. Counselor?"

Cayhill took his cue, saying, "I call Dr. Max Fong to the stand." The mysterious Dr. Fong rose from his seat, and approached the witness stand. Karansky rose to object, but Judge Hernandez cut off discussion in front of the jury, telling both counsel that he would see them in chambers. Karansky waved to Laura to come and the two of them joined Cayhill in the judge's office. "Speak," said the judge to Karansky, "You first. Why do you object?"

"Your Honor," the defendant is springing this witness on us as a complete surprise. Your trial order required each of us to identify in advance all witnesses we knew we would use, especially expert witnesses. They must have known that they intended to use Mr. Fong, and yet didn't disclose it. As you will recall, the last time they were going to use this man, they misrepresented his whereabouts, something we were able to prove because we had time to look into it. I strongly suspect that Dr. Fong is here for a similarly false purpose, only this time I will have no chance to check out his story."

The judge turned to Cayhill. "Counselor, how do you respond?"

"Your honor, the doctor only called my office yesterday because he had seen news accounts of the trial. I did not plan to use him as a witness until I talked with him this morning. Besides, the doctor's testimony will be that Mr. Chapman died of heart failure and did not suffer the agonizing death claimed by plaintiff. Now, Mr. Karansky may not like that testimony but he is and has been well aware of Dr. Fong's view for some time, and cannot legitimately claim surprise."

"I don't buy it, Counselor," the judge said, addressing Cayhill. ""Given what happened during his last, "paper appearance" before this Court, it seems unfair to give Plaintiff no notice." The judge looked sympathetically at Karansky, but then said, "Still, I am going to allow him to testify, provided he sticks to the same topic that was addressed in his letter. If I excluded the witness, I have no doubt but that you," and here he looked at Cayhill, "would be in appellate court seeking a new trial on the grounds that his testimony was essential to your defense. At best, this would cause delays in getting a final resolution; at worst, I would have to suffer through a second trial of this with the two of you. Mr. Karansky, your objection is noted for the record. Now let's get on with it."

Once Dr. Fong was sworn in, Cayhill began his examination.

"Dr. Fong, could you state your complete name for the record," he began.

"Doctor Maxwell S. Fong," the witness said. Several other questions elicited the facts that Dr. Fong was a medical doctor, with degrees from Johns Hopkins, and made his home in Beijing.

"Why, if I may, are you in the United States?" Cayhill asked.

"I am working on behalf of one of the ministries of my government," the witness said. "It's public now so I can say that my government was considering an investment in your company American Auto and asked me to report on the treatment and health of its workforce."

"And how did you do that?" Cayhill asked.

"By making physical inspections of their various facilities, and talking to employees," the witness replied.

"Did there come a time when you visited their facility in Linden?" Cayhill asked.

"Yes," Dr. Fong answered.

"Do you remember when?" Cayhill added.

"It would be impossible to forget. It was March 6, the day of the accident," Fong said.

"Did you witness the accident?' Cayhill asked.

"No, not the actual incident," the witness said. "I arrived just after the unfortunate man had had his fingers crushed."

Cayhill looked extremely solemn as he asked the witness what he had observed next. "The man had his head slumped on his chest," the doctor said.

"He was not screaming?" interjected Cayhill.

"No, not at all. I later determined he had died of a heart attack," the witness replied.

Vampires

"Doctor, did the decedent suffer, in your judgment?" Cayhill asked.

"For an instant, almost certainly. But only for an instant. After that he was with God," the witness replied.

Cayhill thanked the doctor, and looking pleased with himself, turned to Karansky and said, "Your witness."

Karansky began to stand up when Laura put her hand on his arm, and said, "He's mine." It was she who stood up, and approached the witness. "Doctor," she said, her voice laced with the skepticism she felt, "how close were you standing to Mr. Chapman when you observed him being killed?"

"Not too far," the witness replied. "Pretty close, I think."

"Can you put that in actual distance? Use feet or meters, whichever you are comfortable with," Laura said.

"Oh, I'd say about 3 or 4 meters, then," Dr. Fong said.

"That's about 9 – 12 feet," Laura said, facing the jury. She walked over to the jury box, and asked the witness, "About the distance between you and me right now?" The witness said yes. "Was anyone closer than you?" she asked.

"I don't think so," he said. "Sadly, I had the best view of what was going on." He paused a moment, and then added, "I suppose his colleague was closer, but he was not functioning at the time."

"Because he was drunk?" she asked.

"I believe that to have been the case," the witness replied.

Laura suddenly turned combative, asking, "Dr. Fong, being that close, you could have turned the machine off. Yet you didn't. The undisputed medical evidence is that it continued to pull him in and chew him up for almost thirty seconds. Dr. Fong, how could you just stand there and do nothing for that length of time?"

Cayhill stood to make and objection in order to give his witness time to think. But Judge Hernandez headed him off at the pass, saying, "Whatever you were about to say, don't. The question is proper and I will allow it."

The witness fidgeted, and then said, "I didn't know how to turn it off," he tried.

"Come now, doctor. There was a large red lever, with the words 'on' and 'off ' painted right by it. It's pretty hard to miss, isn't it?" While she was asking this, she walked to the jury box with a picture of the machine that had previously been introduced into evidence.

Dr. Fong said, "I also thought he was already dead."

"In your previous testimony, you said you determined only later that he had died of a heart attack. Come doctor, you couldn't have been so certain he was dead that you thought it unnecessary to turn off the machine, could you? Is it your testimony that you, a medical doctor, stood by and watched a man be chewed up for almost a half-minute without making the slightest effort to turn off the machine or help in any way?"

The witness looked at her with obvious hostility but said nothing. She stared back, letting the period of uncomfortable silence lengthen.

Vampires

Finally, she broke it, asking quietly, "You weren't there, were you doctor?"

His voice lost some of its composure, as he said, "That's a lie!"

"Is it, doctor?" she asked. And without getting an answer, she sat down, and said, "Nothing further, your honor."

Cayhill did the best he could on re-direct to rehabilitate the witness, having him affirm that, yes, he had been there. But he made no effort to re-open the discussion of why the doctor had not stopped the machine, leaving a gaping hole in his credibility.

This was Cayhill's last witness, and he rested after his re-direct. Karansky said that the plaintiff also rested, while writing a note to Laura, saying "Excellent!" and sliding it in front of her.

The judge looked at his watch. "That's it for today, I'm afraid." he said. "Closing arguments tomorrow." A few minutes later, as the jurors were filing out of the courtroom, Cayhill came over to where Karansky was talking to Laura, and said, "We need to talk."

Karansky looked up, and shook his head to indicate his agreement. "I don't know what you want to talk about, but I'd like to start with the events of last night."

"Agreed." Cayhill looked up, and saw Fong standing next to Dunlop. They were watching the three of them. Cayhill said quickly, "You know the coffee shop you two go to?" he asked, directing his question to Karansky. Karansky was shocked they would have been observed so closely that Cayhill even knew where they went for coffee, and his face showed it. "Oh, grow up," Cayhill added. "Be there in thirty minutes."

They were. Cayhill didn't show for nearly an hour, and when he did, he seemed distracted. He came in quickly, and ignoring that he was late, he took a sip of Karansky's coffee, and said, "Look, the deal is as follows: American Auto will offer, for today only, fifteen million for the widow. That's it. In return, you agree to stay completely silent about both the Mahoney memo and the fact that the new management is planning to move all auto production out of this country to China in three years, as the documents in this envelope reveal." Cayhill slid an envelope under Karansky's elbow as he said this.

"What-a-a-a-t?" said Karansky.

"Your interrogatory number 36 asked for all plans involving expanded use of such equipment. Well, the Chinese plan to use identical punch presses in their new factories, as many of these documents explain. Is it relevant to this case? Not particularly, but then again, the fact that a document is not relevant does not justify a failure to produce it in discovery." Cayhill gave a little smile, aimed at Laura. "So the right thing to do here is to provide the document in discovery, and then argue against its use. Right?"

"Right," Laura answered, thinking of the irony of her initial interview with this man. "But why start now?"

"Look," Cayhill explained, "It's not exactly safe to have these documents. But there are two reasons why I want you to have them. First, you did request such documents in discovery, and I am obligated to comply, even if it exposes you to danger. And second, I have advised the Chinese that should anything happen to me, you would have no choice but to make these public. Hopefully, that will never happen, but I would appreciate if you would say that's what you would do if you're asked."

After he left, Laura asked, "What do we do?"

"What we were hired to do," Karansky answered. "We represent our client. The rest is interesting but not our concern, at least not now."

What will she want us to do?" Laura asked.

"Based on past experience, she'll look for my advice. My advice will be to take the fifteen million and run. But I'll know for sure pretty soon; I have an appointment with her at the office at five."

Chapter 52

Karansky arrived back at his office roughly ten minutes early, and was unlocking the door when he felt a jab in the back. Karansky, assuming it was a robbery, said, "Look, my wallet is in my back pants pocket. If you want..."

"I don't want your money, man. I want to talk to you about the way you made me look like I was an idiot," the man said. Karansky was so stunned that he forgot about the gun in his back and started to turn around, only to be slammed into the door.

"You are the eyewitness who said that you saw Cayhill here the day of the murder," Karansky exclaimed. "Mr. Stevenson, wasn't it?"

"You got that right," the man said. "And you used your cheap lawyer tricks to make me look like a damned fool and got that murderer freed."

"I did what I did to defend my client," Karansky said, "Who, by the way, is not guilty of the murder for which he was charged."

"Now who's playing the idiot?" Stevenson asked. "Sure you fooled me with your trick questions, but do you really think I would confuse the day when, first, I saw him walk from the building, throw something into the trash behind the building, and drive away in his car, and second, see the news reports about a gruesome murder in the building?

Man, you have shit for brains if you can't put two and two together," the man concluded.

Karansky was shocked by what he'd heard, and said, "Why didn't you say any of this on the stand?" He was bewildered by the seemingly inconsistent facts that he thought he understood about the murder.

"I was waiting to be asked," Stevenson replied. "I was never asked." He shuddered as if suddenly chilled, and seemed to get angry all over again. "Right, now you know why I am here. Open the door and go inside."

Karansky had a very bad feeling about what would happen once they were inside, and he fumbled nervously with the keys. He was trying to think what to do when he heard a familiar voice say, "Young man, don't be a fool. Put your gun down!" Stevenson swiveled, expecting to be attacked from the rear. He was not. But Mrs. Chapman stood her ground, with a defiant and angry look. "You put that gun away," she repeated with great irritation and power. "Mr. Karansky is a good man, and I will not permit you to hurt him."

"You're wrong about him," Stevenson argued. "What he did was unforgivable."

"Young man," the widow said, "does it look like I am easily duped? Whatever he did he must have had good reasons to do, and whatever awful thing you think he did won't be so awful once you understand the reasons why."

"You say this without even knowing what he did?" the man whimpered.

"I don't have to know," she replied. "He has a good heart. It guides his actions. All of his actions."

His gun was no match for her conviction. Stevenson put the gun's safety on and gave it to Karansky. "Sarah, thank you," Karansky said. To Stevenson he said, "Please come inside and tell me what you know. From the top. I want to know everything. "

The maintenance man tied the day he saw Cayhill to his watching of the evening news and the reports of the murder. Cayhill had clearly been here the day of the murder, and had lied about it. Why? Thinking out loud, Karansky said without really meaning to, "If he did commit the murder, why did Wendells try to frame him with that ridiculous story about Cayhill and the Cecelia in a sexual tryst gone bad?" Why too would anyone doctor the tape in a way that could so easily be detected? That made no sense either. The pieces didn't fit.

Unless....

Karansky started sifting facts through various scenarios. It took a few moments but his brain tumbled to a horrible conclusion, allowing all the pieces to fit. He tested it within his own mind and couldn't find the flaw. Again without meaning to, he started moaning, "No," over and over. The widow shook him by his arm, bringing him back to reality. "Are you okay?" she asked.

"No I am not," he answered. "I just had a horrible thought but one that puts all the facts into one consistent mosaic. Oh my God, if this is true then I helped acquit a killer!" Suddenly he needed to talk to Laura, to share this with her, to pick her brain and to be comforted. He called her at home, but there was no answer. He tried her cell with the same result. He began feeling panicked but then saw the message indicator on his cell phone. Maybe she had been calling him while he had been trying to call her. He listened. Thank God, he thought, her voice.

Vampires

He listened to her message, "Hey honey! Well, you do quick work. I just heard from Cayhill who said the two of you had talked and had settled the Chapman case. He said he tried calling you back but like me had been unable to reach you. It turns out that American Auto has some reason for wanting to make the settlement happen today, and he wanted one of us to sign the papers tonight. Don't worry; when I couldn't get you I told him I'd sign for us. I'm on my way back to his office. He said he'd meet me there. Oops, my battery is about to die. See you…" The message stopped abruptly.

Karansky was near panic. He forced himself to think what to do, and after a minute, decided. He asked Stevenson if he could borrow the gun, hugged the widow, and heard her yell to him as he ran from the office to do what he thought best. He ran down the stairs, and out of the building into the street. He hailed a cab, and two pulled over – itself a small miracle in New Jersey. He looked at the drivers, yelling loudly enough for both to hear, "which one of you will ignore speed limits getting me across town? The first driver muttered, "Asshole," and drove away. The second one smiled at him and nodded. Karansky jumped in the cab and yelled out the address, and told the driver to hit it. Again, the driver only smiled. The driver pointed to a piece of scrap paper in his hand and pantomimed writing on it. It took a second for Karansky to realize that the man did not speak English! No wonder he had smiled when Karansky had asked him to speed; he smiled at everything!

Karansky said "Shit!" and jumped out of the taxi. He hailed another cab that he saw in the distance, and when it finally pulled up to him, jumped in. This time his first question was whether the driver spoke English, and only after getting an eloquent "yeah, do you?" did he tell the man that he'd double the fare if he hurried. He gave the driver the address and they were off with a jolt. It was the fastest he had ever made it cross town, but it seemed as if they were crawling.

As they approached the destination, Karansky took the gun out of his pocket without thinking. He was trying to determine whether the safety was on or off, when he happened to look up and saw the agitated face of the driver reflected in the rear view mirror. Karansky tried to calm him but it was too late. The driver pulled sharply to the curb, and jumped out, yelling, "He's got a gun, he's got a gun."

Karansky didn't know what to do. He looked at the gun, decided he wanted to keep it, and put it into his pocket. Then he too ran from the cab, into the building that housed Cayhill's office. He immediately drew the attention of the security guard, a black man who looked like he could play linebacker on a pro-team, and who accosted him in a deep voice with, "May I help you?"

"Yes," Karansky said, "I believe Mr. Cayhill is expecting me. Do you mind if I go up?"

"Just hold on there a minute, friend," the guard said. "I don't think Mr. Cayhill is expecting you, and yes, I do mind if you go up. You see, Mr. Cayhill is entertaining a lady friend and told me explicitly that he did not want to be disturbed."

Karansky's agitation increased radically upon hearing this. He took the weapon from his pocket and after pointing it at assorted other things, he finally got it aimed at the security guard. "I don't want to hurt you but I will if I have to," Karansky said. "The woman upstairs is my colleague and she is in great danger. Take me to Cayhill's office, or I swear I will blow your mother-fucking head off!"

The security guard looked at Karansky without fear, as if he were dealing with a problem child. After what seemed an interminable amount of time to both of them, but was only a few seconds, the guard stood up, said, "Suit yourself," and grabbed a huge ball of keys. He started walking towards the elevators, and when Karansky failed to follow, he turned to him, and said, "C'mon, then, if you're coming. They're on the twelfth floor." Karansky lowered the gun and followed the guard to the elevator. Once inside, the guard looked Karansky over as they rose in the elevator. "Here, hand me your gun," the guard said.

Karansky held it closer.

"Look, you seem like a nice guy who doesn't know the first thing about guns," the guard said. "If you are going to have any success rescuing young ladies, you really need to turn the safety off." Karansky handed him the gun.

The guard handled the gun expertly. He then offered it back.

"Good luck," the guard said. "You'd best be good at bluffing," he added, opening his hand to show the bullets he had taken from the gun. "I'd say you have about ten minutes before the police arrive, in case that affects your plans any," the guard concluded.

Karansky's agitation increased. He wanted the bullets back, but he didn't want to take the time to convince the guard. Feeling suddenly helpless, he stepped off the elevator, and a moment later, the doors swished shut.

Not knowing what to expect, Karansky gripped the pistol tightly in his right hand, while he tested the handle on the front door of the law firm. It was unlocked. He opened the door quietly and went inside. The entry foyer was dark and he stayed there for a moment to let his eyes adjust and to listen for sound. Nothing. There was a light coming from an office down the right corridor. Moving as quietly as he could, he began walking towards the light. About halfway there, he heard voices. He stopped to listen, and then heard the unmistakable sound of a laugh. Her laugh!

His emotions cycled rapidly though relief, concern, and anger. No longer trying to be stealthy, he strode towards the conference room from which both the laugh and light had emanated, and taking a deep breath, moved forward so he was standing in the doorway, still grasping the gun.

Laura was seated in one of the many chairs around a massive table. There was a drink on the table in front of her. Cayhill was standing right next to her, his foot on her chair, with a glass in his hand. They were both smiling, but those smiles began disappearing as they looked at him, and more specifically, the gun he was holding.

Laura regained her power of speech first. "Steven, have you lost your mind?" she asked? "Put that gun away."

"I don't have time to explain now," Karansky responded. "Laura, I need you to leave the room. Cayhill and I have something to discuss. Privately."

"No," she said. "You're acting like a madman. I have no intention of leaving until you come to your senses."

Karansky had not counted on her lack of cooperation. He stammered, starting to argue with her, "Listen, Laura, you may think you know this man…" he started.

Cayhill surprised them both by jumping into the conversation. "Laura, it's okay. I too have some things that I need to discuss with him I would prefer to keep just between the two of us," he said, gesturing towards Karansky and himself. "My office is right next door. Make yourself comfortable. Trust me, no one is going to get shot."

Laura stood for a minute, with her hand on her hip, thinking. Then she made her way to the door, walking right past Karansky without making eye contact. After she walked out, he went to the door and closed it. Then he turned to face Cayhill, and waving the gun at him, said, "Stay away from her. If you hurt her, so help me, I will find you and kill you."

Cayhill remained calm. "You've got it wrong, Stevie. Why would I hurt her? For one thing, I like her – she's got spunk. And more important, she is my insurance policy. I know you are going to behave because, as I proved tonight, you can't prevent me from getting very, very close to her if you don't."

"What the hell do you mean 'behave'?" Karansky bellowed, raising his voice as he was beginning to feel trapped. He fought to remain calm as he talked to a person who he now was convinced was a madman.

Cayhill, on the other hand, appeared totally relaxed. "Please put the gun down and I will tell you. We both know you aren't going to shoot me, and it is unnecessarily theatric. Okay?" Karansky put the gun on the table in front of him. "Thank you," Cayhill resumed. "Now let's see. The meaning of behave is as follows: first, I don't care what you believe, but you retain lock-solid attorney-client privilege on the murder case. Hey, enjoy it – you won! I was found not guilty and can't be tried again. But I don't want you ruining my reputation by spreading gossip about the case. It's history. Do you understand that? Cecelia's death was an aberrational necessity that will not be repeated."

"What about Wendells? When he resurfaces he is going to come after you – you know that," Karansky said.

"He has about as much chance of resurfacing as Jimmy Hoffa," Cayhill said.

"You?" Karansky asked.

"No. Think of it as clients not willing to trust someone who would double-cross his partner."

"You're such a cold-blooded bastard. You killed her, didn't you?" Karansky asked.

"You mean the late Cecilia van Horn, the named plaintiff in the RICO case brought against me?" Cayhill asked sarcastically, an ugly smile breaking through his outer benign façade. "You really killed her by bringing the case. It would have ruined me and my reputation, which I couldn't allow. Yes, I did the final honors, but it was you who made it necessary."

Karansky was aghast at the man's coolness while admitting the commission of an inhuman act. "But how could you? How did you know…?" his questions were stammered, without focus. Cayhill provided it.

"How'd I know I'd get away with it?" he asked. "I didn't know for sure. But I knew the district attorney was a pompous ass who would rush in if he thought he could secure a quick conviction. I knew you were a far better attorney who would push him into making a mistake. And I knew that Wendells was just looking for an opportunity to stab me in the back. So the only thing that had to be done was to feed the district attorney some material that would lead him to believe he had an open-and-shut case. And, of course, convince you to take the case."

"I still don't get it," Karansky said. "The tape…"

Vampires

"Lucky for me that you are a better lawyer than detective," Cayhill said. "Want to guess?" Cayhill smiled, literally beamed.

"No, I don't. Please enlighten me," Karansky replied.

Cayhill was nearly bubbling over, he was so eager to share what he had done. "It was brilliant," he began, beaming. "Wendells was telling the truth! I gave him the package containing Cecilia's underwear, which I had taken from her place right after I killed her, and a tape that had been doctored, somewhat clumsily, to insert my picture into a tape that Cecilia had made of herself and her boyfriend. I also told Wendells that I'd had an affair with her, and needed to keep the stuff safe but didn't want to throw it out for sentimental reasons. It was entirely predictable that he'd do what he did --- take the stuff swearing fidelity till his last breath, and then try to stab me in the back as soon as he was sure that the tape was what I told him it was. The DA had a wet dream over the stuff, never suspecting I had in fact framed myself with evidence that would fall apart upon closer inspection."

"So the district attorney rushes to prosecute with a case that falls apart, you are acquitted and now insulated from any further prosecution for Cecilia's death by double jeopardy, Cecilia and the RICO case are dead, Wendells is missing and presumed dead, and the only one who knows any of this is me, who was your attorney and is forbidden by the canon of ethics from divulging what he knows," Karansky summed up.

Cayhill was positively beaming. "Precisely," he said. "But you are a resourceful man, Mr. Karansky, and one I have come to respect. That is the reason for tonight, to remind you that no matter what you do, I can get to Laura. And though it pains me even to think about it, I could and would kill her if absolutely necessary. That is why you must agree to not do or say anything that would reveal what you know about the murder of that poor woman. It is not the only thing you must agree to ensure the lovely Laura survives the night, but it obviously is the most important."

"What are you talking about?" Karansky said. "What else could you possibly want from me?"

"There are two very minor items, trifles really, that I would like you to agree to," Cayhill said. "First, we need to settle the American Auto case today. The company closes its books for the quarter today. Based on my earlier advice, they had reserved twenty-five million dollars for this case. Settling it for fifteen million dollars will make them deliriously happy because after reversing the reserve they actually get to report the other ten million dollars as profit. They want do it this quarter. Laura has already signed the agreement, so all I really need here is your acquiescence.

"And the other condition?" Karansky asked.

"That you and Laura attend as my guests the annual bar association dinner a week from this coming Saturday. Word has it that I am going to receive the award for the bar association's Man of the Year. I want you there so I can tell the assemblage that I could never have achieved what I did without your help," Cayhill said.

Karansky felt nauseous. "And if I don't agree?" he asked.

"If you don't agree, then you can try to kill me, if you are better with guns than I am, which I doubt." Cayhill paused briefly, reached under the table, and placed a gun on the table. "Even if by some miracle you survive, you will face prosecution for my death. Either way, to not agree is to choose death and an end to any chance you have for a decent life. On the other hand, if you do agree, everyone lives, you have a chance to live happily ever after with a fine woman," Cayhill said.

Karansky could think of nothing to say. He finally spoke, saying, "You are a miserable excuse for a human being."

"I really don't care what you think of me," Cayhill said. "But before we bring Laura back in, I need a simple yes or no. Do you agree to the three conditions?"

"Yes," Karansky said at length. "Just make certain that nothing happens to her. The day she dies, you die."

"I'll take that risk. She's young and healthy. We should do just fine," Cayhill said.

"What next?" Karansky asked.

Cayhill waved a document at him, saying, "Laura already signed. I will make you a copy."

Karansky looked at the copy he was handed a minute later, saying, "But this is dated next Tuesday. I thought you needed something done today."

"We just needed to sign today. Now, based on the letter I submit to American Auto, they can reduce their reserve today to the number they will pay you on Tuesday. That entitles them to reverse the excess reserve and declare that as profit today. And, so I understand, it gives you the chance to collect your five million dollars from the settlement, assuming your house does sell at the auction."

"Why are you doing this?" Karansky asked, amazed at the inconsistencies in Cayhill's personality.

"Because, contrary to what you think, I really am a nice guy," Cayhill said.

Vampires

Chapter 53

Karansky was dreading the bar fete. For one thing, he did not know whether he could tolerate the adulation of a man he could not stand. Even worse was the fact that he would be credited with helping this monster become what he was. But by far the most intimidating part of the event in his mind was that he suspected that he would be seated at the same table as Laura.

He had not seen her in the intervening week since the night he had gone over to Cayhill's office. She had told him after the events at Cayhill's office that she would be spending the night at a hotel, and that she expected him to clear out whatever he didn't want thrown out by the morning, at which time she was having the locks changed. She also had not shown up for work. Not able to share the truth without putting her in jeopardy, he didn't know how to explain his behavior. As a result he didn't try.

The day before the event, he received a call from Cayhill that can only be described as exceedingly strange. Cayhill called to complain that Laura had given her regrets, saying she did not plan to attend the bar dinner. Karansky stayed silent so Cayhill filled the void by saying, "She says it is because of you," Cayhill said.

"Goddamnit!" Karansky exclaimed. "What do you expect? I haven't been able to tell her the truth, and without it, she is convinced I am a total lunatic."

"And that is a problem," Cayhill said. "Perhaps not now, but if you two go your separate ways, over time the degree of your affection for her may go down, and that means the value of her life as my insurance policy goes down with it."

Karansky was totally exasperated. "So what would you have me do?" he asked. "You have tied my hands and I can't even explain why I can't explain things to her."

"Exactly," said Cayhill, "which is why I decided to do us both a favor. I played Cupid."

"You what?" asked Karansky.

"I told her the truth. Or at least some of it," Cayhill said. "Now she wants to kill me, but the good news is that she is once again ready to spread her legs for you."

"Don't be crass," Karansky said. "It doesn't suit you."

"Very well. Think about it how you want. The fact remains that if you'd like, you have a perfect opportunity to resume whatever relationship you had with her. Of course, I had to make it clear to her that with understanding comes responsibility." Cayhill smiled as he said this last part.

"Meaning?" Karansky asked.

"Meaning she knows that if any of this stuff leaks, I kill you," Cayhill said, "right before I kill her," he added. Karansky was thinking how to respond when he lost interest in the conversation. Laura had entered his office and put a hand on his shoulder. He jumped at first, but when he saw who it was, his face melted into a broad smile. He said, "Got to go," into the telephone and hung up. Then he turned to face Laura who had stood between him and his desk, with her arms draped around the back of his neck. She showered him with kisses, on his cheeks, eyes, neck and mouth. "You know?" he asked. "He said he told you."

She put her finger on his lips to quiet him. "I know," she said. "But you must promise never to mention that horrid man again. Steven, I am sorry. I had no idea…I mean, he is evil…"

It was his turn to silence her. He first put his finger on her lips. Then, saying "deal," he replaced his finger with his lips.

Chapter 54

The bar fete was truly an event to remember. Following a rousing introduction by his partner Preston Dunlop, Cayhill was awarded the bar association's man of the year award. Dunlop reviewed recent events, before concluding that he was "proud as punch" for having as his partner a man such as Cayhill, who "never stopped believing in himself" and had weathered the storm, emerging intact at the top of his chosen profession.

Cayhill's speech was even better, thanking the two people who had inspired him and made his revival possible: Steven Karansky, whose legal skills and acumen had resulted in his acquittal, and Laura Simon, whose insistence that integrity was the foundation on which one should build one's career as an attorney, had inspired him to keep going even when things were darkest. He got laughs when he admitted that he had foolishly chosen not to hire her when he'd had the chance, apologizing to American Auto for making such a costly blunder.

It was, in short, an evening to remember. At the end of Cayhill's acceptance speech, the press wanted pictures of Cayhill, Karansky and Laura. The latter two eventually were persuaded but looked distinctly uncomfortable. Immediately after the pictures were taken, Laura pleaded fatigue and they left. To those who pressed she reminded them she had just finished the bar exam earlier that day and that she was exhausted. Still, it seemed strange for the two heroes to leave so quickly after Cayhill revealed their roles in the saga. Their departure might have even drawn comment, had the newspapers not become preoccupied with another slant on the story.

It was a tragedy, the papers reported, having been through so much, and having come out on the top of his profession, that Lester Cayhill, aged 44, died, the victim of a senseless hit and run driver as he was leaving the event. Preston Dunlop, his partner when asked for comment said only that, "Cayhill loved the law. It is truly a shame that his own life should end this way, a victim of a cowardly and lawless act."

Karansky appeared at a hastily called press briefing, hosted at the Marriott Hotel right after that. He started out by saying, "Those of us who knew him will notice his absence every day. He was, to say the least, a unique individual." He stopped, and the press representatives wondered whether they were going to get anything more than platitudes. Then, with the perfect timing of a good stand-up comedian, Karansky added, "Oh, and one more thing: Mr. Cayhill had asked us that should anything happen to him, we make public certain documents he had obtained revealing that the joint venture between American Automobile and the government of China plans to move all manufacturing from the United States to China in three years."

He had brought twenty copies, which disappeared in the first seconds following Karansky's revelation. The room erupted into chaos, as some tried to shout questions, while others fought to get a copy of the documents. Karansky saw Preston Dunlop among the reporters trying to get out of the room without being noticed. Karansky held up his hand for silence, got at least a break in the noise levels, and added, "I really don't know anything else about this document. But he does," Karansky said, pointing to Dunlop. As I recall, he was the person who negotiated the document with the Chinese government in the first place…"

Chapter 55

The next day was Sunday. Steven hung up the phone, and was smiling ear to ear. He walked into the bedroom where Laura, who had been trying to read in bed but had given up, was restlessly trying to find a position she liked. She saw his smile, and said, "God, Steven, what on earth is there to be that happy about?"

"I am smiling because I am taking you somewhere for dinner tonight that is going to be a total surprise," he replied. "Want to guess?" he added.

"Not really," she answered. Her words were inconsistent with her tone, into which some small measure of enthusiasm had crept. After a minute of silence in which she had expected him to spill the beans, she couldn't resist asking, "Okay you've got me. Tell me where we are going. I need to know how to dress."

"Just wear light, tropical weight clothes," he said. "Casual is fine. Oh, and we need to leave here by one. It's a bit of a distance."

She gave him a full smile now, calling him a silly man, and protesting that they had an early client meeting in the morning.

"I cancelled it. It was at ten a.m., and I figured we wouldn't be up till eleven."

"Why?" she said. "You never sleep past five anyway."

He did his best to leer at her suggestively, which wasn't very good. He found it easier to convey the same message with his hands, which he did by placing them on the backs of her legs, and moving them up in the general direction of her bottom. "Who said anything about sleeping?" he deadpanned.

"Would you stop?" she said. She shook off his hands, but the moodiness was gone. "One last question: do I need to pack a suitcase?"

"Nope," he said. "Now please, no more questions! You'll ruin the surprise."

She looked at her watch, and gave a theatrical groan. "What am I going to do for the hour until we leave?" Her eyes danced happily as she came up with a solution to her question. "I think I am going to take a bath. Alone!"

Not quite an hour later, they went downstairs to a waiting taxi. "Newark Airport," he said, beginning to unravel the mystery. He turned to Laura and said with a smile that tested the elasticity of his face, "If the plane isn't too late, we will just have time to check into our room before we go to dinner – at the Ritz Carlton in St. Thomas, the US Virgin Islands."

"Oh Steven," throwing her arms around his neck as prelude to a kiss, "how wonderful." Then she thought a moment and asked, "But why did you say I didn't need to pack? I don't have anything to wear. Not even a bathing suit!"

Steven held up a finger to indicate that he had some response, and opened his satchel, an old leather bag that was too small to hold much of anything. He unbuckled its top and proudly showed off its contents. "We have here," he said, "two toothbrushes, one pink and one blue; his and her bathing suits" – and here he first held up his, a substantial suit that offered coverage from the waist almost to the knees and then hers, a few small triangles of material held together by the skimpiest of straps, suntan lotion, and even something for you to put on at night should you get cold." The piece of lacy material he held up made her laugh out loud.

"Yes," she said, "I can see how that would keep me warm."

The flight, a direct one from Newark to St. Thomas, was uneventful. He rented a car to avoid using the local taxis and this too was uneventful, except for the one turn where he accidentally ended up on the right hand side of the street, which would have been correct on the mainland U.S. but nearly got them killed there. Finally, they arrived at the Ritz. He had been there once before and knew what to expect; it was her first time.

"Oh, Steven," she said. "I thought you were exaggerating, but it is every bit as beautiful as you said." The temperature was at its usual near-perfect blend of warmth and humidity. What set the Ritz apart from other, lesser places were the gardens, perfectly manicured and designed to accentuate the natural beauty of the place, and the people who worked there, well trained, smiling people who made their guests feel special. Steven and Laura checked into their room without problem, and were given a rum and fruit juice drink to begin the relaxation process after their trip.

One of the staff asked where their luggage was; Laura countered by asking where they could buy clothes. The man checking them in looked at his watch and said, "If you hurry, the clothing store right here at the Ritz is open for another twenty minutes. But once you are there, they won't kick you out until you have bought everything you want. Here, let me give them a call and tell them that you are on your way."

Steven didn't argue; there would have been no point. They went to look at the clothes. It was not a large store, but he was amazed at how much they seemed to have that suited Laura, and how costly each item was. He noted this mentally but uttered no word of protest. This was no time for frugality.

Laura had bought two outfits already and was trying on a third when his cell phone rang. He looked at the number of the calling party on his phone and, not recognizing it, sent the call to voice mail. A few moments later, the phone rang again. He was torn between answering and turning off his cell phone. The fact the caller had called back again so quickly influenced him. He doubted Laura would miss him for a few minutes, so he stepped out of the shop, and picked up the call, saying "Karansky here."

"Thank God, I thought I wasn't going to get you," a familiar voice said. "Am I speaking to the same Stephen Karansky who defended Les Cayhill?"

"Mr. Dunlop?" he guessed."

"Yes, it's me," Dunlop said.

"Listen Preston, this is not the best time. May I call you back later?" Steven asked.

"No! I won't be here. Listen, this won't take long," Dunlop said. Stephen said nothing and for a moment there was silence. Then Dunlop spoke again, his voice friendly in a very insincere way, "Mr. Karansky, I wanted to share some good news with you. I have instructed a banker friend of mine to submit a bid on your house during the auction tomorrow. By the end of the auction, you shall again own the interest in the fees from the American Auto case."

"Thank you," Steven said, meaning it, "You are a gentleman and a scholar."

"Thank you. Now perhaps you can return the favor," Dunlop said.

"You want me to buy your house?" Steven asked, trying to keep the conversation light.

"No, although that is very funny," Dunlop said in a voice devoid of humor. "No, I really would like you to issue a statement to the effect that you don't know anything about the rest of the American Auto/China agreement, and that you can't comment on the overall…"

"Why would I ever issue such a statement?" Karansky asked, having heard enough.

"Because it's true, and because the Chinese, who you really pissed off, might take that into account in deciding how to handle the current situation.

"What the hell does that mean?" Karansky demanded angrily. "That sounds like a threat!"

"I'm not threatening you," Dunlop said. "But, so you know, the last person to piss the Chinese off was Les Cayhill. And come to think of it, he asked me whether I was threatening him when I tried to give him a similar warning."

Vampires

"Fuck you!" Karansky said, as he severed the connection. He felt angry and wondered whether he had really put their lives in jeopardy. He looked back at the shop and saw Laura looking toward him through the window, a look of concern on her face. She was signing for her purchases and in a moment, came out of the door, looking to him like a goddess.

"Is everything okay?" she asked.

He thought a moment, and looked into her guileless face. "Just fine," he said. "Sorry, that was a wrong number."

She looked at him, her head cocked, but didn't press.

"Then, I want to show you how I look in all my new clothes," Laura said gaily. "Starting with a certain piece of lace that will get your mind off your wrong number, and on me where it belongs."

Steven smiled then, and they walked hand in hand toward the room. He unlocked the door and breathed a sigh of relief. There lying on the floor just inside the room was the envelope he had been expecting. He handed the envelope to Laura, saying, "Here, it's for you." She looked at him strangely, but took it and opened the envelope. It was a facsimile, from Pam to Laura, which contained one word: "Congratulations!" It took awhile for Laura to focus not on the message, but rather on the letter head the message was printed on. It was legal letterhead. Across the top of the page were the names "Karansky and Karansky," and underneath were the individual names of Steven Karansky and Laura Karansky. She looked at Steven, not saying anything.

"Marry me?" he asked.

"Yes. Of course I will," she said. "Only…"

"Only what?" he asked.

"Only why do you have to have the name Karansky? Ugh! I really don't know what to do. I love the name "Simon" but then our children would have different last names than I."

"Children?" he said.

"Oh, at least three. Do you like big families?" she asked. He began to look apprehensive, and she broke into laughter. "What is going on?" he said.

"Did you really think that Pam would keep your secret? I have known that you were going to propose and have been waiting all day for it.

"So you don't want three children?" he asked.

"I want ten," she replied. "So long as they are with you." She dragged him over to the bed, and began taking off her clothes. "Let's start tonight."

Vampires

Epilogue

The Minister had received the briefing and was angry. His anger was directed less at that lawyer with the funny name (Car-something, it sounded like) who had done exactly what the Minister had expected him to do, but at Preston Dunlop who had personally assured the Minister that the awkward publicity that had just occurred could and would be prevented.

He could no longer trust that man. For the second time, Dunlop had requested the Minister arrange a violent solution to what was essentially a business problem. But, while the Minister had reluctantly acquiesced the first time, this second request to do harm to the lawyer was different. He was an insignificant player who had already done whatever damage he was capable of. He obviously knew nothing other than what he had already disclosed; otherwise he would have used it by now. As a result, the Minister thought that to do violence now would be punishment for past behavior, but would not fix or prevent anything further.

It was the Minister's experience too, that the use of violence ran the risk of making things worse. The Minister was a pragmatic man, and thought Dunlop's request for approval to arrange some violent end to the lawyer was emotional, and not at all well thought out.

That led the Minister next to consider Dunlop himself. Emotional people caused the Minister concern. He decided to send a message that such reckless attitudes would not be rewarded by not only denying the request for action against the attorney, but also rejecting American Auto's proposal to use the Dunlop law firm as the joint venture's American counsel. As he thought of alternatives, the Minister smiled for the first time since the briefing. His assistant came in, saw the smile, and the Minister chose to explain.

"Liu," the Minister said, "What would you do if your wife became much more important than you?"

The assistant became quite fearful, not knowing whether his career were over. "I would be most unhappy, Minister," he answered nervously.

"Oh, relax Liu," the Minister continued. "I don't mean you, literally. I am talking about someone in the West. Do the men there have enough self-respect not to be happy with women more successful than they?"

"I don't know, Minister," the assistant said.

"It is an interesting question," the Minister said, thinking out loud. Then, to himself, he thought that it was time to start learning what Westerners were really like. "Liu," he said, "In my email, you will find a message from William Gamble, American Auto's general counsel, proposing that our new venture use Dunlop & Schmidt as its U.S. counsel. Prepare a response from me saying no, that I lack full confidence in that firm. And find me the name of the girlfriend that the lawyer with the funny name is traveling with. Thank Gamble for his suggestion, but tell him as the majority partner, it's my choice and I choose her."

It is another reason why, he thought to himself, the east would eventually conquer the west. Not only are we more patient; but we also appreciate subtlety. By choosing her, he wounded and taught a lesson to Dunlop, and also made the attorney's girlfriend far more successful

than the attorney, even though she had just barely finished her school-
ing. He was a student of human nature, and suspected the attorney
would act as if he were happy about things, but (like any other man)
he would secretly want to provide for his wife, and wear the pants in
the family.

Even if he were proved wrong, which the Minister thought unlikely, it
would be instructive to observe. He had much to learn about the west,
and was pleased that his education was about to begin.

THE END